The Geneva Trap

The Liz Carlyle series
At Risk
Secret Asset
Illegal Action
Dead Line
Present Danger
Rip Tide

Nonfiction
Open Secret: The Autobiography of the
Former Director-General of MI5

The Geneva Trap

A Liz Carlyle Novel

Stella Rimington

BLOOMSBURY

NEW YORK · LONDON · NEW DELHI · SYDNEY

Published by Bloomsbury USA, New York

All papers used by Bloomsbury USA are natural, recyclable products made from wood grown in well-managed forests. The manufacturing processes conform to the environmental regulations of the country of origin.

LIBRARY OF CONGRESS CATALOGING-IN-PUBLICATION DATA HAS BEEN APPLIED FOR.

ISBN: 978-1-60819-872-6

First U.S. Edition 2012

1 3 5 7 9 10 8 6 4 2

Typeset by Hewer Text UK Ltd, Edinburgh
Printed in the U.S.A. by Quad/Graphics, Fairfield, Pennsylvania

I T ALL BEGAN BY accident.

Early one evening, Dieter Steinmetz of the Swiss Federal Intelligence Service was at Geneva airport, seeing off his daughter Anna who was flying to Florence on a school exchange visit. Mireille, his wife, had seized the opportunity to go and see her mother in Basle, and had left the day before. So now he had a week on his own, and as he emerged from the departures hall, he was wondering whether he should go back to the flat, put a pizza in the oven and watch the football on television, or eat something more interesting in his neighbourhood café and watch the football there. He was pondering the choice when he spotted a familiar face coming out of the arrivals hall.

Steinmetz clocked him right away. He didn't remember the name, but he did remember the face and the figure. Steinmetz rarely went out with the surveillance teams nowadays – he had twenty years' seniority in the job and most of his work was done in the office – but they had been a man short recently, and he'd been happy to make up the numbers, glad to keep his hand in.

The man he was looking at now had been the target of the surveillance; a member of the large Russian Trade

Delegation in Geneva and a suspected intelligence officer. The teams had watched the Russian for two days, and though nothing of particular interest had emerged on that occasion, there had been some suspicious sightings in the recent past – he had been seen twice with a Pole they strongly suspected of drug running – so he was still very much on their target list, along with at least half a dozen other Russian so-called 'diplomats' posted to Geneva.

Steinmetz filed this sighting away in his mind, resolving to report it the next day, then bought a paper and walked across to the short-term car park where he climbed into his ancient Renault and drove off to join the back of the queue at the exit. As he was waiting, he noticed with admiration the car in front of his, a large, shiny, black Mercedes saloon. An arm emerged from the driver's window and pushed a ticket into the machine, but it must have been the wrong way up because it fell out of the slot on to the ground. The car door opened and it was the Russian who got out, picked up the ticket and impatiently stabbed it back into the machine. Steinmetz watched as the barrier lifted and the Mercedes accelerated fast out of the car park.

The Russian seemed bad-tempered and in a hurry; Steinmetz wondered why. He pushed in his own ticket and, as the barrier lifted, drove off towards the airport exit. To his surprise he saw that the Mercedes was heading towards the motorway leading north, rather than back into Geneva.

This seemed odd to Steinmetz, who was in the business of noticing unexpected behaviour. On a sudden impulse, he also took the northbound exit, hanging back a little to make sure he wouldn't be spotted by the Russian.

The Mercedes joined the A1, skirting the lake's edge and heading towards Lausanne. Steinmetz hoped that wasn't where he was going; it would be a nightmare trying to follow him on his own in that town's narrow streets. But less than a quarter of an hour later, about five miles short of Lausanne, the Russian turned off the Swiss autoroute, and headed north. On the outskirts of the small town of Aubonne, he stopped at a petrol station and filled up, while Steinmetz parked discreetly off the road a hundred yards behind him.

While he waited, he looked around the car for a pen and a piece of paper. He found a pencil stub in the door pocket but no paper. Searching further, he discovered a paperback novel in the glove compartment. Anna had left it behind. *To Kill A Mockingbird* – one of the set texts in her English class. On a blank page at the back of the book he scribbled down the licence number of the Mercedes saloon: **GE 672931.** If he lost his target, at least he'd be able to check whether the car was registered to the Russian Trade Delegation or whether it was privately owned, information that might be some use to the surveillance teams in future. He'd just finished when the Mercedes pulled out, so he stuffed the book back into the glove compartment, and slammed it shut.

The Mercedes drove into Aubonne, through the square with its ancient *hôtel de ville*, past a pretty church and a turreted castle, leaving the village on its north side. It would be getting dark in an hour or so; surely this couldn't be just a sightseeing trip. Anyway, why would he come straight off a flight and drive up here? He must be meeting someone. The more Steinmetz thought about it, the more likely this seemed. What had been casual impulsiveness, triggered by the appearance of the Mercedes in front of his own car at the barrier, was now growing serious. Steinmetz wished he wasn't on his own. Single-handed surveillance in this terrain was very difficult. There was not much other traffic around so he'd have to hang back, but he was determined not to lose his quarry.

Yet he almost did – the black saloon was moving quickly through the countryside, and Steinmetz had to struggle to keep up. As he passed the Aubonne arboretum, the road entered a pocket of dense woodland. When he emerged from the trees the lowering sun came straight through the windscreen into his eyes. He pulled down the sun visor, blinking to help his eyes adjust to the sudden brightness, and realised that there was no sign of the Mercedes ahead of him. Damn! He pushed the accelerator down to the floor as the road climbed sharply out of the valley.

As he crested the hill, he was relieved to see the Mercedes again. It had slowed down dramatically, so much so that although Steinmetz braked sharply, he was soon only a hundred yards behind the other car. They were on an unusually straight stretch of road; nothing was coming from the other direction. Any normal driver would take the opportunity to pass the dawdling Mercedes, and Steinmetz realised that if he didn't do that his cover would certainly be blown. It would be obvious that he was following.

There was nothing for it, so he started to swing out to overtake. The road here ran like a causeway on top of an embankment, with the land sloping away to form a steep drop on either side. Mireille would hate this, he thought – his wife had a terrible fear of heights.

He kept his eyes straight ahead as he started to overtake. But as he did so the Mercedes picked up speed; it was taking Steinmetz longer than expected to pass. Then suddenly he saw a shadow coming from the passenger's side, and he realised that the Mercedes was pulling out on to his side of the road.

Steinmetz hit his horn and jammed on the brakes. But it was too late – the Mercedes's front wing smashed into the Renault, knocking the smaller car towards the flimsy barrier on the left side of the road. Steinmetz desperately swung the steering wheel to the right, but the Mercedes was still pushing against his car, making a terrible grinding noise of clashing steel. As his car slid left towards the barrier, Steinmetz saw with a helpless sense of dread what was going to happen next.

The Renault hit the thin barrier like a bullet going through a paper bag, and hurtled off the road. The front of the car dipped in the air, lifting Steinmetz up in his seat. The Renault landed and flipped on to its side. It rolled over once, twice, and then a third and final time, until it sat crookedly upright on its one remaining wheel. It had lost both front doors, and its roof was crushed like a concertina.

Forty minutes later, a fireman attending the scene remarked to a colleague that it was a miracle that the car hadn't caught fire. His colleague looked at the body being removed from the Renault's front seat, and said softly, 'Some miracle.'

2

RUSSELL WHITE SAT IN the locker room with his head in his hands. Though he played tennis regularly twice a week, today for some reason he felt exhausted. His heart was racing and he was still breathing fast ten minutes after the game had finished. He must be putting on weight or perhaps it was just his age – forty-five next week. But that wasn't old. The game on the indoor courts was always faster than on grass, but it would be weeks before the Geneva spring was far enough advanced for the outside courts to be used. He must cut down the alcohol and change his diet.

His tennis partner and colleague Terry Castle emerged, whistling, from the showers. 'You OK, old chap?' He nodded and Terry went on whistling as he put on his clothes – the informal uniform of soft wool jacket, open-necked shirt and slip-on shoes which the younger diplomats favoured.

'If you're sure, I'll rush off. Got a meet in twenty minutes. See you back at the Station.' He slung his bag over his shoulder and strode out.

White watched the younger man go, envying him his lean figure and jaunty attitude to life. He got up slowly, showered and dressed carefully. He himself still favoured the traditional Foreign Office style – a well-cut striped cotton shirt from Hilditch & Key in Jermyn Street, a blue worsted suit made by a tailor he'd been frequenting for years, and polished brogues.

He was standing in front of the mirror adjusting his Travellers Club tie when he saw the reflection of a man in tennis whites emerge silently from between the line of lockers behind him. Something about the man's sudden appearance made his back crawl. He swung round to face the man, surprised he hadn't realised there was anyone else in the room. The tall figure had prominent cheekbones and dark hair brushed back from a high forehead. He walked straight towards White, who drew back slightly against the mirror as he approached. The man just brushed by him before turning towards the door to the courts. As he passed he said in a low voice what sounded to White like, 'I want to speak to Lees Carlisle.'

'I beg your pardon?' said White to the man's receding back, wondering if he'd been mistaken for someone else.

The man turned, with his hand on the door, and said again, 'I want to speak to Lees Carlisle. Only her. No one else.' Then he left the locker room and the door swung shut behind him.

Russell White stood for a moment, fingering his tie and thinking hard. He could have sworn he'd never seen the man before. What did he want? And who on earth was Lees Carlisle, if that was what he'd said? A woman. He'd definitely said 'her'. It seemed utterly bizarre.

Unless . . . it was an approach?

'Of course it was an approach,' said Terry Castle, when White told his story. Terry was junior to Russell White in the Service, but he was never slow to offer an opinion. 'He's trying to make contact.'

'Funny way to make it, but you may be right.' They were sitting in White's office in the small suite of rooms in the British Mission in Geneva. Though relations between Foreign Office staff and MI6 officers in the Station were excellent, the Station's first line of communication was to the green-and-white MI6 Headquarters building in Vauxhall Cross in London.

White thought himself lucky to have been left as Geneva's Head of Station for five years. Though it wasn't everyone's ideal posting, he loved it. He loved the old town; he loved the easy access to the countryside and the mountains, where he rented a small chalet, ideal for skiing weekends or summer walking. And he enjoyed the diplomatic round and the ease with which you could pick up gossip or inside information, which could be turned into intelligence reports for home consumption. The Station was regarded as a success and he flattered himself that he contributed a good deal to its reputation. But this style of approach, if that's what it was, was new to him.

'Did you recognise the guy?' asked Terry. 'He must know who you are. He's not going to make an approach to just any old Brit.'

'No. I'm sure I've never seen him at the club before. Or anywhere else that I can remember. Pass me the Mug Book and I'll see if he's in it.'

Terry reached into the open safe in the corner of the room and plonked a large leather-covered album on White's desk. Inside, each page held rows of photographs, with identifying captions typed on labels underneath. The people caught on camera, usually without their knowledge, were individuals either known to be or suspected of being intelligence officers. Unsurprisingly, given its importance as an international hub, there were a great many of these in Geneva.

Most nations were represented. Many of the recent photographs were of the Chinese, whose trade delegation had swollen disproportionately in recent years – a transparent cover for industrial espionage. But there were Middle Easterners, Russians, even other Europeans – the Station liked to know its friends as well as its competitors and targets. White leafed through page after page without pausing, then suddenly stopped.

'Here we go. That's him,' he said, jabbing a finger at a black-and-white photograph. He was pointing to a small group of people, some sort of a delegation perhaps, one of the countless number that went in and out of the various international organisations which Geneva hosted, their buildings dotted around the lake. UNESCO, the WHO, the ITO, the UN itself – so much activity, thought White, with so little result.

'Third chap from the left,' he said as Terry Castle came round the desk to have a look.

Castle peered at the picture and the caption below it. 'So, he's a Russian. Looks it too.'

The man in the photograph was wearing a suit rather than tennis gear, but the receding hairline was in evidence, and the same high Slavic cheekbones. White read the caption aloud. 'Alexander Sorsky. Second Secretary, Soviet Trade Delegation.'

'I bet he is,' said Castle sarcastically. 'So what does he want to talk to us about? Talk about a blast from the past. It's just like the old Cold War days, huh?'

White gave him a look. Terry Castle was less than ten years his junior, but he liked to pretend that Russell White was a dinosaur from the pre-*Glasnost* era. White said pointedly, 'I wouldn't know. The Cold War was before my time. Anyway, that identifies our mysterious stranger. I'd better get on to Vauxhall pronto.'

'What about this person he said he wanted to talk to? Are you sure you got the name right? Lees something, wasn't it?'

'Yes. Lees Carlisle, it sounded like.' White shook his head. 'I've checked the Service Directory, but there's nothing that looks at all like it. There's Lees Armstrong in Bangkok, but he definitely said "her" and it certainly sounded like "Carlisle". I don't know who the hell he's talking about.'

3

Geoffrey Fane knew exactly who Liz Carlyle was, and sitting in his third-floor office in Vauxhall Cross, he could look out of his window across the river to the building where she worked. Thames House, headquarters of MI5.

Elizabeth Carlyle – what a pity she insisted on being called 'Liz'. He had known her for almost ten years and had worked with her on many operations. She was intelligent, incisive, direct – and also, Fane acknowledged, very attractive. He respected her, admired her, and might have felt even more warmly towards her if she had shown any sign of admiring him.

But then women were inscrutable to Fane, and right now deeply annoying. Just that morning a letter had arrived at his flat in Fulham from the solicitors of his ex-wife, Adele. It seemed they wanted to reopen the financial settlement that had already drained his coffers irreparably. In particular, they were making noises about his family house in the Dorset countryside, the house which he and his brother had inherited. Its value, the lawyers were arguing, was appreciably higher than that declared by Fane during the divorce negotiations. It seemed Adele felt she had been cheated.

Bloody women, thought Fane. They always wanted to have it both ways. Some insisted on having careers – Vauxhall Cross now positively swarmed with women, many alarmingly competent, and some nearly as senior as Fane himself. They wanted equal pay and equal consideration, even if half the time they were off on maternity leave. They wanted to be part of things but on their own terms: if you tried to treat them as one of the chaps, they laughed at you. If you treated them like ladies, in the way he'd been brought up to do, complimenting them on their appearance, their clothes or their hair, you risked being accused of sexual harassment.

Not that Adele was like that. In fact, Fane wished she were more of a modern woman with a career of her own. Instead, Adele enjoyed playing the role of a high-born lady in a nineteenth-century novel, content to lie on a chaise-longue all day, nibbling chocolates at someone else's expense. Fane's expense for years, until a rich French banker had come along to take her off his hands. After the divorce, Fane thought the problem had gone away for good. But now here she was again, Oliver Twist-like, saying *I want some more.*

As if that weren't enough for one day, now there was another woman disturbing his life. Fane looked with irritation at the communication from Geneva that had arrived on his desk a few minutes earlier. It seemed mildly amusing that a woman he knew so well was unknown to the Geneva Station. But he was not amused at all to read that the Russian who had approached Russell White had said he would talk only to her. Fane was always reluctant to hand over a potentially interesting case to the people across the river, but the Russian's request had been unequivocal – he would only speak to Liz Carlyle. And not even Fane could pretend that Liz Carlyle didn't know what she was doing.

But why was this Sorsky approaching the British now, and in such a covert way? How did he know Liz Carlyle's name? He must have been posted in the UK at some stage – but even so how had he come across Elizabeth, and under her real name too? Let's hope she can provide some answers, thought Fane. Because whatever lay behind the approach, it couldn't be ignored. After the Cold War ended, relations with the Russian Intelligence Services had thawed momentarily but various events had turned the temperature frosty again. The Russians had reverted to their old tricks: it would be useful to know more about their operations, not least in Geneva.

Fane buzzed his Secretary. 'Could you do an urgent look up for me on Alexander Sorsky, Second Secretary at the Russian Trade Delegation in Geneva?'

'Yes, Geoffrey,' replied a youthful, female voice. Fane knew he could have retrieved the information he needed himself from the database on the terminal on his desk but he was set in his ways, and preferred hard copy on his desk, printed paper rather than a screen. He also liked having young Molly Plum bring the files in. She was sweet and very pretty, and young enough to be his daughter. Better still, she seemed slightly in awe of him, which was not an attitude he was inclined to try and change.

As he waited, he stood at the window, looking out at the Thames, sparkling in a flash of spring sunshine, and thinking about the Cold War; recalling the efforts each side had made to infiltrate the other, and the deep satisfaction he and his colleagues had felt when the Soviet Union had collapsed and the game had seemed over.

Molly came into the room, carrying the cup of tea he

always had at this time of the afternoon. 'The Swiss have reported Alexander Sorsky as suspected SVR, but they haven't confirmed it. We have no other traces,' she said as she handed him the cup and saucer.

That was odd. It meant that not only had Sorsky never served in the UK but he also hadn't crossed MI6's radar anywhere else in the world. So how did the man know Liz Carlyle? Geneva had sent over a photograph, which Fane now examined. It was a low-resolution snap of a group of people; someone had drawn an arrow over the figure of Sorsky. He had unprepossessing features, was losing his hair, and in general looked more like a junior bureaucrat than an intelligence officer. Well, it took all sorts, as Fane knew. At least he's not another bloody female, he thought grumpily, as he buzzed his intercom again and asked Molly to tell Liz Carlyle he wanted to come and see her.

4

Liz was sitting in a Eurostar train somewhere under the Channel. She had caught an early train so that she'd be back at her desk in good time to face the backlog of phone messages and emails that would have accumulated while she'd been away. But the train had been stationary for the last twenty minutes and, in the absence of any explanation, uneasy conversations had begun as people asked each other what they thought was happening.

She'd gone to Paris to be with the man she had met more than a year ago, when an operation that had begun in Northern Ireland had unexpectedly taken her to France and close collaboration with Martin Seurat of the DGSE, the French Military Intelligence Service. The professional relationship had become something more, and they now spent most of their free time together. They had just passed a happy week, spending a couple of days staying at Martin's flat in Paris, then going off to a small country hotel in the Loire, where spring was just arriving. Good food, good books to read, and each other's company. It had been perfect. Until now.

Three hours later Liz arrived at Thames House. The train had stop-started its way to St Pancras after a disembodied voice had explained that the one in front had broken down. She dropped her bag in the corner of her office and sat down at her desk with a sigh to face the rest of the day. She had just turned on her screen when the phone on her desk rang.

'Good afternoon,' said a chirpy female voice. 'It's Molly here from Geoffrey Fane's office. He's coming across to Thames House for another appointment in an hour and would like to look in on you, if that's convenient.'

Liz groaned to herself. The last person she wanted to see right now was Geoffrey Fane. 'What's it about? I'm rather snowed under today.'

'He didn't say,' replied Molly, 'but he did say it was urgent. I think it's something to do with a message that came in from Geneva this morning. But don't tell him I told you,' she added cheerfully. 'You know how he likes to play things close to his chest.' Bye now.'

Liz smiled as she put the receiver down. Molly's got the measure of him all right, she thought. Poor old Geoffrey. But Liz was also intrigued. What could a message from Geneva have to do with her?

An hour later she was still working her way through emails when Peggy Kinsolving stuck her head round the door.

'Hi, Liz. Good holiday? Can I come and brief you on a few things when you've got a moment?'

Liz liked the young researcher and was always pleased to see her. 'I'd say come in now but I'm threatened with an imminent visit from G. Fane. I'll give you a buzz when he's gone.'

'Lucky you.' And Peggy's head disappeared, to be replaced after a short time by another.

'Good afternoon, Elizabeth. Sorry to disturb you on your first day back. I'm here to see DG but wanted to tell you about something rather intriguing that's just come in.'

How typically Geoffrey, thought Liz, to remind me that he's a big fish accustomed to swimming with other big fish, and that he's doing me a favour by letting me into his pond.

'How was France?' he went on. 'I hope our friend Seurat was in good form.'

A second Fane ploy: he loved to show that he knew everything about everyone's private life – particularly hers.

Ignoring this, Liz said sharply, 'Molly said something urgent had come up.'

'Have you had much to do with the Russian Services in recent years?'

She'd worked on a Russian case a few years ago, in which Fane had also been involved. He knew about that, especially as it had ended disastrously for him. She didn't want to remind him of it.

As though he was reading her thoughts he said, 'I don't mean the oligarch. I was wondering about other cases.'

'I helped uncover a British scientist who was selling secrets to the Russians a few years ago. I had to give evidence in court. He got ten years.'

'What about earlier on in your career? Weren't you in counter-espionage in your first years here?'

What on earth is this about? thought Liz. But she knew Geoffrey Fane too well to try to hurry him. He would tell her in his own good time.

'Yes. In my first three years. Then I moved to counter-terrorism,' she replied.

'You didn't deal with an approach from any Russian intelligence officer? Or run anyone here who'd been recruited?'

'No. I was far too junior. I didn't do agent running until I went to counter-terrorism.'

'Hmm,' said Fane. Then he went on, 'Some people thought the end of the Cold War would mean the end of espionage. How naïve. Motives change, allegiances change, but spying goes on . . .' Liz listened impatiently as Geoffrey droned on, expounding his familiar theme about the perennial need for intelligence work. I don't know why he's telling me all this, she thought. I agree with him. Perhaps sensing her impatience, he said suddenly, 'Anyway, this chap Sorsky says he wants to speak to you. In fact, he won't talk to anyone else.'

'I don't know anyone called Sorsky. Are you sure he really meant me?'

'He's reported to have said "Lees Carlisle". There is only one Lees in either Service, and the only other Carlyle, Rex, has been our man in Uruguay for the last sixteen years. And in any case, Sorsky clearly indicated his Lees Carlisle was a woman. So yes, I rather think he does mean you.'

'But how's he got my name?'

'I was hoping you could answer that. You must have met him somewhere.'

Liz racked her brains, but nothing emerged. Fane was looking at her sceptically, but she could only shrug. 'What can you tell me about him?'

'We don't know anything more than that he's suspected SVR, under commercial cover at the Trade Delegation in Geneva. As far as our records go, he's never served here, though you'll want to do your own Look Up.' Fane reached down for his briefcase. 'I have a photograph. Not a very good one but perhaps it will jog your memory.' He handed over the group shot from the Geneva Mug Book. 'We could improve this, of course, but have a look at it and see if it means anything.'

She stared at the small group of men, standing on the steps of a large institutional-looking building, and in particular at the figure that had been arrowed. A man a little older than she was, wearing a dark suit and looking sombre.

'Mean anything?' asked Fane. His tone was light but he was staring keenly at her.

She shook her head. 'I don't think so.'

But she kept looking at the photograph, and in particular the eyes. They were dark and unusually large. There was something familiar in the gaze, something she had seen before.

Fane started to say something, but she shook her head for silence. Memories were stirring, a confused collection of them slowly starting to take form in her mind. It had been a long time ago – a world away. But where? She'd joined the Service straight after university and had come to London. Apart from a posting in Belfast, she hadn't lived anywhere else for longer than a month or two. Surely she couldn't have met him at home, when she'd been visiting her parents in Wiltshire. But she had the feeling she had been young when she met him. Could it have been before she joined the Service?

5

OTTO BECH LIKED TO come into the office on Bern's Papiermühlerstrasse very early. He got up at five each morning, walked the dog along the shoreline of the Wohlensee, ate a healthy bowl of muesli, kissed his still-dozing wife goodbye, then sat reading the paper in the back of his Audi saloon as his driver took him to work. Bech's office was on an upper floor of a small complex of modern buildings known as the Egg Boxes, from the dimpled indentations in the external concrete along the line of the windows. The name reminded him of when he was a boy growing up on his father's farm in the foothills of the mountains outside Geneva.

Bech thought that coming in at the crack of dawn set a good example to his staff; it showed that their boss worked longer hours than anyone else and if they wanted to get on they must work hard too. But the real reason he was usually at his desk at 6.30 was that it was quiet; no one else was around except the security guard and the night duty officer. He had peace and time to think.

Thinking, planning, analysing situations was what he did best. Not that he was bad at management – the staff of the FSI found him approachable and fair for the most part; and he had led them effectively through the disruption when this new intelligence service had been created by merging the two existing agencies.

It helped that Bech hadn't come originally from either of them; he was an ex-policeman, though that had not been a recommendation in the eyes of most of those he now led. But he wasn't an ordinary cop. He had run the National Fraud Squad, working for over two decades in the labyrinthine world of hidden bank accounts and anonymous tax shelters. Bech knew his way through his country's arcane rules and banking practices, and in twenty years he had learned when to keep his eyes shut and when to investigate. But things were starting to change now, he reflected, looking out of the window across the Mingerstrasse at the parkland beyond. Terrorism had seen to that. Swiss banking laws had toughened, and there was unprecedented cooperation with foreign authorities, tracking down and freezing suspect bank deposits. It was difficult work; money could be moved at the click of a mouse, and keeping pace took foresight and speed.

This morning Bech was examining an interesting case. He was used to watching strange transfers of funds in and out of his country, but the movements recorded in this file seemed especially baffling. Twelve months ago an account had been opened in Switzerland's second largest bank by a foreign national, and a significant deposit was moved into it from another Swiss bank. Checked in a random audit, the money had been traced back to a holding fund in one of the ex-Soviet Republics, Belarus. The bank had put an audit tag on the account, which meant that each deposit (and they came in monthly from various reputable European banks) was traced to its origins, which turned out to be other former Soviet Republics: one month

Azerbaijan; the next Kazakhstan, and so on until eventually six or seven seemed to be involved, and the total sum in the account was over 5 million Swiss francs.

There the money had sat, drawing the negligible interest on offer during the worldwide recession. Then it started to be moved, initially in a series of transfers to the branch of a French bank in the city of Lyons. Then withdrawals from the Geneva account started to be made by a man who came into the Head Office and showed credentials proving him to be the same individual who had originally opened the account. He had made four withdrawals, each for 100,000 Swiss francs, before Bech's officers had been alerted under money-laundering regulations. The identity details of the man, passed over by the bank, showed him to be one Nikolai Bakowski.

There was just one problem: when Bech's officers attempted to trace Bakowski, they found that he didn't seem to exist. At the Geneva address he had given, no one had heard of him; the mobile phone number had been terminated, and Swiss Immigration had no record of anyone entering the country under that name. All of which suggested that the Polish passport he had shown at the bank was false, and that it had been used only to create the account.

Bech idly scratched his cheek. The whole thing smelled, and the bank seemed to have been very casual in not checking Bakowski's credentials properly. If this was 'funny' money – the receipts from drug trafficking or mafia activity in the old Soviet bloc – investigation would get them nowhere. The Belarus authorities weren't going to cooperate in an investigation of the sort of activity that half their own government was probably involved in, nor were the Kazaks nor the Azerbaijanis.

But this felt different, Bech thought. Why had this Bakowski character started to show up at the bank in person instead of continuing to transfer money electronically? For a man with a false identity he was taking a big risk. How could he be sure that the bank was not on to him? He must know that at the very least the CCTV cameras would have photographed him as he withdrew the money. Perhaps he was relying on traditional Swiss banking secrecy. If so, he was out of date. He must need clean cash for some purpose. It must be for paying someone, and it wasn't his window cleaner. An intelligence operation of some kind perhaps, brooded Bech.

This wouldn't have bothered him very much if he could have been sure that whatever he'd stumbled on was being carried out somewhere else, but that seemed unlikely – after all, the cash was being withdrawn in Geneva.

The next step, Bech decided as he looked out of the window and saw members of his staff starting to arrive for work, was to find out who this Bakowski really was. The bank had supplied a very blurred CCTV photograph – their camera looked as though it could do with some attention – but he needed something better.

'Monsieur Bech?'

He looked up with annoyance, since people knew he didn't like to be disturbed this early. It was the night duty officer, Henri Leplan.

'What is it?'

'Forgive the interruption but I thought you should know. There's been an accident.'

The man paused, ill at ease. Bech prompted him, 'What kind of accident?'

'A car ran off the road last night, not far from Lausanne. It was being driven by Dieter Steinmetz.'

'Is he all right?' Steinmetz was a good officer, thoroughly reliable, very experienced.

Leplan shook his head. 'He's dead, I'm afraid. There was a long drop off the side of the road, and the car rolled over several times.'

'Good Lord. Was anyone with him?'

'No. And it doesn't look as if another car was involved.'

'There were no witnesses?'

'None. A local farmer discovered Steinmetz's car. There's no way of knowing how long after the accident. We've sent a team to assist the police, but right now we think Dieter somehow lost control of the vehicle.'

'Has his family been notified?'

Leplan nodded. 'We've managed to contact his wife. She's in Basle seeing her mother. She says Dieter had taken their daughter to the airport and should have gone straight home.'

'I thought he lived in Geneva.'

'He did.'

'So what was he doing near Lausanne?'

'That's what we're trying to find out. Madame Steinmetz says she can't understand it.'

Bech raised a suggestive eyebrow. 'Maybe he'd planned a rendezvous while his wife was away.'

Leplan stiffened and shook his head. 'I've known Dieter for years, sir. You couldn't find a more devoted husband. We even used to tease him about it. There has to be another reason why he was up there.'

6

THAT YEAR SPRING HAD come early. Even before
Easter the lilacs on campus were showing their first
blush and at home Liz Carlyle's mother said the bluebells
were already out in the woods. Liz, just turned twenty-one,
was in her last year at Bristol University and preparing for
her Finals. When she looked ahead, she wondered what
she was going to do with her life.

She was half-frightened, half-excited. So much seemed
to be happening in the outside world. The Berlin Wall had
come down a few years earlier, and now the Soviet Union
– once an impermeable bloc – had suddenly fragmented.
The glacier of the Cold War, which as Liz grew up had
seemed permanent, was melting away: Democratic move-
ments had sprung up in the states of the Soviet Union, and
new governments had taken over in the Warsaw Pact
countries after free elections; censorship was lifted, private
enterprise encouraged – all measures which formerly
would have brought in the tanks from Moscow.

As a History student, Liz had learned enough to realise
that it was too early to tell if the promise of *perestroika*
would be fulfilled and a new, safer world would emerge; or
if instead all the changes would bring fresh dangers. Either

way, she watched the fast-moving events and waited impatiently to get her degree and a job that would enable her to be part of it. She was working hard; she wanted to do well because she knew that a good degree would open more doors than a poor one – though she hadn't as yet worked out which door to knock on. One thing she knew for certain was that she didn't want to stay on at university. Academic research held no interest for her. She wanted to be involved on the front line of something that was happening – something relevant to the changes in the world.

For the short thesis that formed part of her degree, she had chosen to write about the significance of the break-up of the Soviet Union. Her tutor, Dr Callaghan, had invited her to the postgraduate seminars on twentieth-century European history that he held every week. She had found some of the topics pretty obscure, but she was flattered to be included, and one week the guest speaker had seemed particularly relevant to her thesis.

Dr Callaghan had introduced the serious, dark-haired young man at the end of the table as Alexander Sorsky, a visitor from Moscow State University where he was a lecturer in political theory. Sorsky looked little older than the postgraduate students, in his turtleneck pullover and jeans. He smoked unfiltered cigarettes the colour of maize, and spoke in excellent, accented English. He had high cheekbones and a prominent forehead, and though he wasn't exactly handsome, his large, dark eyes made for an attractive, even exotic appearance.

'I would like to speak of my own experiences during the recent upheavals in my country,' he began. Then, talking without notes, he described how he had watched with mounting excitement as the new wave of freedom swept across the countries of the Warsaw Pact, moving inexorably towards the epicentre of the empire that had once contained them. He said that for months he had felt like a child waking up on his birthday morning.

At his own university in Moscow there were student protests against the Communist regime. They had been timid ones at first, then buoyed by events in East Germany and Czechoslovakia they had grown bolder; there was even a series of 'teach-ins' – inspired, Sorsky noted proudly, by those held in American universities during the Vietnam War. People started to speak out for the first time in their lives.

The guest speaker brilliantly conveyed the excitement of those days, and the uncertainty – no one knew when the Party might crack down on this new dissident movement, or if the military would intervene. It was only when the Republics of the Soviet Union broke away that it became clear there would be no counter-revolution. At one 'teach-in', in fact, a KGB officer had appeared in the lecture room and taken a seat. Out of habit everyone grew nervous in his presence, and the discussion – usually lively – was muted and restrained. But then the KGB man politely raised his hand and asked to speak. He rose, looking slightly nervous, and announced that he was not there in any official capacity. He came simply as a citizen, one who wanted to acknowledge that the time for change had come, and could not be denied. His listeners had applauded him, and to their astonishment the KGB man had burst into tears. To Sorsky this seemed the ultimate symbol of the Communist state's demise.

He ended his talk on an optimistic note, saying that however difficult the immediate future might be, there could be no return to the heavy-handed days of Party control. Looking at her watch, Liz was surprised to see that the Russian had spoken for more than two hours – yet her interest had never flagged.

Afterwards Sorsky had stayed on to answer questions and several of the students then persuaded him to join them in the bar of the Student Union. Feeling a bit of an outsider among the postgraduates, Liz was about to leave, but Sorsky saw her and said, 'You come too, please.'

In the smoky student bar, they had all talked until late in the evening, bombarding Sorsky with questions about Russia and his life there. He was entertaining, telling them funny stories about the ridiculous ways of the old bureaucracy, but also asking them about their lives, and insisting on paying for more wine. When they moved on to bottle number three, he had even sung a Russian folk song. As the party finally broke up, he shook hands with the boys and kissed the cheeks of the girls, and said he hoped to see them all again.

As Liz walked back to the hall of residence with Sylvie, a postgraduate who lived on the same floor, she said, 'That was fun.'

Sylvie agreed. 'Wasn't it just? And isn't that Sorsky a charmer? He certainly seemed to take to you.'

Liz would have thought no more of it or of him, but a week later she ran into Sorsky coming out of the Library. He seemed pleased to see her, and suggested going for coffee. Liz hesitated – she was revising hard – but it seemed churlish to say no. So they went into a nearby café, where after some initial awkwardness they talked easily.

Liz found herself describing where she had grown up – Bower Bridge – and realising how much she missed the contryside. Which Sorsky seemed to understand at once – he told her he was from a small village himself, and that however much his professional life lay in the capital these days, his heart was always in the country.

Liz had warmed to him; so much so that she'd told him how her father had been diagnosed with cancer the year before, and how she had had to spend time at home helping her mother run the estate while her father underwent first chemotherapy then radiotherapy. He seemed better now, she said cheerfully, though inwardly she knew her father's remission might prove all too temporary. Sorsky had been sympathetic, but tactful too; sensing Liz didn't want to say much more about her father, he had changed the subject to the seminar he'd addressed. He'd been surprised when she explained she was still an undergraduate, and had asked what she was going to do next.

'I don't want to be an academic,' she said firmly.

'Good,' he said, and waved one hand dismissively, 'that's the last thing you should do. You seem very interested in the world – you should do something that makes you part of things.'

Which was exactly what Liz had been thinking. The problem was, what? He must have seen the doubt in her face for he said, 'There are lots of opportunities for someone like you – you just need to find them. We need people who think clearly about the world – you could work in business, looking at foreign events and interpreting them. Or do something with the UN, if you want to travel. Or for your own government.' He was looking at her appraisingly now. 'The Foreign Office, or perhaps something closer to home. I will be interested to hear what you choose.'

'Or more likely what chooses me,' said Liz with a laugh, beginning to feel embarrassed that she'd told him so much about herself. She glanced at her watch, 'I had better get back to my books,' she said.

Sorsky stood up. 'I understand. But perhaps before I go back we could meet again.' He was watching her face.

'That would be nice,' said Liz. Would it? Yes, it would; she liked this man.

'Let me give you my phone number – I'm staying in one of the university flats. Perhaps after the Easter break you would ring me, and we could meet again.'

Liz took the slip of paper and they said goodbye. She couldn't really make him out. Was he interested in her? It seemed odd to have given her his number, instead of asking for hers. Perhaps that was the Russian way. But she decided she would call him after the break.

And she almost certainly would have, especially since just two days later a friend happened to show her an advertisement in that day's *Guardian*.

Are you interested in doing
something completely different?
Something important – even if you can't crow about it?
Are you decisive, level-headed, logical, and calm in a
crisis? Then we might be for you . . .

Liz had never even remotely contemplated joining the Security Service, since everyone knew MI5 and MI6 were filled with Oxbridge public-school types, and very few women.

But something in the ad spoke to her, and she wrote off for an application. When the form arrived, she broke off from her last-minute cramming and filled it in. As she licked the stamp and posted the envelope, she realised that if she hadn't had coffee with Sorsky she would never have answered the ad – *You should get a job that makes you part of things.*

But after Easter, while Liz was still at home in Wiltshire, her father took a sudden turn for the worse. She stayed an extra week, trying to study when she wasn't helping her mother keep him comfortable and making sure that his instructions for the estate were carried out. Only when his illness plateaued did she go back to Bristol where, with only ten days left before her exams began, she revised frantically.

And when she finished her Finals she felt so washed out that she didn't do anything for days. She thought at one point of ringing Sorsky, but then she received an answer to her application – she was wanted for interview on the following Tuesday in London. The letter warned her that this was just the first step in a long process, and reminded her that she should keep the fact of her application to herself and very close members of her family.

The interview had gone well, and then there had been another, and another after that. By then she had forgotten all about Alexander Sorsky, who must have returned to Moscow when the term ended.

7

'AND I NEVER SAW him or heard from him again,' she finished.

Fane sat silent for a moment, leaning forward in his chair, elbows on the desk, fingertips meeting steeple-like. Liz had omitted any mention of her own feelings towards Sorsky at the time he was showing an interest in her. She knew only too well what Fane would make of that.

Lifting his head to look straight at her, he gave a sardonic smile. 'So Sorsky's the reason you joined MI5?'

'Hardly,' said Liz. 'Apart from that one conversation, we didn't discuss my future plans. And the Service was never mentioned at all.'

'I don't mean he recruited you.' Fane gave a short laugh. 'But he put the idea into your head. He obviously made an impact on you – and you on him. It explains things.'

'Does it?' It was true enough, she thought, that without Sorsky's encouragement to look further afield, she would probably have ended up as a teacher or working in business; certainly something quite different from the intelligence world. But it was very difficult to see how Sorsky's casual piece of advice of twenty years ago could have triggered this situation. His insistence that he would speak to

Liz and only Liz was most likely a calculated move to ensure that his approach was taken seriously and was passed on by the Geneva Station. Though how he had learned not only that she'd joined MI5, but that she was still there, was a mystery.

Fane must have been asking himself the same question. 'Did Sorsky know that you applied for MI5?'

'No. I told you that the last time I saw him was before I'd even seen the advertisement in the *Guardian*.'

'Could someone else have told him? Someone you'd confided in?'

'I didn't tell anyone else.'

'Not even family?'

'Oh, don't be ridiculous. I didn't tell the family, but even if I had, my family have never been in touch with Sorsky or any Russians.' The truth was that with her father so ill at the time, the last thing she'd wanted to do was to worry him or her mother by telling them that she was applying for a job that they would have considered dangerous.

'And you never saw Sorsky again?'

'No, I didn't. I've told you that already. I don't have any idea why he's mentioned my name.'

Fane nodded. 'Well, you'll find out why soon enough.'

'What do you mean?'

He raised his eyebrows. 'He asked for you. No one else will do – he said so himself. I can hardly send Bruno Mackay, for example, to fly over and see the man when he's made it quite clear that he'll only talk to you.'

Liz knew that he had not picked Bruno Mackay's name at random. Fane knew very well that she and Bruno were old rivals. They typified the different cultures of the Services they worked in and the different jobs they had to do. Liz was careful, analytical, with a direct, straightforward and very determined style. Bruno was the opposite – his flashy exterior covering a subtle and, in Liz's view, devious approach; he was no less clever than she but reached his goals in a much more oblique manner. They were like chalk and cheese, and Geoffrey Fane knew that suggesting he might put Bruno in to do a job that Liz was balking at, was bound to wind her up.

'Are you saying that you want me to go to Geneva and meet Sorsky?'

'Yes. We can't afford to ignore his approach and since Sorsky is hardly in a position to come over here to see you, you'll have to go and see him. Don't worry. The Geneva Station will look after you. Russell White is very sound.'

Liz nodded slowly. Fane was right of course. If Sorsky had asked specifically for her, it would be stupid to try and fob him off with someone else, at least not until they'd found out what he wanted to say. And Liz had to admit that she was intrigued by his unexpected reappearance in her life.

Fane stood up. 'Good, that's settled then. I'm seeing DG now, so I'll mention it. Then I'll get Russell White to contact you and fix all the details. Meanwhile,' he added, 'I'd give a little thought to how this Sorsky character might know that the girl he met at university is now an MI5 officer. We don't want any nasty surprises, do we?'

8

'ENJOY YOUR STAY IN Switzerland, Ms Falconer.'
The immigration officer handed back her passport and Liz walked on, pulling her small overnight bag past the desk, through the baggage hall and the Customs post, emerging into the arrivals hall of Geneva Airport.

She paused for a moment, scanning the sea of waiting faces for anyone who looked as though they might be meeting her. It was 11.30 in the morning; her flight had landed on time. She didn't know if she was being met; she'd changed her travel plans the previous afternoon, in response to a message from Geoffrey Fane. There had been a second contact with Sorsky and the meeting was arranged for this evening. So here she was, twenty-four hours earlier than she had planned.

She waited a few minutes more, but when no one approached her, she started walking towards the taxi rank. She was just nearing the terminal doors when a man appeared at her side.

'Ms Falconer?' he asked, slightly breathlessly.

She nodded and he offered his hand. 'Russell White from the Embassy. Sorry to cut it so fine – traffic's unpredictable this time of day.'

He was wearing a smart blue suit and one of the striped ties that Liz knew that Englishmen used as a sort of signal. The corner of a paisley silk handkerchief was poking out neatly from his jacket's breast pocket. He made friendly small talk as he led her outside to the short-term car park where a small grey Mercedes saloon sat parked near the exit. 'Hop in,' he said, unlocking the doors. 'Shove your bag on the back seat.'

As they drove out of the airport, White said, 'I'm getting rather fit thanks to you.' Liz gave him a questioning look and he laughed. 'I usually play tennis twice a week, but since your friend emerged, I've been on the courts every morning. Didn't want to miss him. And yesterday he showed. We've agreed a meet with you at 18.30 in the Old Town. It'll be twilight but not dark. It depends how long he wants to talk for. I'm glad you could make it at such short notice. Do you know Geneva?'

'Not really. I've been here for a conference, but I came one day and left the next. I didn't have time to look around much.'

'Ah, then let me make a few detours. Give you a bit of a feel for the place, and I can show you where your meeting will be. We can talk over all the details back in the office, but I can tell you he's given us some pretty precise instructions. He's clearly scared.'

Liz nodded. She was beginning to get that familiar sense of excitement, the tension in her stomach that front-line operational work produced.

They were driving along the lakefront now, passing a mix of modern glass-and-steel towers and grand old-fashioned hotels. Turning away from the lake, White drove down a street of baroque stone-and-brick houses, originally the mansions of the rich but now apparently housing the offices of law firms, accountants, small businesses.

'Geneva's a strange city,' he went on, 'stuffed with international organisations and banks, of course, but it's also a big industrial centre: pharmaceuticals as well as hi-tech and IT companies of all kinds. But it's by no means all modern and soulless. The cultural life here is very strong; you can't turn a corner without running into a museum or gallery. As you can imagine it's also a hotbed of intelligence gathering, industrial espionage: political and military, agents of influence – it's all going on here. A bit like Vienna in the Cold War. The place is heaving with the opposition and our American friends – all trying to get one up on each other. And then there's the local Security Service, trying to keep the lid on things, never quite sure where to focus their attention.'

They crossed the river, and White parked on the edge of the Old Town. The buildings were smaller, the streets irregular and narrow. 'We have to go on foot from here. But the meeting point's not far.' They walked through an ancient stone arch and on to a cobbled street. To Liz it looked like a Central European version of Stratford-upon-Avon, little houses with bulging white plaster walls and black beams, overhanging the narrow streets.

'It gets a bit touristy here in the summer,' White said. 'People holidaying in the Alps often come down for the day. Now, do you see that park over there?' He pointed to the west.

'Just,' said Liz, catching a glimpse of green beyond a long high stone wall.

'That's Parc des Bastions.'

'Was it once a fort?'

'Originally, though more recently it was the city's

botanical garden. Now it's part of the University of Geneva. That's where chummy wants to meet you this evening. We'll go over the details when we get back.'

'Looks awfully exposed.'

'That's what we thought. On the other hand, it means he can tell if anyone's watching him.'

'Or me,' said Liz. 'Speaking of which, I don't want any surveillance from our side when I meet him.' She saw White hesitate and said firmly, 'None at all. I don't want anything to alarm our man. It's not as if I'll be in any danger. If he wanted to murder me, he wouldn't pick the middle of a park.'

9

A T SIX O'CLOCK THE café in the small square known
as Place du Bourg-de-Four was half-empty. It was
too early for dinner, and there were just a few people
enjoying an after-work *apéritif* before heading home. Liz
sat at a table under the outside awning, with a glass of
Campari and soda and a copy of *Paris Match*. She hadn't
touched her drink: she wanted to be completely clear-
headed. She had taken a taxi from the Embassy along the
shore of Lake Geneva, then walked the half-mile inland,
stopping from time to time to look in shops with wide
windows which she could use as mirrors to check her
back. She went into one or two of these, and at one stage
retraced her steps back to a place she had been in before,
as if she had left something behind. By the time she'd sat
down at this small café, she was pretty sure that she wasn't
being followed.

Unless . . . there had been a man in a dark winter over-
coat and hat who'd been walking ahead of her as she'd
turned away from the lake. It wasn't particularly his clothes
that she'd noticed so much as his build – squarely broad-
shouldered, almost grotesquely so, as if he had once spent
many years as a weightlifter.

She'd spent the afternoon with Russell White at the Embassy, going over every detail of the two contacts with Sorsky: how he'd looked, exactly what he'd said. Liz had looked at the mug shots of the Russian intelligence contingent in Geneva and listened to White's debating with Terry Castle whether Sorsky was SVR or FSB. 'The Swiss think he's part of the Security Department,' said Terry Castle.

Castle had produced a collection of large-scale maps of the area of Parc des Bastions as well as a laptop computer on which he had brought up Google Street View so Liz could rehearse the route she would take for the meet. At their second contact, Sorsky had given White an envelope which contained detailed instructions as to how to approach the rendezvous. He clearly had some plan of his own for checking that she was not under surveillance.

Over the top of her *Paris Match*, Liz saw a man walking across the square towards the café. He didn't look in her direction, and he wasn't wearing an overcoat or a hat. But his build looked familiar – he was broad and square. He stopped at the edge of the pavement and gestured for service. A white-aproned waiter went over to him and the man began speaking – loudly in bad French. It appeared that he wasn't asking for a table but for directions. The waiter pointed up the street, the man nodded and set off in the direction indicated. Liz noted with relief that he was heading away from the park.

She waited until he had disappeared from sight, then gestured to the waiter for the bill. She paid, stood up and crossed the square.

The route she'd been given took her through a medieval stone arch on to Rue St-Léger, a narrow twisting street with a long stone wall on one side– the 'Reformation Wall' she'd learned that afternoon at the Embassy, built to commemorate the city's die-hard Protestantism. As she neared the park gates, she glanced around and was relieved to see that there was no one else on the little street.

Once inside the park, she strolled along the wide tree-lined avenue which divided the park into two halves. She was carefully controlling her pace now, forcing herself to resist the urge to hurry. Ahead of her on the left was a complex of buildings which she recognised from the maps. They were built in what looked like a light-coloured marble to a classical design. These, according to the maps, had formerly been the headquarters of the botanical society, and now housed the administrative offices of the university.

It took her ten minutes to walk the length of the park. As she neared the wide gates at the far end, facing Place Neuve, she saw an array of life-sized chess pieces. A group of tourists were standing watching as several young people slowly moved the pieces at the direction of two older men – clearly the players. Liz scanned the small crowd gathered around the chess board, looking for anyone whose attention was not focused on the game. Nothing.

Going through the gates, she waited on the edge of Place Neuve. Traffic swirled around the square, horns blaring and brakes squealing; a smaller version of Place de la Concorde in Paris, and equally terrifying. She waited for the nearest lights to turn red, then dashed for the sanctuary of a small island in the middle of the square. Here she paused as if to read the inscription on the immense statue of a local general, but all the while her eyes were looking for signs of surveillance.

A woman emerged from the park. Would she wait to see where Liz was going? No. She walked off and disappeared down a side street. A tall man in a yellow sweater was buying a paper at the kiosk over by the park gates; he looked across in her direction, then quickly looked away again. This made her feel uneasy, but he took his change and walked away from the square.

Following Sorsky's instructions, Liz took her life in her hands and dashed back across the street to the park gates, drawing only one blast of the horn from an irate driver. She retraced her steps along the avenue, but halfway down she turned right, on to a broad path leading to the university's marble buildings. After fifty yards she stopped, as instructed, and sat down on a solitary, unoccupied bench under a tall tulip tree.

She sat there for almost ten minutes, pretending to read her *Paris Match*. She was debating how long she should wait when out of the corner of her eye she saw a man come out of the shadow of a copse of trees to one side of her, at one corner of the university buildings. He was walking quickly, looking straight ahead towards her, and as he drew closer, she recognised him. Not from their meetings almost two decades before – he looked quite different, thinner, older, balder – but from the photograph she'd seen in the MI6 Station Mug Book.

His face was expressionless as he came up to the bench and sat down at the far end from Liz, taking a folded newspaper out of his raincoat pocket. She continued to stare at a page of *Paris Match* as he unfolded the paper on his lap and fixed his eyes on the front page. After a moment he said quietly, 'I am sorry for the complicated instructions but they were necessary. I am confident you were not followed.'

She hoped he was right and that he was as confident about himself.

'Do you remember me, Liz Carlyle?'

'Of course I do, Alexander. It's good to see you again. I've never forgotten your talk at that seminar.'

'Thank you. I also remember the other time we met. You were about to take your final examinations, and I gave you some advice. Which you seem to have taken.' He smiled wryly. 'You have not perhaps chosen the career I expected, but it has certainly kept you out of academic life.'

She smiled, wondering how much he knew. Presumably quite a lot, otherwise why would he have asked for her? But though she was very curious to know how he had kept abreast of her career, this meeting was for him to talk to her, so she said nothing and waited.

'You know I am in the same business as yourself?'

She nodded. 'Yes.'

'I have information that should be of interest to your government. Of great interest, in fact. I asked to see you because I knew nothing of those I'd be dealing with here – perhaps someone low-level who might not understand the significance of what I have to say. Then it could all go nowhere and I would have taken the risk for no benefit at all.'

'Well, I can guarantee you that whatever you tell me will be heard at the highest level.' She felt this sounded rather pompous, but it appeared to reassure Sorsky, who nodded and seemed satisfied. Then he began to talk.

'About three months ago my Station learned about a project that is being developed jointly by the United States and your country. Its object is to create a new military communications system for drones that will be used by the armed forces of both countries. The project is not being shared with other NATO members. It will work via a special satellite system, which will be concealed behind complex encryption. I do not know the details, which I suspect neither you nor I would understand. The Pentagon and your Defence Ministry are driving the project but the development work on the encryption systems is being done in England. The project is called Operation Clarity.'

Liz was not surprised that she had never heard of it – there was no reason for her to know about top-secret defence programmes – but how did Sorsky know? Russell White had told her that Sorsky was thought to be on the security side of the intelligence component in the Russian Embassy, so not part of the scientific and technical group.

She could not resist asking, 'How did you learn this?'

'Well, not from the British or the Americans, be assured.' He laughed, but then his expression sobered. 'I am not telling you this to boast that we know about your secrets. In fact, we don't know much more about Clarity than I've just told you. My Station and a few key others were tasked with finding out more about the programme – difficult since it is so hush-hush even in the US and UK. The most effective way would be to recruit one of the computer scientists working on the project, but that has proved easier said than done.'

'That's a relief.'

Sorsky shook his head. 'Not so fast. We have discovered that another country – not one of your NATO allies – has managed to infiltrate the development. They are acquiring enough technical information about this system to sabotage it once it's in operation. It will be a cyber-attack. Before you ask me, I do not know what country it is that is doing this. But my Government and those higher in my Service do, and they have decided not to inform your Government. Or the Americans. They are holding on to the information for whatever use they can make of it.'

'I see,' said Liz, though she was beginning to feel rather confused. 'Let me just be clear what you are saying. A third country – you do not know which – has mounted an operation to infiltrate a US/UK top-secret development programme called Operation Clarity. Have I got that right?'

'Yes. Those are the bones of it.'

'My Government will be interested to hear this, Alexander, and very grateful to you. But I'm sure you'll understand that they will also want to know why you are telling us this. Particularly as you say that the authorities in your country have decided not to pass on the information. You are taking a big risk. Why are you doing that?'

'I am not a traitor.' He was looking straight at her now and she could see his face clearly for the first time. Age lines were etched deeply into the pallid skin; his eyes were intense and beneath them dark pouches of skin sagged. 'I disagree with the hard-line elements in my Service who are advising our Government. To these people the potential disruption of Western military communications would be a positive thing. But they have not thought it through. If the kind of cyber-attack that is intended took place, Russia might well be suspected. We could have another Cold War, or even worse – some kind of cyber-war, where each country is trying to disable the infrastructure of the others. That would not be in Russia's or anyone's interest.'

Liz had heard versions of this statement before. It was the classic rationale of the spy, the double agent, as he justified his actions to himself. She knew that her role was to listen while he worked out his sense of betrayal to his own satisfaction. So she merely nodded and stayed silent. He went on.

'I love my country. But I love the world even more and I cannot see any value in keeping this information from you. On the contrary, I think it could cause very real harm and possibly bring about conflict between our countries. And if anyone could survive such a conflict, it would not be Russia. That is why I am here. Not as a traitor, but a patriot.'

He stopped talking and slumped back on the bench as though he had exhausted himself. Sweat was standing out on his forehead and he brushed his hand back over his balding crown.

'Yes,' said Liz. 'Now I understand.' She paused. She had to go carefully here. She must get more out of him, but it was quite clear he was in a fragile state and it would be easy to say the wrong thing and send him away dissatisfied. 'You are right about the importance of preventing this plot, Alexander. Is there anything more you can tell me that might help us do that? Do you know how they are acquiring the information? You said they have infiltrated the team. Have you any more information about that?'

'All I know is that there is an agent based in the Ministry of Defence in London who is relaying critical information about the software that will control the satellite.'

'Do you know what nationality he is?'

'No. But I do know he is not British or American.'

That would help track down this infiltrator – Liz couldn't believe many foreigners could be working in the MOD, but surely none would have access to such sensitive information.

Sorsky was looking at his watch nervously. 'Have you got to go soon?' she asked.

'I am due at the theatre in twenty minutes – it's an evening with other colleagues and their wives, so I could not avoid it. And I must not draw any attention to myself.'

'Of course not. But we'll want to meet you again. In the meantime ...'

He finished her sentence. 'In the meantime, I will try and find out which country this threat is coming from. That is what you need to know.'

Liz nodded. She saw that Sorsky had his hands clasped tightly together now, perhaps to keep them from shaking. 'How can we contact you?' she asked.

'You can't.' He took a deep breath. 'Tell your colleague Mr Russell White to continue to play tennis on Mondays and Wednesdays; I will make the arrangements through him when I am ready. But I will not deal with his partner Terry Castle. He is too young to be reliable.'

So Sorsky knew Castle's name; clearly, Russian intelligence in Geneva was on the ball. In an effort to reduce the tension, she said, 'Russell White told me he's getting fitter from playing so much tennis.' She paused a moment, then added, 'You know, he is a senior member of his Service and it might make sense for you to meet him next time. He is based here.'

'No!' Sorsky's voice was sharp. 'The information I give you needs to be investigated in the UK. It would be coming to your Service in any case. So better to deal direct with an officer of MI5 – and one I have known for a long time.' He smiled at her briefly.

Liz said nothing. Sorsky sighed. 'You have not escaped my attention since we met so many years ago in Bristol. I have followed your career with interest. I heard that your work with Brunovsky was noteworthy.'

Liz was amazed that he knew about that operation. Several years ago she had joined the household of a Russian oligarch in London, who had asked for protection. But it had turned out that he was very far from needing protection, and it was Liz herself who was in danger.

Recovering her cool, she said, 'Noteworthy is one way of putting it.' As far as she was concerned that case had ended in a debacle. She had done her best, but it hadn't been good enough.

Sorsky sat up, pushing his back against the bench and stretching as though throwing off a burden. 'I will leave first. You wait a few minutes and then go out through the gates to Place Neuve.'

'Okay.'

'I will say goodbye for now.' He stood up, without looking at her.

'Goodbye, Alexander, *à bientôt*,' she said, and she watched him as he strode off towards the university buildings.

Liz gave him three minutes, then rose to her feet and walked towards Place Neuve. Dusk was falling, and the oversized chessmen had been returned to the board's back rows – the game was over. Cars in the Place had their lights on, and the pavements around the square were full of couples bustling off to restaurants or the theatre.

How, among the flurry of movement, Liz managed to spot the man who half an hour before had been buying a newspaper at the kiosk across the crazy confluence of streets, she didn't know. But she was certain it was the same man – he still wore a yellow sweater – and she was troubled by what she didn't believe was a coincidence. She was even more troubled when she saw another man on the steps of the Grand Théâtre across the street. The overcoat was missing, and so was the jacket he'd worn in the Place du Bourg-de-Four. But the width of his shoulders and the stocky build were still the same.

10

L IZ FLEW OUT EARLY the next morning. She had
stayed the night in a small, elegant hotel near the
Embassy, though she had barely had enough time to
appreciate her room's décor before falling asleep, utterly
exhausted. After leaving Sorsky she had gone back to the
Embassy to brief Russell White and Terry Castle, and by
the time they had gone over every detail and sent off a
message to Vauxhall Cross, it was midnight.

One thing had continued to trouble her. At the end of
the session, she had tackled White about it. 'I asked for no
surveillance of the meeting, but I'm pretty sure there were
people around. Was it your lot?'

White looked uncomfortable. 'I'm sorry. Orders from
Vauxhall Cross, I'm afraid – they insisted we keep an eye
on you. But I am very surprised you saw him. He was
convinced he hadn't been spotted.'

Liz shook her head. She was cross, but not with White.
He had only been following orders; orders from Geoffrey
Fane himself, she was pretty sure. The man couldn't keep
his fingers out of the action, she thought wearily. But
something still nagged at her. 'I saw your man first in the
street and then again in the Bourg-de-Four – before I

went into the park. Then I saw him again afterwards. And there was a guy in a yellow sweater, which I thought was pretty unprofessional since it made him stand out a mile.'

White looked at Castle; it must have been the younger man who'd set things up. Castle shook his head, and White said, 'That wasn't us. We had someone in the university buildings. He watched while you were talking to Sorsky. He didn't see any other surveillance.'

'I didn't see anyone in the park. Just in the street and the square outside. Sorsky said he didn't think I had been followed so perhaps I was imagining things.'

But Liz didn't think so. As she looked out of the aeroplane window and down at Mont Blanc, its snowy cap glistening in the sun, she knew that the thick-set man could have had a perfectly innocent reason for his stop-start walk around Place du Bourg-de-Four. But why had he come back and hung around Place Neuve? And why did he change his coat? Not to mention the 'coincidence' of her twice spotting a man in a yellow jersey. And if it wasn't the MI6 Station, who were these people working for? Sorsky had been at pains to make it clear that his own people had no reason to suspect him of anything. The only conclusion she could draw was that these people were not interested in Sorsky or the meeting; they were watching her.

11

'I t's a great story, Elizabeth. But is it true? Or is something else going on here?'

'Good question, Geoffrey, but I can't answer it. I just don't know.'

They were sitting in Geoffrey Fane's office in MI6's headquarters building in Vauxhall Cross. The wide greenish-tinted windows looked down on the sweep of the Thames as it flowed by, past the long MI5 building with its shining copper roof, towards Parliament. Today a sharp breeze was whipping up little waves on the river and the tourist boats were rocking in the swell as they turned underneath the bridge to return to their starting point.

On Fane's desk was the message that Liz and Russell White had composed in Geneva the previous evening. He picked it up and stabbed his finger at it.

'What do we know about this friend of yours anyway? He says he's a patriot not a traitor. Wasn't that exactly what all defectors used to say in the Cold War? It was difficult enough to believe it then – and most of them turned out in the end to be pretty self-seeking – but it's even more difficult to believe it now.'

'Look, Geoffrey. I agree with everything you say . . .'

'Well, that's unusual for a start,' he broke in.

Liz smiled. 'It's true. We don't know anything about Sorsky. Or what his motives really are. Asking for me by name was certainly a weird way of making contact. But it worked. Whatever he is, he's not a fool. And even if he is the front man in some complicated deception operation, what could it be about? Designed to set us against a third country perhaps or cover up something real that the Russians are doing? Who knows? But we can't afford to ignore what he says. We are going to have to look into this Operation Clarity, if it exists.'

She sighed. She had some experience of searching for infiltrators – moles – and it was a hard, messy business. Any mole as well placed as this one must have covered his tracks very cleverly, which meant that innocent people would become suspects, and distrust and disruption would be rife.

Geoffrey Fane stood up and walked over to the window. He turned his back to the view, leaned on the window ledge and surveyed the room – and Liz in particular. She looked tired today, he thought, not surprisingly. She'd done a good job in Geneva. Russell White had told him that she thought someone had had her under surveillance as she went to the meet. White thought she'd been imagining it, but he didn't know her. Fane did know this girl and if she'd suspected surveillance, it was very probably there. They would need to look after her – though she was very difficult to look after. He wished she were more malleable. Together they could be a great team. But now she seemed to spend all her spare time in Paris. He sighed and Liz looked up, her grey-green eyes reflecting the light from the window.

'Even though it may be a bluff, we'll have to tell the Americans,' she said.

Fane eyed her. 'Why don't you leave Bokus to me? I think I've got his measure by now'

Andy Bokus was the CIA Station Head in London. He was a big, blunt Midwesterner, an ex-American football player, who enjoyed pretending he was stupid when in fact he was very shrewd. Liz wasn't at all sure that Fane had got his measure – he tended to respond to Bokus's pretence of stupidity with his own 'English gentleman' act, which meant that they both got embroiled in role-playing and ended up merely annoying each other. Liz would have much rather gone home at this point in the day, but she thought she'd better go with Fane and try to hold the ring. She said, 'I'd prefer to be there.'

'Suit yourself,' he replied sourly. 'Let me try and get Bokus on the blower now.'

12

Andy Bokus was in a bad mood. He didn't much like London, and after four years he wasn't about to develop a sudden affection for the place. But his hopes for reassignment had just been dashed – his boss at Langley, Tyrus Oakes, had told him the previous afternoon, 'Sorry, Andy. You're there for another year.'

The weather didn't help. He couldn't get used to the dispiriting greyness of England: its overcast sky in winter, the enervating drizzle in spring, summer's inevitable failure to materialise, and the lack of sugar maple trees to give colour to the fall.

The people here struck him as equally unappealing – snobbish, undemonstrative, sometimes downright devious. His counterparts in the British Intelligence Services were clever, there was no denying that, but he never enjoyed the times he had to work with them.

Like this evening, when he had heard that Geoffrey Fane was coming over to Grosvenor Square in twenty minutes. At least he hadn't summoned Bokus to Vauxhall Cross. He hated that place; it seemed to be a mixture of understated gloom and grandiose pomp. A bit like Geoffrey Fane himself. Fane acted as though he didn't recognise

Britain's diminished role in world affairs; he tried to treat Bokus as though their dealings took place on a level playing field – sometimes, in fact, he acted like he occupied the higher ground.

In some ways, Bokus didn't mind this: he rather enjoyed playing dumb with the likes of Geoffrey Fane. He found it elicited more information than competing with them would ever do. And, personally, Bokus didn't give a damn if Fane thought he was an uncouth simpleton. Bokus's grandfather had dug coal in the Ukraine with a pick, and Andy Bokus was proud of it. It wasn't England which had welcomed his father when he'd refused to follow Grandfather into the mines. It was America where Bokus's father had landed at the age of sixteen on Ellis Island, with nothing but his muscles and the clothes on his back. It was a classic immigrant's story, and if it hadn't quite gone from rags to riches – Bokus's old man had ended up running a gas station in Ohio – it beat a life spent five hundred feet underground in front of a dwindling seam of anthracite. The America the Bokus clan was loyal to was a true melting pot – with opportunity for all. Not the half-baked imitation of a declining British nation which some of his WASP colleagues seemed to want to create.

Decline – that was a British disease, though Bokus was bothered by the nagging feeling that the virus was coming his own country's way as well. He stretched out one leg under his desk and rubbed his aching knee, a college football injury. He might have played pro ball if it hadn't been for that. Instead he was looking at a fifth year as Station Head in London.

At least he was kept busy here: in a post-7/7 Britain, the world seemed to be a dangerous place and getting more so by the day. Bokus had no time for those of his associates

– especially his British counterparts – who liked to suggest there was an ethical complexity to their work. When it came to his job, Andy Bokus only worked in black and white.

The phone on his desk purred, and he picked it up. 'Your British guests are here, Andy,' said his secretary.

Guests? He'd thought Fane was coming alone. He must have something important to say if he's bringing a delegation, thought Bokus, as he left his office and walked out into a large open ground-floor room, normally full of people waiting for visas but empty this late in the day. Across the room he saw Fane standing with a woman whom Bokus recognised as he drew nearer – it was Liz Carlyle from MI5. Her presence made him uneasy. He found her much more difficult to deal with than Geoffrey Fane. She didn't rise at all to his crude simpleton act, just ignored it and got on with business. She could show a relentless tenacity, which was awkward if you were keeping information from her. They'd crossed swords before.

'Geoffrey,' he said, with a pretence of pleasure he didn't feel. 'Good to see you. And you've brought some extra ammunition along.'

Fane shook hands. 'You know Liz Carlyle, of course.'

The Carlyle woman smiled politely.

'Sure,' said Bokus, taking her hand. 'I never forget a face. Especially a pretty one.'

Fane raised his eyebrows and Liz Carlyle didn't react at all. Good, thought Bokus to himself grumpily; now they'll think I'm not only a right-wing pig, but a sexist one as well.

They went down a wide flight of stairs and along a corridor that ended at a steel security door. Bokus swiped a card and the door clicked open. 'You said this was confidential, so I thought we'd better use the Bubble.'

Like most major Embassies, Grosvenor Square contained a purpose-built room designed to foil any electronic eavesdropping. Down in the bowels of the basement, the 'Bubble' was lead-lined and windowless. Inside it the air resonated with a faint hum – like an air conditioner, but actually the by-product of a high-frequency wave baffler.

The door closed with a pneumatic hiss behind them, and they sat down on padded benches around the grey walls. Bokus nodded. 'Okay, we're secure now, Geoffrey. Shoot.'

Fane took his time, hitching a trouser leg, crossing his ankle across one knee and tugging at a cufflink. He's getting used to me, Bokus thought. He's doing it on purpose. 'Do you know anything about Operation Clarity?' the Englishman said at last.

Bokus shrugged. 'I've heard of it,' he said, which wasn't true. 'But I don't know much about it' – which was.

Fane elaborated: 'It's a joint programme between our two Defence Departments to develop a communications system for unmanned aircraft. It uses very hi-tech encryption, designed to obscure its existence. Part of the work is being done in the States; the encryption work is happening over here.'

'Okay,' said Bokus. Let's get to the point, he thought.

'We've learned from a source – a well-placed source we've codenamed Bravado – that there's a problem at this end. Apparently, the programme has been infiltrated by someone working for a third country – a foreigner, he says, not a US or British citizen. Someone who's been seconded to the Ministry of Defence.'

'A foreigner working on a top-secret programme. Doesn't seem very likely. Can you give me more detail?'

'Elizabeth. Why don't you carry on?'

Liz Carlyle explained how an approach had been made in Switzerland, and that she had flown out to Geneva and met the source they were calling Bravado.

'I don't get it,' interrupted Bokus. 'Why were you sent?' He turned to Fane. 'Geneva's your territory, right?'

Liz leaned forward. 'Bravado asked specifically for me.'

'Why? Does he know you?'

'Not really. He met me long ago, before I'd even joined the Service. But apparently I have appeared on his radar since then – he knew I was with MI5. He's an intelligence officer himself so perhaps that's not surprising.'

'What nationality is he?'

Fane started to protest, 'I really don't think it's rele-vant—'

Liz cut in, 'He's Russian. A mid-level intelligence officer, we think.'

For the first time Bokus was glad she was there, since Fane wouldn't have told him – not because there was any reason to keep it secret, but from his addiction to keeping the cards close to his chest. Close? thought Bokus cynically. The guy had them tattooed on his skin.

He said to Liz, 'Okay. So tell me about your meeting.'

And as she described her rendezvous in a Geneva park, Bokus stared at the wall. It was an old habit of his, which allowed him to focus on what was being said, not the gestures and expressions that accompanied it. He knew it seemed rude, but it worked for him.

When she'd finished, he said, 'This sounds interesting.'

'We think so,' said Fane, adding smoothly, 'and that's why I wanted you to know about it straight away.'

'Where do you think the threat's coming from?'

'China, I'd say,' said Fane.

The Chinese were the modern-day Bogeyman, thought Bokus. If a thirty-year-old Defense Department computer belched twice in South Dakota, everybody attributed the problem to dirty doings emanating from Beijing. Bokus clenched and unclenched the fingers of one hand. Some days they hurt too, though unlike his knee he'd never used them much playing football. Just age, he'd decided.

He ignored Fane and looked at Liz. 'Couldn't the leaker here in London be Russian too?'

'Well, anything's possible at this stage,' she conceded.

'Very unlikely, I'd say,' said Fane, avoiding Liz's astonished gaze. After all, he'd made the same suggestion himself only an hour or so ago in his office.

Bokus sighed. 'Geoffrey, however cosy we are with Moscow these days, I don't think we'd let them join us on a top-secret project. If they found out about it, they might well have an interest in infiltrating it. I was thinking actually of an illegal – somebody the Russians planted here long ago. If your guy Bravado is telling the truth, and the leaker's foreign, then he could be posing as a national friendly to the West. Christ, he could be Canadian, for all I know. He could be anything, but his real identity would be Russian.'

Liz intervened. 'Our source was pretty clear on this. It's not a Russian operation; according to him, the mole is working for some other country. But Bravado doesn't know which one.'

Bokus didn't buy this. 'I think it's far more likely that it's the Russians who have somebody in place. And your guy is looking for some pay-off for the information.'

'That would be the *obvious* way of looking at it,' Fane said. He gave a deprecating sniff.

59

Bokus snorted back at him. 'In my experience, the obvious wins nine times out of ten. Sure, you can always start navel-gazing, but this looks to me like a no-brainer. The Russians have infiltrated an agent into this Clarity programme. Simultaneously, and for whatever reason, one of their intelligence officers wants to turn – but he knows he's got to bring something with him. So this is the dowry.'

When Fane and Liz Carlyle looked unconvinced, Bokus felt exasperated. Why did these Brits always want to make everything so *complicated?* He said, 'Come on, if it's not a Russian planted in the MOD, then how the hell did this source of yours find out about it?'

Fane looked to Liz, who said, 'He says he only learned by accident.'

Bokus made a sarcastic tut with his tongue, but Liz shook her head impatiently. She said, 'Don't you see, that's exactly why it rings true? Bravado didn't claim to be in the know about everything; he didn't bring us secret files all neatly wrapped in a box with a pink bow.'

Bokus replied, 'He's not giving us anything very concrete. He can't think we'd pay much for something so vague. What's his motivation?'

'Funnily enough, he thinks he's being patriotic. He's only telling us because his superiors decided not to. They don't want us to know: they're happy for this third party to infiltrate the programme, and give themselves the capacity to control it – either to screw it up or turn it back against us or use it themselves. There's no end to what you could do if you could get through the encryption and manipulate the software. But Bravado thinks his side is making a mistake in not telling us what they know. He thinks that if the system is sabotaged we might well blame the Russians, the Russians will blame the Chinese, the Chinese will blame us ... et cetera. And eventually, all hell could break loose.'

Maybe, thought Bokus. But it still seemed overly elaborate to believe this Russian Bravado was betraying his own side because they knew about a third-country threat to this Clarity programme.

Liz said gently, 'I know it all looks very strange at this stage, Andy. But it's early days. I have to believe Bravado until something proves I'm wrong, and that's the starting point. We can't ignore the information.'

Bokus noticed that Fane was staying quiet, which suggested he had another agenda. Bokus knew better than to ask what it was: Fane would never tell. Bokus looked at Liz, and decided there wasn't any point arguing with her; besides, he had to admit her argument made sense. He nodded but also let a slight sigh escape, to show his agreement was reluctant. 'Okay, so what do you want me to do?'

'Alert your people. I suppose the Bureau will need to be told as well.' It was clear she'd come knowing what she wanted out of this meeting. 'Tell them we're on the case over here but I'm sure they'll want to look at your part of Clarity, though Bravado was clear it was the British end that had been penetrated. I need to know I can get help from you over here if I need it.'

'Count on me,' Bokus said. And he meant it, for the time being.

13

E ARLY ON SATURDAY MORNING, Liz drove down to
Wiltshire, to the Bowerbridge Estate where she had
grown up in the gatehouse. When her father died, just
after Liz finished university, her mother Susan had gone
on living in the house and had eventually been allowed to
buy it. She now managed the garden centre, which occu-
pied the old kitchen garden. For many years she had hoped
that Liz would give up what she thought of as her danger-
ous job in London and come back to live in the house and
marry a local man. But she had abandoned that ambition
a few years ago, realising that, though Liz loved to visit her
old home, her heart lay in her work, and that the last thing
that would make her happy was rusticating in Wiltshire.

Susan had been helped to come to terms with reality by
Edward Treglown, whom she had met at a friend's house
and to whom she was now very close. Liz and Edward got
on well and, just as importantly for Liz, Edward and
Martin Seurat got on well too. Both had been in the mili-
tary, and they had discovered contacts in common from
when they had served in Kosovo in the eighties.

As she stop-started in the traffic on the M4, Liz thought
about her meeting with Sorsky and wondered whether

Fane and Bokus were right in their suspicion that there was something more behind Sorsky's offer of information. It was not as if she could really assess the man. Despite the Russian's easy familiarity with her in the Parc des Bastions, she hadn't seen him before that for almost twenty years, and even then had barely known him at all.

Yet it was hard to see his approach as anything other than what he claimed it to be. In particular, his lack of specifics seemed convincing to her. If for whatever reason he wanted to seduce her into believing something that wasn't true, surely he would have had more information on offer.

As she neared the Newbury exit, she felt herself gradually starting to relax. Martin was in Paris this weekend, helping his daughter move apartments, and though she'd rather be spending the time with him, his absence might make it easier to take her mind off work. She was looking forward to the weekend, to walking in the Wiltshire countryside, and seeing the hyacinths and the late tulips that would be colouring her mother's cottage garden.

When she arrived, Susan seemed unusually preoccupied. Normally she would have come out into the yard as Liz was parking her car and there would have been a freshly baked cake on the kitchen table. But Liz found her standing in the sitting room, listening tensely to a conversation Edward was having on the telephone.

Liz frowned. 'What's wrong?' she whispered. Judging by the anxious tone of Edward's voice, something was clearly upsetting him.

Her mother sighed. 'Come into the kitchen.'

As she put the kettle on Susan explained: 'Poor Edward. His daughter Cathy's come back to live in England, but it's all proving rather . . . *difficult*.'

Liz's mother was old school, trained to take troubles on the chin and just get on with it. So 'difficult' meant things were serious. Liz knew Edward's daughter had been living in France; by all accounts she was a kind of latter-day hippie – Liz vaguely imagined her playing the guitar with flowers in her hair. She had a little boy, whom Edward adored but rarely got to see.

Liz took three mugs down from the dresser, while her mother stood in the middle of the kitchen, tapping her foot nervously.

A moment later Edward Treglown came in. Seeing Liz, he gave her a smile. 'Hello, stranger, or should I say *bonsoir?*'

Liz laughed, acknowledgment that she had been in Paris for many of the weekends she would formerly have spent here. She gave Edward a big hug. He was a tall, loose-limbed man with a lived-in face that could seem stern, until it creased into a warm smile. Despite Liz's initial suspicions (she remembered how pompous she had been, asking her mother if Edward's motives towards her were 'honourable'), she had come to like him very much, a feeling enhanced by the obvious fact that he made Susan very happy.

After leaving the Army, Edward had become chairman of a charity that provided operations to cure some of the simple diseases that caused blindness in the Third World. Now, having turned seventy, he claimed to be cutting back on his involvement, but his energy showed no signs of flagging.

'Cuppa?' Liz asked, but he shook his head.

'Stiff whisky more like,' said Susan sympathetically, and he nodded with a deep sigh.

'Problems, I gather,' said Liz. 'Anything I can do to help?'

Edward smiled but there was sadness in his eyes. 'It's Cathy,' he said. 'Your mother's probably told you that she's moved back to England with my grandson. Teddy's seven now and he's a nice boy, if a little out of hand. I know single-parent families are nothing unusual these days, but I have to say, I do think there are times when a boy needs a father and Teddy's hasn't been seen for six years.'

'But you're a wonderful grandpa, Edward,' said Liz's mother loyally.

He shook his head. 'Not the same thing, I'm afraid. I do what I can, but I'm too old to play football for hours with the boy – a few minutes is the most I can manage. And besides, I'm not there most of the time.'

'Why has Cathy come back to the UK?' Liz asked.

'That's the problem,' said Edward. 'I'd hoped she was doing it to get away from those people she's been involved with.'

Susan said, 'She's been living in a commune in the South of France.'

'How long has she been there?'

Edward sighed. 'Five years or more. Teddy's father, Paul, introduced her to the place when they were living in Cahors; the commune's not far from there in the Lot-et-Garonne. When Teddy was born and Paul took off, her mother and I urged Cathy to come home. But she wouldn't – she's always been very independent. Still, it couldn't have been easy on her own with a baby in a foreign country, and eventually she went to live in the commune. I thought she might come back when her mother died, but she didn't.'

'When did she leave France?'

'About three months ago. I have the feeling the commune leaders didn't want her to go.'

'Is it some kind of a cult?' asked Liz, imagining a hippie-style enclave, with a charismatic, controlling guru at its head.

'Not really. They style themselves anarchists: none of this love and peace stuff for them – their activities can be pretty violent. They've clashed with the police on several occasions, though thank God Cathy has never been arrested. They like to disrupt G8 summits – that sort of thing.'

He sighed, and Susan said, 'Why don't you two go next-door and sit down and I'll see about supper.'

They went into the sitting room and, equipped with a stiff whisky, Edward told Liz more. He had been pleased that his daughter had come back to England, happy that he could see her more often and get to know his grandson better. And at first things had seemed to pan out – Cathy had found work three days a week with a software company within walking distance of the flat she'd rented in Brighton; Teddy had adjusted to English school (and English) very well; and the upheavals of Cathy's life in France seemed well behind her.

'But then?' asked Liz sympathetically.

Edward shook his head. 'These wretched anarchists contacted her again.'

'What did they want?'

'Money, I think. You see, my wife set up a trust for Cathy, and I'm one of the trustees.' His face darkened. 'But the trouble is she's twenty-eight now and she's entitled to the money.'

Recently, she'd asked for some of it, to buy a house she'd found on the Hove side of Brighton. 'The solicitor, who's the other trustee, and I were happy with this – not that we could have done much if we weren't. We told her to go ahead and make an offer, and we gave her enough for the down payment.

'But then the French people she'd lived with got in touch, and since then nothing's happened – Cathy's still in her small flat with Teddy, and there's no sign of her buying anything. Since she's got some money now I'm worried she's going to give it to these anarchists. It's impossible to talk to her. She won't explain anything or come here to tell us what's going on.

'If I push too hard, she just threatens to go back to France, and take Teddy with her. We're barely on speaking terms, I'm afraid. When I rang last week and offered to take the boy out for the day, she said no and put the phone down.'

His distress was obvious. Liz realised it must be made worse by his feeling of powerlessness. From the sound of it the boy could use a strong paternal figure like Edward in his life.

'It does sound very difficult,' she said. There didn't seem to be any useful advice she could offer.

'The thing is, if Cathy wants to go and live with these people again, there's nothing I can do to stop her. It's her life after all. And ultimately the money's hers ... not just the ten thousand she's already had, but the rest as well. I'm legally as well as morally obliged to give it to her.'

He hesitated for a moment. 'But ...?' prompted Liz.

'Well, I may be kidding myself, but I don't think this is one of those classic scenarios – you know, where someone's daughter goes off and joins the Moonies and the parents say the child's been brainwashed and the daughter says not at all, she's doing what she wants to do.'

'How is this different?' asked Liz gently, since it didn't sound very different to her.

'I think something else is going on. When I last saw Cathy, I got the distinct impression that she's scared of these people. It wouldn't surprise me to learn they were threatening her.'

'Threatening her?'

'Edward's already spoken to the police about it.' Susan Carlyle had come into the room.

'They were very sympathetic,' he said, but gave a resigned shake of his head. 'The problem is, I didn't have any hard evidence, and these people are all in France. The police here said there wasn't anything they could do.' He sat back gloomily in his chair, looking despondent and uncharacteristically vulnerable.

Liz thought for a moment, wondering if Edward was right about this. Or was it merely wishful thinking? Like any parent, he probably couldn't bear the thought of his daughter choosing to get mixed up with a bunch like these French anarchists.

She tried to sound encouraging, 'Why don't I have a word with Martin? He could probably find out a bit about these people. If they are as violent as you say, they are sure to be known to the police in France. Then at least you'll know what you're dealing with.'

'Would you?' said Edward, brightening up. 'Then I'd feel I was doing something and not just sitting back helplessly.'

'Well, if you're feeling helpless,' Susan said cheerily, 'you can come and set the table. Supper's ready.'

14

L IZ CARLYLE DISLIKED VISITING the Ministry of
Defence. Its building, white and cold, sat at an
awkward angle between Whitehall and the Thames. All
those stiff-backed men walking smartly up the steps to its
grand door made her feel like an alien. And once inside,
there was a certain disapproving hostility about its security
arrangements, which made it the least welcoming of all the
government departments.

Now, having survived the first layer of security, and with
her pass pinned to her lapel, she sat waiting to be collected
by someone who would take her inside the Secretariat of
Operation Clarity. Except that it wasn't called that here. It
had turned out that the codename itself was top-secret and
she had been told to ask for Sy3A.

She watched as a military officer, dressed in what looked
to her like a musical-comedy uniform, was ushered through
the security barrier by a young Major who had greeted the
visitor in a language Liz didn't recognise. Serbo-Croat
perhaps? she wondered idly as they disappeared up a long
escalator.

Eventually, a voice at her elbow asked, 'Miss Carlyle?'
and she got up to follow an attractive young woman,

dressed surprisingly casually in trousers and a flowing top. She looked as though she might be pregnant. No uniform, Liz noted with relief.

They rose up through the building via escalator and lift to a floor near the top where the corridors were long, narrow and silent. Her escort stopped at a windowless, unmarked door, which clicked open in response to some numbers she tapped into a keypad.

The door gave directly on to a small foyer, containing a plain brown Government-issue table and four chairs.

'Sit down, please,' said the girl. 'I'll tell them you're here.'

Liz waited again. She had been told that access to the Clarity Secretariat was extremely restricted, and she didn't even know the name of the person she'd come to see. But at least they seemed to be expecting her, which was a step in the right direction.

After a few minutes, another, much more formally dressed woman appeared, carrying a folder.

'Good morning. I'm Miranda Braithwaite,' she said.

I bet you are, thought Liz. Just like I'm Jane Falconer when I choose to be.

'I'm to take you through the indoctrination. When I've done that, you'll sign this form and then you'll be Clarity Blue, which is the first level of clearance. We'll decide later if we need to up your clearance to Silver or Purple. But Purple is only for the top brass – and all of us, of course.'

You may be in for a surprise, thought Liz, but she didn't say anything.

Miranda Braithwaite then told her rather less about the Clarity project than she had learned from Sorsky, and when she had finished, Liz solemnly signed 'Liz Carlyle' on a sheet headed 'CLARITY INDOCTRINATION LIST. BLUE'.

Miranda nodded, looking satisfied, and got up. 'Henry Pennington will see you now,' she said, and motioned Liz to follow her.

Not Henry Pennington, thought Liz. What on earth was he doing here? She had last come across Pennington several years ago in the Foreign Office. It was at his instigation that she had gone undercover in the household of the Russian oligarch and almost been shot for her pains.

The figure sitting at the desk didn't look up as Miranda and Liz came into the room, but went on reading a document on his desk.

'Liz Carlyle is here,' said Miranda. There was no reaction, and she left the room.

Liz looked round her. This was nothing like as grand as the room Pennington had inhabited in the Foreign Office on the last occasion she'd encountered him. She remembered a high corniced ceiling, marble fireplace and a large antique desk with chairs to match. Now he was sitting at a desk, large but much more ordinary, in an office with unadorned walls and no fireplace.

She wondered if he'd been demoted – probably not. The carpet was thick, the meeting table against the wall large, and the window wide. It was probably just that the MOD building was nothing like as grand as the Foreign Office. As she looked round her eyes fell on something she recognised. Propped up against the wall under the window, where a visitor couldn't miss it, was a violin, the symbol that this was the office of a truly cultured man.

Liz did not like Henry Pennington. He was patronising but, worse, he was a panicker. When unexpected events occurred to disturb his vision of how things ought to be, he could be relied on to flap and do something unhelpful, as when he had suddenly offered Liz's services to the Russian oligarch. So she was wary of anything that Henry Pennington was involved in.

Having established how very busy and important he was, Pennington looked up at last from his desk and acknowledged Liz's presence.

'I have a conference call in fifteen minutes,' he said, by way of opening the conversation. 'I hope this won't take long.'

Same Henry, thought Liz as she looked at his thin, bony face with its prominent nose. You're in for a shock, Mr P, she thought to herself.

'I think you'll find that what I have to say is just as important as your conference call.'

He frowned as Liz went on. 'What I have to tell you is very much "need to know" so I must ask you to sign this indoctrination list for Operation Bravado.'

Henry flushed and tutted irritably. She was playing him at his own game and he knew it. He signed reluctantly on the form Liz presented and said rudely, 'Let's get on with it.'

'We have learned from a well-placed source,' Liz began, 'that the existence of Operation Clarity is known to the Russians and also to another foreign power.'

Henry flopped back in his chair and started to rub his hands together in a washing motion. He said, 'What do you mean? It can't be true. Our security is top-notch.'

'I'm afraid it is true. I didn't know anything about Clarity until I was told by this source, who is himself foreign. What's more important is that it's possible that Clarity itself may have been infiltrated.'

The hand-washing accelerated. 'That's impossible. Everyone is vetted to the highest level. I just don't believe it.'

'For the moment we have to assume it's true. My job is to follow this lead, and to find out what if anything is going on in Clarity. What I need from you is a list of those employed on this project.'

'They are all either American or British,' he broke in. 'There are no foreign powers, as you put it, involved.'

She ploughed on. 'As I understand it, this is the Secretariat. The development work is being done elsewhere. Where is that?'

'I can't tell you,' said Pennington desperately. 'You're only cleared to Level Blue.'

'Well, you'd better get me cleared to Level God. Because I not only need to know where the project is, but I or one of my colleagues will need to visit it and talk to whoever is in charge.'

'You can't. Access is totally denied to outsiders.'

'Look, Henry, you can try to block me if you like, but you're just wasting your time – and holding up an important investigation. This is already at DG/PUS level and may shortly go up to Ministers. So let's stop all this and give me the information I need so I can get on with the job.'

Pennington slumped in his chair. His thin face had gone very pale and his large nose seemed even more prominent. He said nothing for a second or two, then muttered in a broken-sounding voice, 'Our security can't have been breached.' Liz could see that visions of his shattered career were floating before his eyes.

'Don't worry, Henry,' she said soothingly. 'It may not have been. We don't know for sure that Clarity itself has been infiltrated. Only that there's someone working for a foreign government who has some sort of access to Clarity material.'

But Pennington had given up. 'What do you want from me?' he asked weakly.

'The details of the UK Head of the Project and an introduction. Believe me,' said Liz, looking at his slumped figure, 'no one hopes more than me that this information is wrong.'

'*More than I*, I think you mean,' said Pennington with a sniff.

15

Peggy Kinsolving was beginning to panic. Holding the steering wheel with one hand and her map with the other, she was driving slowly along a track between wide fields where bright green shoots of some sort of crop were just beginning to emerge from the ground. 'You have reached your destination,' her SatNav kept repeating, though she could see no building of any kind, not a barn or farmhouse, far less anything that could be Brigham Hall. The last town of any size that she'd passed through was Brandon and then, as instructed by the charming-sounding lady on the SatNav, she had turned off down a narrow road. Then the road had turned into little more than a track and here she was, lost, miles from anywhere with the useless SatNav shouting at her.

The track entered a small dark wood and out of the corner of her eye Peggy spotted what looked like a drive on the left, with an open five-barred gate. Nothing ventured, nothing gained, she thought to herself, and turned the car through the gate and proceeded up the drive, bumping and rattling over the cracks in the asphalt. After about fifty yards she saw, ahead of her, a security fence and a barrier next to a small wooden guard post. Made it, she thought to herself, as she got out of the car, clutching her Ministry of Defence pass.

But the guard post was empty. The only sound was the cooing of wood pigeons and the occasional creaking call of a pheasant.

So much for security, she thought, wondering what to do next. She wished Liz had come with her, but Liz had felt obliged to stay in London, in case a call came from Geneva and she had to leave at a moment's notice for the next rendezvous with Bravado. 'You'll be fine,' she'd reassured Peggy. 'This should be right up your alley. Just don't let anyone try and push you around.'

Peggy hoped Liz was right. By choice she preferred deskwork, intelligence analysis and research, to dealing with people. She had always been like that. As a girl she'd been teased for her owl-like glasses and bookish ways – she used to hide in the library when it was time to play netball. But her studiousness had paid off: she'd gone to Oxford, where she'd read English and taken a good degree. After that she'd found a job in a private library in the North. At first this seemed ideal for her: there was lots of new material to catalogue and plenty of time for pursuing a research project of her own.

But after a bit it had begun to pall. The work had started to seem dry as dust, and even her own research largely pointless. Moving to London and a bigger library hadn't helped; by then the whole world of libraries and research projects had lost its appeal. When a chance remark by a friend had led to the invitation to an interview with MI6, she'd swallowed once, swallowed twice . . . and gone for it. The rest was history. She'd joined MI6 as a researcher, been temporarily seconded to MI5 to assist Liz Carlyle in an investigation, and had stayed – something she didn't regret for a moment. She liked working on cases in the UK, liked the feeling she could make a difference, and both liked and respected her boss. Liz was clear, direct, sometimes tough, yet always encouraging and supportive.

As she stood outside the guard post, considering her options, Peggy noticed a CCTV camera mounted on a metal post. Presumably someone was monitoring the camera and would turn up in a moment to find out who she was. She peered ahead down the drive, to see if she could see Brigham Hall – she had no doubt now that she'd arrived at the right place – but the drive curved sharply and all she could see was a mixed stand of oak and ash. As nothing seemed to be happening, she pushed open the guard-post door and reached for the phone.

Simultaneously a voice called out, 'Hello!' Looking up, Peggy saw a man coming round the bend of the drive towards her. He was slightly built, dressed in a Harris tweed jacket that had seen better days, with a tie sitting slightly askew on his blue shirt.

'Miss Kinsolving?' he asked, sounding breathless as he approached the booth. 'I'm Charlie Fielding.'

'There was no one here,' she said, pointing vaguely at the guard post.

'Jim's at lunch,' he said, looking apologetic. 'I'm afraid we only run to one guard. Budget cuts – you know how it is. We don't get many visitors.'

I'm not surprised, she thought, even if she *was* surprised about the apparently casual attitude to security. Though given the remoteness, the difficulty of finding the place, and the security fence and camera, perhaps it wasn't as casual as it seemed.

'Have you had lunch?' he asked.

'Yes, thanks. I got something at a service station.'

'Sounds a bit grim. But to be frank, you wouldn't have done much better here,' said Fielding with a smile. 'We're pretty much sandwiches and crisps only at midday. Leave your car. There's no spare parking space up at the house. It's not much of a walk.'

The drive ran through the woods for a couple of hundred yards until suddenly the trees stopped and the asphalt gave way to a circle of flattened gravel in front of a large Victorian house. Cars were parked all around it. The house had two Gothic gables and was built of brick that over the years had turned the colour of burned oranges. Dormer windows jutted from the heavy tiled roof, with intricate fretwork decoration. On the ground floor the wooden porch shielding the entrance was ornamented with delicately carved bargeboard trim.

'Golly,' said Peggy. 'What an unlikely building to find in this spot.'

'It was put up by a brewer who liked peace and quiet. More Betjeman than Pevsner,' said Fielding. 'Though neither would have approved of what we've done inside.'

They went through the porch into an entrance hall with a colourful tiled floor. On one wall coats hung from wooden pegs, and in the centre a dusty mahogany table stood below an elaborate crystal chandelier that dangled from a fraying cord. At one side of the hall a dark oak staircase ascended to the house's upper floors.

Fielding opened a door and they went into a large front room that looked like an old-fashioned parlour – except that against the far windows two modern desks were covered with print-outs and several computer monitors. A man in a sweater and jeans sat at one of the desks. He turned in his swivel office chair as they came in.

'Hugo,' Fielding called out cheerfully, 'meet Peggy Kinsolving.' He turned to her. 'Dr Cowdray is my deputy, for his sins.'

The other man stood up and shook hands. He looked to be about forty, with regular features and striking blue eyes. His hair was the colour of summer corn and very neatly cut, almost military-looking with its sharply trimmed edges. 'Welcome to Brigham Asylum,' he said with a smile.

Peggy laughed. 'Well, it's certainly got more character than most government buildings. Do you all live here as well?'

Fielding said, 'Not really. The team's usually based in London. They mostly drive up when they need to. If the weather gets too bad in the winter, people can stay in the upstairs bedrooms. Jim's wife does the housekeeping.' He pointed to Dr Cowdray, saying, 'Alas, Hugo and I have to be here for longer hours than most of the others. We're sharing a rented house in Downham Market. Sometimes Mrs Cowdray joins us, which improves the level of cooking dramatically,' he added with a laugh. 'Anyway, let me show you the rest of the place.'

Fielding opened another door and they walked down a passage towards the back of the house. What might formerly have been a study and a dining room had been gutted, and the space divided up by white shoulder-high partitions to form cubicles, most of which were occupied by serious-looking young men and women peering at computer screens. Fielding nodded as they passed, but few of them even looked up.

At the rear of the house they came to a very large room, visible through two massive new windows set either side of a door. This must once have been the kitchen, Peggy thought, but now instead of an Aga a bank of computers, each the size of an American-style refrigerator, stood lined up against the back wall. In the middle of the room a pony-tailed man, dressed in a programmer's uniform of blue jeans and Glastonbury T-shirt, stood at a lectern, writing in a log book. Peggy noticed that he wore paper slippers on his feet.

'That's Luke, the data manager,' Fielding explained. 'And this is the machine room – MR as we call it. Dust-free, in theory anyway.'

He gestured to Luke to come out and then introduced him to Peggy. The data manager was soft-spoken and looked very young – mid-twenties, she thought, despite a trendy attempt at growing stubble on his chin. Peggy pointed to the machine room. 'I thought computers that size went out in the nineties.'

'Most did. But these are super-computers,' Luke explained. 'Not everything can be done on a PC, regardless of what Microsoft tells you.'

Fielding laughed and added, 'Encryption in particular needs an incredible amount of calculating power.'

They said goodbye to Luke and retraced their steps to the front hall. Upstairs, on the first floor, normality returned – Fielding's office was a former bedroom that had not been refurbished. The curtains were of faded chintz and the carpet was thin with age. He waved Peggy to a chair and they sat down on either side of a large walnut desk that was covered with stacks of paper.

Fielding said, 'I know you're from the Security Service and here to discuss our own security. But that's all I know. Perhaps you could fill me in.'

His voice remained friendly, but now it had a briskness to it that belied the abstracted air he'd shown before. This might be a boffin, thought Peggy, but he had a level-headed, business-like side that explained why he was running the place.

Liz and Peggy had agreed that there was no point in obfuscating; it would merely hinder their investigation. So Peggy explained MI5's concern that information was being leaked about Clarity, though she didn't explain how they knew this.

'Who's doing it?' asked Fielding. He looked alarmed.

'It's our understanding that the infiltrator is a foreign national. Unless I've been misinformed, all of your staff are British, so we don't think it's someone actually working here.'

Fielding still looked worried. 'They say everyone's a mongrel in this country of ours. Including yours truly,' he added. 'My father's name was Feldman; he left Germany as a child on the last of the *Kindertransport*. So couldn't someone have been placed here who wasn't British, but just pretending to be?'

'You mean an illegal?'

'Yes. Weren't there lots of those during the Cold War, especially in West Germany? I read somewhere that Willie Brandt had an aide who turned out to be East German.'

'That's all true,' said Peggy, rather surprised that Fielding was so quick to take the situation on board, but also pleased that he was clearly concerned. 'But I don't think that's an issue here. Illegals can only get by with a cover story if it isn't scrutinised too closely. If you say you were born in Auchtermuchty when actually it was Kiev, enhanced vetting will eventually unmask you.'

'If that's the case, how is there a security problem here?"

'I'm hoping there isn't one. But we're worried that someone at the MOD in London has somehow accessed information about Clarity.'

'It's not possible.' Fielding was shaking his head, and he seemed relieved. 'Let me explain.'

There followed a ten-minute technical overview of the networks and systems used at Brigham Hall. To Peggy's relief, Fielding managed to speak in ordinary English for most of the time. Aided by an intensive briefing the day before from MI5's own computer expert, 'Technical Ted' Poynter, in his lower-floor den at Thames House, she found she could follow most of what Fielding was saying, though there were lengthy descriptions of 'botnets' and 'attack vectors' that made her mind reel.

'Let me just make sure I understand you,' said Peggy finally. 'Because of these security provisions you've made for communications, it's technically impossible for anyone to access your system here.'

Fielding hesitated almost imperceptibly, then said, 'I can't see how it could be done. The system here was specifically designed for Clarity. It cannot be accessed from outside – not by the Chief of the Defence Staff himself. It's deliberately sealed off.'

'But how do your people communicate with the MOD? Not to mention the outside world.'

'There's a second distinct MOD network we are part of – we sit as an extra nodule on it, a bit like a new wing on a house. As for the outside world, we have standard internet access, but we insist it takes place on completely different computers, in designated places. That way it can't affect our security system.'

'So it's impossible for anyone to get in from outside?' Peggy insisted.

'Well,' Fielding said with an uncertain laugh, 'I wouldn't say impossible. I just don't myself see how it could be done.'

'I've been told that there isn't a system in the world that can't be hacked into, and that your average fourteen-year-old hacker in his bedroom in Slough can get through most of them in no time.'

'But that's because they pose a challenge.'

'And yours doesn't?'

Fielding gave a mock-groan. 'I don't imagine there's a hacker anywhere who even knows we exist. And if one did get in somehow by accident, I doubt they'd understand anything they found.'

'But an infiltrator who was a computer scientist might?'

She could see Fielding was resistant to this, but it seemed right to persist. Especially when he sighed and said, 'All right, you win. Theoretically it might be possible. I don't know how it could be done, but that's not a good reason to assume it *can't* be done.'

Peggy admired his honesty. He went on, 'I think if it were happening, the only way to tell would be from the outside.'

'How do you do that?'

'We need to look across the entire MOD network, and see if there has been any illegitimate contact between it and our system here. I will scan the internal Brigham Hall logs for any sign, but if someone's managed to penetrate us – and as I've said it's extremely unlikely – they will almost certainly have made sure there's no evidence of it at this end.'

He was looking depressed now. Peggy tried to lighten things, saying, 'I'm not trying to ruin your day.'

He smiled. 'It's not the day I'm thinking about – it's the week, possibly the month. It will take at least that long to make a system-wide check of the MOD network. I'd better go down to London first thing in the morning.'

16

THE PHOTOGRAPHS SPOKE FOR themselves. Bech leaned forward in his chair in the office on Papiermühlerstrasse, and looked again at the glossy prints on his desk. He shook his head in exasperation. 'Do we know who the woman is?'

Gollut, the veteran Head of the Surveillance Section, looked sideways at Patrick Foehning from Analytic Research. Foehning was young – barely thirty years old. He had been recruited from a risk assessment consultancy personally by Bech, something that had put a few noses out of joint, for there had been a popular internal candidate for the post. But Foehning had caught on fast, and had won the respect of even his most hostile new colleagues.

He said, 'We have a name, but I don't think it's real. We checked with our London people and they found no one of that name who could plausibly be her.'

Bech nodded. It had to be a working alias then, a common enough piece of tradecraft. He said, 'All right, I'm glad you've brought this to my attention. I think I'd better have a word with the British about it. They've obviously got something going on which they should have told us about.'

After the two men left, Bech's PA came in. 'Henri Leplan's waiting outside, and would like to see you for a minute.'

Leplan had been night duty officer when Steinmetz had had his accident. 'Send him in. And could you also see if Mr Russell White can fit me into his busy schedule?' Bech was rarely sarcastic, but he was angry with the British. They think we're the Botswana Special Branch, he thought to himself. Well, they're about to learn we're not. If Mr White's not careful, he'll find himself PNG-ed.

When Leplan came in, his expression was grim, though he was never a cheerful-looking man. 'I thought you'd want to know about Dieter Steinmetz, sir. We've examined the wreckage of his car, and discovered paint on the passenger-side door.'

'Well, so what? He'd probably had a scrape somewhere.'

'That's what we thought at first. But Madame Steinmetz said no. He loved the car, apparently, which is why he was still running it when most people would have traded it in long ago. She said he spent every Sunday morning washing and waxing it, and that if someone had run into him, she'd never have heard the end of it.'

'So what are you telling me?'

'We think there was another car involved in his crash.'

Bech considered this for a moment. 'Are you suggesting that this was not a straightforward accident?'

'Well, sir, it's made us wonder. We couldn't see why he should have driven off the road at that particular point – unless he fell asleep. And we still have no explanation for why he was there in the first place. We're hoping we'll be able to trace the paint.'

Good luck, thought Bech, but he nodded, not wanting to discourage the younger man. It was a long shot by any standard, but it wasn't as if they had anything else to go on.

The thought that someone might have murdered one of his officers was so upsetting that by the time Russell White arrived, half an hour later, Bech, normally a calm, measured man, had worked himself into a towering rage. The sight of White, strolling into his office in a blue pinstripe suit and club tie, only inflamed him further. What was it with the English and their suits? he thought, as they shook hands. They wore them like uniforms; perhaps that was the point, he decided, they use them to intimidate their opponents. Just try that on me, he thought angrily.

Bech and Russell White had met many times before – most recently at an EU meeting on counter-terrorism a few weeks ago. Now, as White settled in his chair, he seemed relaxed, if curious about why he had been summoned. 'Well, Otto,' he said. 'What can I do for you?'

Bech ground his teeth. At any other time he would have taken the casual familiarity for friendliness, but today he was not feeling friendly.

'Let me start with these,' he said shortly, throwing the photographs down on his desk.

White said nothing as he picked up one after the other of the four enlarged black-and-white stills. Each photo showed a woman sitting on a park bench; in two of them she was talking to a man who was sitting at the other end of the bench.

As White looked at the pictures, his expression didn't change. Bech asked, 'Do you know who that is?'

'Yes. Alexander Sorsky of the Russian Trade Delegation.'

'I was referring to the woman,' snapped Bech.

White shifted uneasily in his chair, and it was clear to Bech that, for all his surface calm, the man had been caught by surprise. So the Swiss surveillance hadn't been detected

– by the British at least. At last White spoke. 'Why do you ask?'

'Because I want to know why a British woman was meeting Sorsky.'

'Presumably to discuss trade matters,' said White coolly.

'I don't think so. There is no British Trade Delegate here called Jane Falconer.'

'I'm afraid I can't confirm that, but I'll take your word for it.'

Don't dare play games with me, thought Bech, glaring at White as he struggled to keep his temper. 'I think you know perfectly well who she is. I don't, but I know that she flew in last week on a British passport, and the next day flew out – and now she's back again. As for Sorsky, you know as well as I do that he's an undercover Russian intelligence officer.'

White avoided Bech's gaze, his eyes straying to the window. Then he seemed to decide something. He looked straight at Bech. 'We had an approach.'

'From Sorsky?'

White nodded. 'Though he may just be the messenger. We don't know for sure yet.'

'So this Falconer woman flew in from London to meet him. Why didn't you meet him yourself?'

White put both hands up in a gesture of helplessness. Bech growled, 'I know, you were only following orders. Aren't we all? But what did Sorsky want?'

White sighed. 'I'm sorry, but I'm not authorised to tell you that.'

'I see.' Bech leaned back in his leather-upholstered swivel chair. He cupped his hands under his chin, looking thoughtful. Then suddenly he leaned forward, his fists clenched. 'Then I would ask you to contact London and ask for authorisation. You can tell them that we are not at all happy we weren't told in advance about this meeting – and you were obviously not planning to tell us about it afterwards either. This is Swiss territory, and we expect our friends and allies to act like friends and allies, not to go behind our backs. As it was, you could easily have derailed our own investigation.'

'Into Sorsky?'

But Bech was not going to be any more forthcoming than White, so he simply said, 'We will be happy to exchange information once we know it works two ways.'

'All right. I'll talk to London.'

'Good. And in the meantime, I expect to be kept informed of any developments. Is that clear?' He was watching White very carefully. 'I assume another meeting is planned between this woman Falconer and Sorsky.'

Reluctantly, White gave a small nod.

'When is it taking place?' asked Bech.

White was looking very uncomfortable. 'Tomorrow. I'll get authorisation to brief you, and in return I must ask you not to repeat your surveillance. It could be very dangerous, not only for Sorsky but also for my colleague from London.'

17

A NOTHER PARK, ANOTHER BENCH. Sorsky was late; Liz had been waiting for almost half an hour, feeling very exposed sitting by herself in Parc La Grange near the shores of Lake Geneva. Summer was still months away and a breeze off the lake lent a sharp edge to the evening air. The sailing boats heading for harbour before sunset were tacking fast.

She suppressed a yawn. Having got up in London at the crack of dawn to catch an early flight, she was tired now. Still, she could catch up on sleep at the weekend. Unless something happened to detain her here, she would fly back to London tomorrow. She was having lunch with her mother and Edward on Saturday, but otherwise she had the weekend clear. Martin was in Paris; when she had spoken to him earlier in the week they had arranged to meet in two weeks' time.

While they were chatting, she'd mentioned the difficulties Edward was having with his daughter.

'Do these commune people have a name for themselves?' Martin had asked. 'Or would that go against their anarchist principles?'

'I don't know, but I'll see if Edward does. Relations with

his daughter are a bit tricky at the moment. She doesn't appreciate that he's trying to be helpful.'

'Sometimes people of her age don't want to be helped. But it's very frustrating when it's your own child.' A sigh came over the line, and Liz knew he was thinking of his own daughter. 'After my divorce Danielle got very upset – but she wouldn't talk about it. Not to me anyway.'

Liz knew things had got better since Danielle had gone to the Sorbonne and stopped living with her mother. Martin tried to see her regularly, at least once a month, and recently when she'd changed her digs, she had actually asked him to help.

'I am going to give Isobel Florian at the DCRI a call,' Martin had said. 'She's taken on the job of monitoring violent groups, so she may know something about this lot. I'll let you know what she says.'

A man came through the gates of the park from Quai Gustave Ador and Liz's mind snapped into the present. It was Sorsky all right. In the distance the city's famous fountain, the *jet d'eau*, was shooting water high into the air where the lake met its inland river.

Watching Sorsky coming towards her, hunching his shoulders as he walked, she remembered how he'd looked all those years before. Funny how it came back to her, even though she'd barely known the man. He took the gravel path that would bring him past the bench she was sitting on; he was walking slowly, not looking in her direction. While she waited for him to reach her, Liz scanned the park yet again. Across a broad stretch of lawn two women were sitting chatting together, keeping a casual eye on a couple of toddlers. Near them a gardener was scarifying a patch of grass with a metal rake, its tines flashing whenever they caught the rays of the lowering sun. Late for a gardener to be working, she thought. Further back from the gates, a young couple canoodled on a picnic blanket spread under a large plane tree. It all looked innocuous enough though she knew that any or all of it could be surveillance.

Sorsky did not seem particularly concerned; he kept walking along the path towards her, but when he arrived at the bench and sat down he was breathing noisily. For a minute or so he said nothing as his breathing gradually slowed. Then, 'So we meet again, after rather less time than before.'

He looked weary as he went on, 'I'm disappointed that I haven't found out as much as I would have liked.'

'That's okay,' said Liz. She waited for him to say something else. The daylight would soon be gone, and she was afraid the park might close, so trying to push things on she said, 'When we met last week you said your Station had been asked to try and infiltrate Clarity. But then you were told this had already been done by another country. How did your people find that out?'

'I don't know.' Sorsky seemed troubled – not as nervous now as he'd been at their first meeting, but somehow weighed down, burdened. He pursed his lips for a moment. Then he shrugged and sighed deeply, as if to say, to hell with it. 'We were briefed about Clarity two months ago – one of the high-ups flew in from Moscow. But that is not how I learned about this other country.'

He paused and Liz resisted the urge to press him, since he seemed so fragile. Eventually he started to speak. 'One night about six weeks ago,' he began, 'my section all went out for a night on the town.'

It was an annual outing, he explained, and they liked to splash out. That night was no exception: Sorsky and four others dined in a fine French restaurant in the old town where they had nothing but the best – foie gras, Chateaubriand, a perfect Camembert, and finally Crêpes Suzette. There was champagne before dinner, bottles of Château Margaux during the meal, and a fine Sauternes with the dessert.

It was a real blow-out, and by the time the meal ended Sorsky was more than ready to go home, but one of them – 'I'll call him Boris,' said Sorsky, 'but that is not his real name' – wanted to go on to a club.

'What sort of a club?' asked Liz at this point.

'A nightclub. Not a good one.'

It was called the PussKat Club. You went down some steps, tipped the doorman, signed any name you liked in a book, then went into a cavernous, smoke-filled room, with disco music blaring from speakers in the ceiling.

The place was full of international businessmen, sitting in little groups on vinyl banquettes, drinking exorbitantly expensive champagne or – in the case of the Russians – bottles of Stolichnaya. From time to time, semi-clad 'hostesses' approached the tables, offering lap dances and the possibility of a whole lot more.

It wasn't Sorsky's scene at all and he wasn't surprised when the others swallowed down their vodka and peeled off home – they were all family men. Sorsky was about to go home too, but Boris refused to leave – he had his eye on one of the women. Sorsky didn't want to abandon him. Boris had had a lot to drink and was beginning to get aggressive, and Sorsky was afraid that if he stayed there by himself he'd end up either getting fleeced or beaten up by the bouncers, or both.

Fortunately, after another drink, Boris was starting to flag and when Sorsky said firmly that they should leave, he didn't argue. Once outside, it was obvious Boris could hardly stand and that Sorsky would have to take him home. Twenty Swiss francs were enough to persuade the doorman to leave his post and flag down a cab at the corner, while Sorsky propped his colleague up against the wall.

The man lived alone in a new high-rise block on the edge of the financial district and it took only a few minutes to get there, heave Boris out of the cab and into the lift, and then open the front door. Once he'd dumped him on a sofa, Sorsky was ready to go home, but Boris, slightly sobered from the ride, insisted he stay for a drink, and fetched yet another bottle of vodka from the fridge. Sorsky reluctantly joined him, thinking he'd have just one small nightcap and then get out of there. But Boris had found his second wind. Putting on some loud rock music, he suggested, to Sorsky's alarm, that they phone an agency and get some girls to come over. Sorsky was no prude, but when he found out that the girls Boris had in mind were fifteen years old, all he wanted to do was get out of the flat and go home.

To distract him from this new idea, Sorsky began talking about work, asking about other postings Boris had had and how they compared to Geneva; telling a few stories of his own about some escapades he'd had when he'd been stationed in the Ukraine in the year the Soviet Union had broken up. Then, with no particular intention but probably because it was at the front of his mind, he found himself mentioning the recent briefing they'd had on Operation Clarity from the Moscow bigwig who'd flown in. He said to Boris that it was all very well being asked to find out more about the British–American defence programme, but the chances of infiltrating it seemed virtually nil. How could they be expected to put an agent in there? Or, even more unlikely, to turn someone who was already working inside?

Pausing for a moment then, Sorsky turned and looked at Liz. 'You know the history. In the thirties the threat of fascism was enough to make Communists out of a whole generation of young Englishmen – including many who were working in the very heart of the Establishment. But now the only lever we've got is money – blackmail or just pure cash. And first you've got to find the person with the right access. The security for a programme like Clarity would be buttoned up tight.'

He'd said as much to Boris, but his colleague had shaken his head, saying that British security wasn't all it was cracked up to be. When Sorsky started to argue, Boris cut him off, and it was then that he said something startling – he said that another country had already managed to plant an agent in the British Ministry of Defence. Not in the Clarity programme itself, but close enough. Sorsky remembered the exact words – *close enough*, Boris had said.

Sorsky had been astonished by this, and had asked which country had managed this remarkable feat. But by then Boris seemed to be past talking. He was either pretending to be comatose or he really was. After waiting for a short time to see if he'd say any more, Sorsky left the flat and went home.

His story finished, he leaned back on the bench in silence. Across the lawn the two women were packing up and putting coats on the children. Liz said, 'So that's how you learned about the spy?'

Sorsky nodded. 'Unfortunately, I haven't been able to learn anything more.'

At work the next day, Boris had acted as if their drunken conversation hadn't happened; when Sorsky had made some passing remark about the infiltrator, he'd just looked blank. He clearly didn't want the subject brought up again.

'What is Boris's job?' said Liz hopefully.

'I'm not prepared to tell you any more about him,' said Sorsky. 'Except that his name is not Boris.'

Damn, thought Liz, they seemed to have reached a dead end. At least Russell White at the Geneva Station should know who Sorsky's colleagues were and perhaps there would be CCTV outside the PussKat Club which the Swiss could get hold of. It might show who Sorsky left the club with.

But he wasn't finished. 'I have managed to find out something else . . .'

Liz looked at him. 'I hope you were careful.'

He shrugged. 'Nothing to be careful about – it landed in my lap. You see,' he said, 'Boris has a secretary.' He hesitated. 'For a time, we were friendly. Not so much any more.'

A faint flush was settling over Sorsky's cheeks. You old Russian smoothie, she thought, as a capsule version of the affair ran through her head: the junior secretary, pretty but unsure of herself, falling for the veteran intelligence officer who took such an interest in her when no one else paid attention. The office chats by the proverbial water cooler, then the 'accidental' bumping into her outside work; the innocent drink, the second time for drinks (by then less innocent), the invitation back to his place; the initial infatuation of the man followed by gradual detachment; until it was over – the girl/woman left dumped, feeling bruised and used. Could that have happened to Liz herself with the younger Sorsky, if she hadn't left Bristol when she did?

Now he was looking mournful, even embarrassed. Finally he said, 'It wasn't what you're thinking. I was in love with her – but she wouldn't leave her husband. God knows why – the man is obviously a complete pig. But there it is.'

Liz didn't say anything. Sighing, he went on, 'She came to me last week and said she was worried about something Boris was doing. He'd been away – he often travels – and he was supposed to be in Paris, talking to our Station there. Yet Svetlana said she'd found a receipt for petrol on his desk. The petrol station was in Marseilles.'

'Marseilles? What was he doing there?'

'I don't know. But I do know you don't drive to Paris from Geneva via Marseilles.'

'He may have had some other reason for going there – to meet a relative or else a source. It could be any number of things.'

'Perhaps. I would have thought the same thing, but then something else happened. It was earlier this week, and this time Boris was supposed to be in Zurich.'

'Don't tell me he left another petrol receipt lying around,' said Liz.

'Actually, it was a newspaper. She found it on the floor of his car. He'd given her the keys to have it picked up by a garage. He'd had a little scrape apparently and wanted the paint retouched – Boris loves his car. She was checking to make sure he hadn't left any personal stuff inside when she found a copy of *Marseille Plus*. That's the local paper down there.'

'Couldn't it have been from his earlier trip?'

Sorsky shook his head. 'She's not stupid. The date was this Monday.'

Liz nodded. One odd occurrence she could understand – it might just be a change of plan. Two suggested there was something going on. 'Did she ask him why he was in Marseilles?'

'No, she told me instead. She didn't want him to think she was prying, and she thought I might know if there was some reason for him to be there. Then she could stop worrying. But I didn't. He hasn't said anything about it to any of the rest of us so, whatever it is, he doesn't want anyone else in the Station to know. That means it must be top-secret – orders direct from Moscow, I'd guess. My one thought is that it may be connected to this Clarity project. From what he said the other night, he seems to know more about it than the rest of us do. He said some other country had succeeded in getting close to it. How did he know? Could his visits to Marseilles have something to do with it?'

'Perhaps,' said Liz. 'But it would help if we knew Boris's real name.'

Sorsky shook his head.

'If we knew who he was, we might find out what he's doing in Marseilles. We could — '

Sorsky cut in. 'I told you, I'm not here to betray my country or my colleagues. His name doesn't matter.'

Liz looked up and saw that the two women and the children had gone. There was no sign of the gardener either. In another quarter of an hour the sun would go down and it would quickly get dark.

Seeming to take her silence for tacit agreement, Sorsky continued: 'Now he's away again. Which gives me an opportunity to find out more. Perhaps I can find out which other country is involved.'

'How?'

'His secretary has the keys to his office and to his filing cabinet. At least, she thinks she does.' He jingled something in his hand. 'I managed to borrow them without her knowing – I don't want her involved. So when we're done

97

18

As Peggy stood at the bar of the Angler's Arms, for the very first time in her young life she felt old. The pub was a stone's throw from Hoxton Square and most of its clientele looked as though they'd come straight from the galleries and studios that were sprouting up in the area like well-watered seeds. Among the jeans and designer T-shirts, her office skirt and jacket felt drab, and she envied the loudly cheerful mood of the Friday evening crowd which contrasted with her own feeling of anxiety. Charlie Fielding had asked to see her urgently and had chosen this pub because it was nowhere near the MOD. It was only two days since Peggy had seen him at Brigham Hall and, whatever he had to say now, she couldn't imagine that it was good news.

She took her glass of Diet Coke over to a small alcove at the back of the pub where there were two free stools. Plonking the glass down on the little round table and her *Evening Standard* on the other stool, she sat down to wait for Fielding.

Peggy had been busy since her trip to Norfolk. She'd spoken to a contact in the HR department at the Ministry of Defence, who was clearly under orders to help her with any request. On the vague information that Liz had got out of Sorsky, she hadn't really known what she was looking for or where to start. So, making a stab at it, she'd asked for a list of all the foreign nationals seconded to the Ministry of Defence whose work was in software or hardware development, since it seemed obvious to her that anyone trying to infiltrate Clarity would need considerable technical expertise.

Her contact had come up with a list of six people. There were five men and a woman: four including the female were from three NATO countries – Belgium, Germany and Canada – one was from Taiwan, and one was a South Korean. All of them had spent time in the United States, either at the Pentagon or at a military installation – two had been at the Air Force command centre in Colorado Springs.

So they must all have been thoroughly vetted already, and though Peggy was trying to double-check their credentials as best she could, it was a thankless task and she knew she was unlikely to find any discrepancy that countless pairs of FBI and US Defense Department eyes hadn't spotted.

'Sorry I'm late,' said Fielding, putting a pint glass down on the table. He was wearing a raincoat, though the evening was mild and dry, and he took it off, folding it carefully and tucking it under the table as he sat down. He looked around the pub. 'What a jolly bunch,' he said, but there was little joy in his voice.

'I was surprised to hear from you so soon,' said Peggy.

'I know. I expected it to take a lot longer. More fool me.'

Peggy raised her eyebrows. 'You mean you've found something?'

'I started by surveying the email traffic out of Brigham

Hall. I never expected to find anything out of the ordinary, but I found a breach almost right away. An unauthorised email.'

'Where was it going? What did it say?'

Fielding shook his head regretfully. 'I can't tell you what it said – not because I don't want to, but because it was wiped from the Brigham server. I know it went to an intranet at the MOD, which it should never have done, though it was wiped there as well – double-wiped in fact, both from the server and from the laptop where it would have been read.'

He saw Peggy's disappointment and said, 'There's a chance we can reconstruct it. But that *will* take some time.'

'Do you know who sent it?' Peggy tried to keep her voice down, though there was enough noise around to be confident no one could overhear her.

'I do. And it's almost unbelievable – to me at least.' Fielding picked up his glass of beer, and held it for a moment, then put it down again. It was obvious to Peggy he was very upset. 'The email was sent by Hugo Cowdray.'

She remembered the good-looking blond man she'd seen at Brigham Hall. 'I thought he was your deputy.'

Fielding nodded. 'He is. And my colleague and friend for the last twelve years. I would never have dreamed it . . .'

'Let's not get ahead of ourselves,' Peggy said gently. 'It may not be too bad – we haven't seen the email after all.'

'I know. But it's not necessarily what was in the email. It's the fact that it was sent at all. In the security protocol we wrote, what we stressed most was that there should be no direct contact with the MOD servers from the Brigham Hall system. It's not as if Hugo could have forgotten that – he wrote the bloody thing with me.'

'Who did he email?' asked Peggy.

'That's even odder still. A woman called Belinda Duggan – she works at the London end of our project.'

'Are they friends?'

'Not as far as I know. They know each other, of course, because we're a fairly tightly knit outfit, but there are one hundred and seventy-five of us and they've never worked together before – I checked that right away. I'm sure they'd recognise each other, and know each other's names. But that's it.'

He picked up his beer again, and this time he took a long swig. Then he said morosely, 'I just don't understand it.'

'It does seem very strange. And very stupid of him.'

'Yes, but he must have been confident he wouldn't get caught. What he didn't know is that we put a secret eye on all the machines at Brigham.'

'What's that?'

'It's a tiny application we attached to every computer – it keeps track of keyboard strokes.'

'And Cowdray didn't know it was there?'

'No.'

'But hang on, if it records keyboard strokes, then can't you see the contents of the message?'

'Not easily. We were worried about unauthorised traffic and therefore simply wanted to keep track of who was being emailed, not what the emails said. The application puts the addresses into a file for easy retrieval – that's how I found Cowdray. The messages themselves just get dumped, along with all the headers and HTML coding, into a big pot – something like an average user's Recycling Bin. To reconstruct that may be possible, but it won't be easy.'

Peggy was thinking. This was clearly serious but did she need to act on it urgently? Her forte was assembling and analysing information, not taking direct action. That was Liz's business, but she was in Switzerland and the last thing Peggy wanted to do was go running to her. So she told herself to think how Liz would have proceeded – calmly, without fuss, but decisively. Obviously the first thing to do was to ensure that this discovery stayed secret. She said to Fielding, trying to sound friendly but firm, 'Does anybody else know about what you've found out?'

He shook his head.

'Wasn't Hugo curious about why you'd come down to London so suddenly?'

Again a shake of the head. 'It happens all the time. I get called to meetings at very short notice, especially budget meetings. Hugo would have assumed I was going to one of those.'

'Didn't he ask what I was doing at Brigham Hall the other day?' This was important; if Fielding had never had any reason to distrust his deputy, he might well have mentioned that someone was coming to see him about security.

'He did, but I just said you were from the Foreign Office.'

'What about afterwards – when I'd left?'

'I said nothing to Hugo.' Fielding managed a thin smile. 'If you remember, though I pooh-poohed your concern at first, our conversation opened my eyes to the possibility of a leak.' He added bleakly, 'I never thought I'd find it on Hugo's PC.'

'Well, please keep it to yourself. I expect we'll need to speak to him next week.' She saw how worried Fielding looked. 'Don't worry – he won't know it has anything to do with you. We'll want to talk to this Duggan woman too. What can you tell me about her?'

'Very able, very sharp. There aren't many women in the field, and the ones there are have to be extra-clever – for all its pride in being cutting-edge, the computer industry's rife with sexism. But don't get the wrong idea – Belinda's not your stereotypical computer nerd.'

'What is she like then?'

'Well, for one thing, she's quite stunning – I don't think anyone in the department would contest that. Not the male members of staff anyway.'

'Hugo's good-looking himself,' Peggy mused.

'Yes, and he's got a wife and even more children than me.'

'How many's that?'

'Four for me; five for Hugo.'

Hmm, thought Peggy. Maybe he is a great husband and father, but she wasn't going to leave it at that. She said firmly, 'Tell me a bit more about Belinda. I'll ask HR for her file, but can you give me a quick rundown?'

Fielding thought for a moment. 'She's a Senior Systems Analyst, quite high up in the department; she has several teams reporting to her, working mainly on logistics. Some analysts can be a bit bogus – all flannel and no real experience of programme development. They deal in generalities their own bosses can understand, but they don't actually know the nuts and bolts. Not Belinda – she spent five years writing code.'

'She was a programmer?'

'Yes, but not on any factory line. She worked in Intelligent Search – real futuristic stuff. Like having Google search for something before you've even asked it to.'

'Neither sounds related to what you're doing at Brigham Hall.'

'They're not,' Fielding said. But he was looking troubled

again. 'The problem is, Belinda's background is rather different. She's a Cambridge graduate, took a Starred First in Pure and Applied Maths, then stayed on to do post-graduate work.'

'In computer science?'

'Well, not a million miles away from that. She worked on cryptography.'

'As in encryption techniques?'

'*De*-encryption techniques. She specialised in breaking codes.'

19

DICK COTTINGER YAWNED. IT had been a rough
night. His old schoolfriend Joey Pettleman was
getting married, and the stag night had been an hour's
drive to a club south of Las Vegas. They'd gone in a rented
minivan so nobody had to worry about driving. It had been
a lot of fun, until one of the guys had vomited all over a lap
dancer and the manager had thrown them out, but it would
have been better if it had been any other night than Friday
since Cottinger had drawn the short straw and was work-
ing the Saturday/Sunday shift.

He looked around to see if there was anyone he could
cadge an Advil from, but none of the nearby seats was occu-
pied. This station at Creech Air Force Base was 24/7, but the
weekends were kind of slow. A far cry from when they'd first
started these tests three weeks before. Then this vast commu-
nications room, the size of half a football field, had been full
of top brass. At the briefing he'd learned that he was helping
to test some new software that regulated communications
between him, a pilotless drone thousands of miles away, and
a ComSat orbiting 250 miles above the surface of the earth.

Cottinger sat in the second of three rows of desks that
swept almost the entire length of the room. Mounted on

the wall in front of him were banks of oversized television monitors, but now he stared at his own terminal screen, which was showing a map of the earth. He double-clicked his mouse and the screen shifted at once to a real-time view taken from the nose of a drone, which the console told him was flying at an altitude of 1,000 feet. The view from the drone's camera was over 120 degrees, extending from the surface of the terrain below to the thin clouds in front of and above the aircraft. When Cottinger nudged an icon on his touch screen, the focus automatically sharpened.

The trials of the drone were taking place somewhere deep inside the Gulf state of Oman – Cottinger could have supplied the precise coordinates of its location but it didn't mean a hill of beans to him. On the screen, Oman looked as parched as his throat right now – an endless expanse of gravel-coloured desert. The only vegetation visible was the occasional patch of desert grass, little more than large ink dots on his screen; in ten minutes of watching, Cottinger hadn't seen a single tree, or a human being.

He knew that one day soon he wouldn't be able to tell the drone what to do, but for now he was still in charge. Which would have suited Cottinger just fine, if his head weren't throbbing so much.

'Stay at one thousand feet,' he said into the mouthpiece of the mic strapped around his neck.

Now came the one interesting manoeuvre of the exercise – a sharp turn and a communication with a unit on the ground, three soldiers shaded from the blazing sun in a small bivouac in the packed gravel and sand of the Omani heartland. 'Alpha One, turn ninety degrees west and stay at a thousand feet.'

He watched as the drone turned sharply, its long, wide wing dipping to facilitate its turn. He started to nod, but then he realised that the drone had turned completely the wrong way and was descending rapidly. 'West,' he said sharply. 'Ninety degrees west. Not east.' He realised he was talking to the vehicle as if it were human, but after all, that was the point of the exercise. Around him in the open-plan surroundings everyone had gone quiet.

He watched as the drone ignored him and headed east towards the sea – and towards the nearest habitations. It was still descending, without losing speed; in ten minutes it would be on the ground – crashed most likely, it seemed, since it showed no signs of lowering its landing wheels.

'Alpha One, go back to a thousand feet. Climb!' he commanded, resisting the temptation to stand up himself. That wouldn't do any good. To make matters worse, Colonel Galsworthy was striding towards him, red in the face, and already shouting. 'What is it? Cottinger, what's wrong?'

But Cottinger barely heard him. He was busy on his keyboard, entering the drone's current coordinates, its airspeed, and then the calculated rate of its descent. Within seconds a small window appeared at the corner of his screen, showing a magnified area of the corner of Oman, marking one point in particular with a large red star. The projected trajectory of the drone had it landing in eight – no, now it was seven – minutes, smack in the middle of Salalah. *Population 197,169,* read a small line in the window on his screen.

Christ, thought Cottinger. At least the drone was unarmed. But even so, for it to land on some house or shack or hovel – Cottinger had only the haziest idea of how Omanis lived – would be disastrous. Three tons of polymer and a tankful of fuel – the explosion and resulting fire could kill dozens of people. Innocent people, completely unaware that their government – in fact the Sultan himself – had lent their homeland like a game board for the Americans to play war on.

He continued talking to the drone, trying to put urgency into his voice, as if an unmanned aircraft would sense that its master was saying, enough was enough, you've had your fun, now *cut it out*. He realised Galsworthy was standing next to him, and one glance showed that his commanding officer had seen the little window on his screen and taken in its ominous forecast. 'Can we shoot it down?' he asked, his voice only faintly hopeful.

'No, sir. The Omanis didn't grant additional air space. If the drone makes it to the Arabian Sea, we could send something from a carrier, but there wouldn't be much point if it's going to crash in the water anyway.'

'How much time have we got left?'

Cottinger looked at the digital clock on his terminal. 'Five minutes, maybe six.'

'Oh, God,' said Galsworthy helpfully. 'I'd better go call the Pentagon.'

He moved off at speed, and Cottinger kept talking: 'Back off, Alpha One. Turn around, Alpha One.' Then, in frustration, '*Behave,* you goddamn' drone!'

Suddenly, like a naughty child that finally listens to its parent, Alpha One lifted a wing sharply, and began to turn round. Cottinger watched sceptically and decided not to give any orders for a moment. His hopes started to rise, and soon he began to smile in relief – Alpha One was on course again, heading back at speed for the safe environs of the desert.

Three minutes later, now gradually descending, the drone sent a message to the sweltering trio of American soldiers camped out below it, a message which they successfully relayed back to Cottinger at base. And ninety seconds after that, wheels down, the drone landed smoothly on the hard-packed temporary runway created by the Army Corps of Engineers six weeks before.

In relief, Cottinger put a hand on the back of his neck and found it covered in sweat. He turned to Galsworthy and said, 'I don't understand. One minute it was out of control, then suddenly it was a pussycat again.'

20

Henri Leplan sat down at a desk in the SFI office at Geneva airport and signed the attendance book. It was his turn to do the morning shift, a job he disliked; there was rarely much excitement and you could spend the entire shift in the Immigration hall, just waiting for an alert from one of the desks when they thought they recognised a face or a dodgy passport. But too often nothing at all cropped up to relieve the boredom.

Today he particularly begrudged the time spent at the airport since his own inquiry into Steinmetz's accident had reached an interesting stage. The previous evening, just before he'd left the office, he'd had a message from a contact in the German forensic service. The paint scrape along the driver's side of Steinmetz's car had matched a sample in their paint library. It had turned out to be a special hand-blended colour called Black Onyx. Most people would think it was just a shiny black paint, his contact had added, but in fact it contained finely ground gemstone, which made it particularly translucent. It was only available on top-of-the-range models, Audis, BMWs and Mercedes. What interested Leplan particularly was the information that any car with this paint would have had to be ordered specially. If this had been done in Switzerland, it shouldn't be difficult to trace the person who had ordered it. Leplan was becoming more and more convinced that there was something sinister about Steinmetz's accident and he couldn't wait to get on with the next stage of his researches.

He made himself a cup of coffee and sat down at the desk, pulling towards him the log of the night shift. The only thing of interest was the notification at 23.15 the previous evening of an unscheduled private plane coming in from Moscow, due to land at 10.20 this morning. Some bigwig coming for something or other, he thought. Can't be a delegation, or we would have been notified sooner. He looked at his watch: 8.30. He picked up the phone and dialled traffic control. 'Any lowdown on this Moscow arrival?' he asked.

'It's an ambulance flight. Notified last night. Expected to arrive at 10.12. We'll be landing them at the charter terminal. Crew of four, plus doctor and two nurses. Picking up and leaving straight away. Don't think anyone's intending to go landside but Immigration will know.'

Leplan finished his coffee and strolled over to the Immigration hall, weaving his way through a hubbub of excited children. All was quiet in in the office behind the desks.

'It's a diplomatic flight,' said the duty immigration officer. 'One of their guys has had an accident and is being repatriated for urgent medical attention. They didn't give us a name and we have no powers to ask, if that's what you're wondering. It's authorised by their Ambassador. A stretcher case, they said, so we've agreed the ambulance can drive airside to load the stretcher on. No one's landing and they're going straight off.'

'God help them, whoever they are,' said Leplan. 'They'd get much better medical attention here. Maybe it's a fatality. I think I'll go over and watch proceedings. Might have a word with the ambulance crew. I assume they're locals?'

The immigration officer nodded. 'See you there,' he said.

At quarter to ten Leplan and the immigration officer watched as an ambulance was cleared through the barrier of the charter terminal. A dark-suited man got down from the front passenger seat and showed a document to the guard, and the ambulance was waved in. Leplan didn't recognise him from where he stood, but he knew the camera at the guard post would have taken a good shot of his face. Exactly on time a small plane landed and parked. The ambulance drove up to the door, and a stretcher on which was strapped an inert figure wrapped in a blanket was quickly loaded on board by the ambulance attendants, supervised by the dark-suited man. Within fifteen minutes the plane was taxiing for take-off.

Hmm. That was a pretty smooth operation, thought Leplan as he waved the ambulance to a halt by the barrier. I wonder what it was all about.

It was not until Liz sat down in the café in the Place du Bourg-de-Four that it struck her how strange it was that Sorsky had chosen this as a meeting place. Until now their meetings had taken place on park benches with a clear view of the surroundings and she had received the impression that he had taken extensive precautions against surveillance. But this café was in a crowded little square, where it would be impossible to spot surveillance. She wondered why he had changed his operating methods. Did he have some reason to think there was no longer a risk?

She selected a table inside, by the wall at the back, so she would at least see everyone who came in. But the disadvantage was that she could see nothing of what was going on outside. The café was almost empty; it was too late for breakfast, too early for lunch. She ordered coffee, unfolded her newspaper and kept her eye on the door.

Sorsky was late again. She glanced at her watch for the fourth time. It was 11.45, three-quarters of an hour past the time he'd given her. How long should she wait? No longer than an hour, she decided.

At five to twelve she rang Russell White.

'It's no show,' she said. He would recognise her number.

'No show?'

'Yes. Have you heard anything?'

'Nothing.'

'OK. I'm coming back.'

'All right. See you shortly.'

21

L IZ DROPPED HER BAG on the floor, closed the door and leaned back against it. Home, she thought. Through the open door of the sitting room she could see the sun shining in through the sash windows on to the carpet. She'd bought this place a couple of years ago with the proceeds of the sale of her basement flat in the same large Victorian house and a mortgage she could only just afford. She'd loved the basement flat too when she'd bought it – the first property she had ever owned – though it was rather shabby and dark, and for several years she'd had neither the time nor the money to improve it. But when she'd returned from a posting to Northern Ireland, this ground-floor flat had been on the market. She'd viewed it first out of curiosity, with no idea that she might be able to afford it, but the estate agent had surprised her with his estimate of what she might get for the basement, and her mother, who had never liked the basement flat, had encouraged her to go for it, and suddenly to her great surprise she had found herself the owner.

She still had too little time to look after the flat properly, and she hadn't yet got round to employing a cleaner to replace her old one, who had retired to the South Coast;

after several days away the dust lay in a thin layer on the surfaces and last weekend's newspapers were still in the heap on the floor where she'd left them. But it was Saturday and she'd soon have the place tidied up.

As she dusted and vacuumed, she smiled at the contrast between her humdrum cleaning and what she'd been doing twenty-four hours earlier. After waiting fruitlessly for an hour in the little café in the Place du Bourg-de-Four, she had spent the afternoon at the Embassy with Russell White. As soon as he'd learned that Sorsky hadn't shown up, he'd put a surveillance team on to the Russian Trade Offices and another man at the Russian Embassy to try and get a sighting of Sorsky. Each hour they phoned in to report; each hour they repeated that there was no sign of the man. Then White got one of his colleagues, who had grown up in Normandy and spoke French with a regional accent, to ring the Russian Trade Delegation and ask for Sorsky. The receptionist had said that he wasn't in the office, and no, she didn't know when he would next be there.

Liz had cancelled her flight reservation and rung her mother to explain she wouldn't be home in time for lunch the next day. She'd spent a sleepless night in the hotel, kept awake by the uncertainty of the situation. Could Sorsky have had a change of heart? It was always a possibility, especially if he had found out nothing further and felt that he'd already done all he could to alert the West to the threat to Clarity.

Then again – and this was what really worried Liz – he might have been caught going through his colleague's files. But caught by whom? After all, he'd said the man was away from Geneva. Perhaps the secretary had found him rifling the filing cabinets, but would she really have turned her former lover in – since it was she who had alerted him in the first place to his colleague's odd behaviour?

It was a mystery, and no clearer to Liz when the morning came. Russell White had arranged at short notice to play tennis with a friend (Terry Castle, his usual partner was on holiday), but when he rang Liz at 10.30 it was only to say there was no sign of Sorsky at the club. 'I'll go again tomorrow, just in case,' he'd said. 'Though it's always been a weekday when we've met before. Did you want to stay and wait for that?'

Liz decided. 'No. It doesn't sound likely that he'll show up on a Sunday. I think the best thing is for me to return to London. I'll come back right away if you hear from him.'

Now, the cleaning finished to her satisfaction, Liz took a leisurely hot bath while Mozart played on Radio 3 in the sitting room. After she'd dressed she took an inventory of the refrigerator: one-week-old carton of milk, two eggs past their best-before date, a half-full bottle of Australian Chardonnay that she knew had been opened ten days ago, and a head of Iceberg lettuce, brown and wilted. Even by her standards this was grim, so she went to the corner shop on Highgate Road to stock up, and when she got back the message light on the phone was blinking. It was her mother, still up in town. Liz rang back straight away.

'Hello, dear,' said Susan. 'So you got home at last.'

'I'm so sorry about lunch, Mum. I thought you'd have gone back to Bowerbridge by now.'

'Actually, I'm just about to leave. Edward's staying up – he's arranged to see Cathy and Teddy tomorrow in Brighton. I can't say he's looking forward to it – she was perfectly awful to him on the phone when he suggested it. But he's worried about these French friends of hers. When

Edward talked to little Teddy, he said one of them – he called him René – wasn't very nice.'

'To Teddy?'

'No, to Cathy. Teddy said they were arguing.'

'Oh, dear. Is Edward there now? Let me have a word with him.'

While her mother went to get Edward, Liz thought about this French visitor. Could they really be threatening Cathy, or had Teddy just imagined things?

'Hello, Liz. Glad you're back. Everything all right?'

'Everything's fine with me. But I gather it's not so fine with Cathy.'

'No. I'm going down to see her tomorrow. I'm rather dreading it, to tell you the truth.'

'Would you like some company?'

'Do you mean you'd like to come? You must have better things to do on a Sunday, especially when you've been away.' But his voice had lifted.

'I don't actually. I'd love to come, if you'd like me to?'

'Well, if you're absolutely sure, I certainly won't say no.'

'I'm absolutely sure,' said Liz, hearing the relief in Edward's voice.

She rang Martin next. There was no answer, so she left a brief message on his answering machine, letting him know she was back, then made herself a supper of pasta sprinkled with Parmesan, and went to bed. As she snuggled down in her large comfortable bed, she felt she could sleep for ever. She was halfway there when the phone rang on the bedside table.

'Please say I didn't wake you up.' It was Martin.

She said, 'Even if you had it's nice to hear your voice. What have you been up to?'

'I took Danielle to dinner. You know students; they seem to live on dry crusts and a lettuce leaf. So I took her to La Rouge Chemise.'

'Oh, no,' said Liz, with a groan. Martin had taken Liz there on her birthday – it had been a *grande bouffe* with six courses, none of them small.

'Danielle says she won't have to eat again for a week. But how did your trip go?'

'It had some interesting developments,' she said.

'Well, you'd better come over and tell me about them.'

'I will.'

'You sound tired, Liz. I hope you're going to take it easy tomorrow.'

'Actually, I'm going with Edward to see his daughter in Brighton.'

'Okay. I haven't forgotten about that, by the way. I've put a call in and am waiting to hear.'

'Thank you,' said Liz, realising this meant he had rung Isobel Florian, his counterpart in the DCRI. She tried but failed to suppress a yawn.

'I heard that,' said Martin.

'Sorry.'

He laughed gently. 'You can't fool me. Even if I'm not there to see if you can keep your eyes open. Those beautiful big eyes.'

'Flatterer.'

'I'm French, so what do you expect? But now it's time you closed them.'

22

I N THEORY THEY HAD a choice of cars, but though Liz's Audi saloon had served her well, she had to admit that in old age the car had slowed down: its engine coughed when she drove at more than 70 miles per hour, the brakes squeaked like mice if she applied them hard, and all in all the knacker's yard beckoned. So when Edward arrived at her flat in a sparkling new Golf with leather seats, Liz climbed in without a backward glance at the Audi. When she remarked on the splendour of the new car, Edward laughed and said, 'The one good thing about being as old as I am is that if you buy a sporty little car like this, no one can accuse you of having a mid-life crisis.'

Cathy Treglown lived a mile along the coast from Brighton Pier, in the ground-floor flat of a Victorian house that had seen better days. When she answered the door, Liz felt Cathy could use some refurbishment too. Edward had said she was only in her late twenties, but her skin was red and coarsened, her figure was shapeless and her eyes looked tired. All that, along with her unkempt hair and the stained T-shirt and ragged jeans she wore, made her look middle-aged.

She seemed resigned rather than happy to see her father, and though she was civil to Liz, she wasn't friendly. Only the arrival of Teddy lightened the atmosphere. He rushed into the room, and jumped straight into Edward's arms, shouting, 'Grandpa! You're here.'

The sitting room ran the length of the house and had been freshly painted.

'What a lovely room,' said Liz.

'The landlord redecorated after the previous family moved out. It meant he could put the rent up,' Cathy said sourly.

An awkward silence followed which Edward finally broke. 'I'll go and make some coffee. Come on, Teddy. You can show me where things are.'

When he had left the room, Cathy said nothing so to break the silence Liz asked, 'Did you like living in France?'

'I stayed ten years so I must have.'

'But you've come back now.'

Cathy shrugged. 'I'm starting to think it might have been a mistake. Anyway, let's not talk about me. Edward says you live in London. What do you do there?'

'I'm a civil servant,' Liz said, expecting the usual glazed look of disinterest.

But Cathy said, 'Doing what exactly?'

'I work in Human Resources.' This was usually enough to stop further questions.

'Do you mind working for the government?'

'No. In my more idealistic moments, I like to think I'm working for the people.'

'As if.' Cathy seemed about to launch into a lengthy tirade about Liz's employer, when Edward appeared with a tray. As he passed round the mugs he said, 'Teddy's gone out into the garden with his football.'

'You spoil him, Dad,' said Cathy. 'That bike you gave him must have cost a fortune.' But though the words were ungracious, for the first time her voice softened, and it was suddenly obvious to Liz how much she loved her little boy.

Edward said, 'It's the least I can do. The whole point of grandparents is spoiling their grandchildren.' He smiled. 'It's the parents who have to do the hard bit – the grandparents can shower the children with presents and love, then you lot have to make them eat their supper and go to bed at the right time.'

'At least you admit I've got the sharp end,' said Cathy, her sour mood returning. There was a gracelessness about her which seemed almost artificial – as if she were deliberately suppressing a nicer character behind the sulky façade.

Fearing how his daughter must seem to Liz, Edward was looking embarrassed. He said with a forced cheerfulness, 'So, any news on the house?'

'It's on hold. I told you that, Dad.'

He nodded. 'Well, just tell me if I can help in any way.' He smiled, and Liz found herself feeling immensely sorry for him. The strong, confident man she knew was faltering here, walking on eggshells because he was all too aware that his daughter held all the cards – one argument too many and she'd be back in France, at the mercy of her anarchist friends, and taking Teddy with her.

Liz, thinking it would be best to leave them alone for a bit, said, 'I'm going to join Teddy in the garden – I rather fancy a game of football. Is that OK?'

'Be my guest,' Cathy replied.

Liz went into the hall and, on the way to the garden, stopped in the loo. Stuck to the inside of the door was a large poster of Che Guevara, the classic one with fist clenched and a vivid red beret perched jauntily on the side of his head. Was it a joke? Surely no one of Cathy's age in their right mind could still think of the man as a hero. But below the poster was a framed quotation from Ibsen:

> The State is the curse of the individual ... The State must go! That will be a revolution which will find me on its side. Undermine the idea of the State, set up in its place spontaneous action ... and you will start the elements of a liberty which will be something worth possessing.

As Liz came out and turned towards the door to the garden, she saw a large appointments diary on the hall table beside the telephone. It seemed oddly out of place in this ramshackle flat – a symbol of the middle-class life Cathy had so vehemently rejected.

Liz looked at the diary's open pages, which covered the rest of the month. There were a few entries: a doctor's appointment for Teddy the following week, a parents' day, a dentist's appointment the week after, and most interestingly a brief entry for the previous week: *René L. & Antoine 2.30.*

Was this the René who'd been round to the flat before – the man Teddy said had been nasty? Probably. But who was Antoine? René's enforcer? Liz hoped not, but she made a mental note to ring Martin as soon as she got home.

23

'GOOD MORNING, ELIZABETH,' SAID a familiar voice on the phone. 'You're an early bird today.'

Liz closed her eyes and suppressed a groan. Geoffrey Fane was the last person she wanted to hear from just now. It was only half-past seven and she'd come in early to catch up with all the paperwork that had accumulated while she'd been in Switzerland. How on earth did Fane know she was in her office? It was creepy.

She looked longingly at the cup of coffee and the croissant she'd bought as she left the Underground, and hoped she could get rid of him quickly. 'They say the early bird catches the worm, Geoffrey. What can I do for you?'

'I'm afraid I've got some bad news. The Swiss say a charter plane from Moscow landed in Geneva on Saturday, return flight. It took off two hours later with one passenger – on a stretcher, apparently unconscious. The Russians claimed he was ill. But the Swiss are pretty sure it was Alexander Sorsky.'

'Oh, God. No wonder he didn't turn up at the café. He was perfectly OK when I saw him on Thursday.'

'I'm sure he was. I'm afraid that somehow the Russians must have got on to him.'

Liz thought about her last meeting with Sorsky and her unease about what he was proposing to do. Could he have been spotted going through his colleague's files? It didn't seem likely – he'd been very confident there was no chance of his being caught. Even if he had been, he should have been able to come up with some reasonable explanation. But there was one other way he could have been rumbled. 'Was there any surveillance on my last meeting with him in the park?'

'Why do you ask?' Fane said slowly.

He was hedging; he always hated direct questions. 'I want to know if there was surveillance while I was waiting for Sorsky in the park on Thursday. Russell White promised me there wouldn't be.'

'Well, if he gave you his word, then there wasn't. Not from us.'

'That's easy to say, but he told me the very first time I met Petrov that there wouldn't be any surveillance and there was. So how do I know he was telling the truth this time?'

'You don't, Elizabeth. But you have *my* word for it.'

As if that meant anything, she thought. 'Could it have been someone else then? I don't mean the Russians – if they had been watching Sorsky, they would never have allowed him to come to the meeting on Thursday.'

Fane sighed. 'It was the Swiss. Their DG, a man called Bech – competent fellow normally – admitted as much to White. They were there all right, though he said they are certain no one else was watching. Meaning, the Russians weren't following Sorsky – they must have found out some other way.'

'I'm glad you're so sure the Swiss would have noticed if the Russians were there.'

'Well. Perhaps. One can get overconfident on one's own turf. It wouldn't be the first time it's happened – even here.'

Liz, ignoring this barb, went on, 'I need to know who Sorsky's colleagues are. I've asked Russell White to find out.'

'What's that got to do with his disappearance?'

But Liz wasn't in the mood to continue the conversation. Fane could wait for her report on her meeting with the Russian. 'Just believe me, it's important.'

'Well, the Station will have an ORBAT of the Russian Residency in Geneva but I don't know how detailed it will be. Or whether it will show who works with whom'.

'Then please ask Russell to get the Swiss to help find out. If Bech and his crew screwed up their surveillance, it's the least they can do.' And she put the phone down.

At 8.30 Peggy Kinsolving stuck her head round the door. 'What's up?' she asked, seeing the look on Liz's face.

'The Russians have snatched Bravado – took him out on a stretcher. He'll be somewhere awful by now.'

Peggy sat down. 'What happened? It sounds like something out of the Cold War. Do you remember how Philby told the Russians about that man in Istanbul who wanted to defect? What was his name?'

'Volkov.'

'Yes, him. He was taken out all wrapped in bandages by a Russian plane. No one ever saw him again.' Peggy was a keen student of Cold War cases. 'Does that sort of thing still go on?'

'Of course it does. Have you forgotten Alexander Litvinenko? Look what they did to him – and that was here in the heart of London. The Russian services have never tolerated traitors. They still don't.'

'Poor Bravado.'

Liz propped her elbows on the desk and leaned her chin on her hands, looking out of the window. She felt sick. This was the second time in her career she had lost a source. After the young Muslim codenamed Marzipan had died a few years ago, she had hoped it would never happen again. That hadn't been her fault – he'd been betrayed by a mole in the Service. But now she couldn't help wondering whether this time she was somehow to blame. Had she been wrong to encourage Sorsky? Had she done enough to warn him how dangerous his self-appointed mission was? Should she have insisted he wait before trying to find out more? But she knew he wouldn't have listened to her. After all, he knew more about the risks he was taking than she did.

She felt Peggy's eyes on her, and told herself to snap out of it. So she looked at her younger colleague and said, 'Without Bravado we're on our own. We've got to find this mole in the MOD, if he exists.'

'That's what I came to see you about,' said Peggy. 'I think we've made some progress.'

'Really?' Liz's tone lightened. 'Tell me about it.'

She listened intently as Peggy told her about the unauthorised email Cowdray had sent to a female colleague.

'Is she one of the foreigners?'

'No. It's an English woman. She's been in the MOD for fifteen years.'

'So what do you think's going on?'

'It could be nothing sinister, but according to Fielding even sending the thing has broken some sort of firewall.'

'We'll need to talk to them both.'

Peggy gave a small smile. 'I've set it up. Cowdray's on his way down to London. He's been told there's some sort of a mistake in the budget calculations for the programme he's working on – he thinks he's coming down for a three o'clock meeting with Fielding and the auditor. The woman's name is Duggan. She's expecting to talk to Pensions at two o'clock. I thought it would be best if you saw her first.'

'I don't think it will be me seeing either of them. I need to get back to Geneva, to find out what's gone on and put a rocket behind the Swiss. You'll have to deal with them.'

'Me?' said Peggy, her cheeks going red. 'I can't do it. They'll never tell me anything.'

'Come on, Peggy. Of course they will. You've got all the background and to them you'll be the voice of authority. Don't forget, they've done something wrong. They'll be scared stiff of you.'

There was a pause, while Peggy's expression changed from uncertain to determined. 'Oh, all right,' she said, sitting up straighter. 'I suppose I'll have to do it.'

'Yes, and you'll do it splendidly.'

'I hope so.'

'I've got another lead as well.' Liz told Peggy about the mysterious trips to Marseilles which Sorsky's colleague had been taking.

'Has Geoffrey Fane got anyone in Marseilles?' Peggy asked.

'I doubt it. And I'm not sure what we'd be looking for there anyway. I think the first thing is to identify this colleague and then get the French to see if they can find out what he's been doing there. That's why I've got to go back to Geneva – to get things going before the trail goes cold.'

24

THE MOD HR DEPARTMENT had lent Peggy a room to use for the interview with Belinda Duggan. To call it a room flattered it; it wasn't much more than a cubicle, windowless, lit by a strip light and furnished with two chairs and a small table. 'But this interview is sensitive,' Peggy had said on seeing the thin partition walls. 'We'll be overheard in here.'

'We're quite used to secrets in this department, Miss Kingly,' the severe middle-aged lady who presided over the HR Department said. 'There will be no one within eaves-dropping range. I'll send Miss Duggan in when she arrives.' And with that she'd shut the door firmly on Peggy, leaving her feeling as small as the cubicle.

Peggy sat down in the chair facing the door. She was going to be almost nose to nose with Belinda Duggan when she sat in the other chair, and that made Peggy even more nervous than she was already. How was she going to get this woman to tell her anything? She had nothing to go on but the trace of the email that Charlie Fielding had found. 'The secret is to get them to start talking,' had been Liz's advice. 'Then you've got something to build on, and there's a good chance that what you want to know will emerge.'

So Peggy pushed her glasses higher on her nose, sat up straight in her char and waited.

'Jane Falconer?'

A tall, striking blonde stood in the doorway. Peggy rose, but stayed on her side of the table, waving the visitor to the other chair.

'I'm not Jane Falconer. She's had to go away on urgent business. I'm Patricia Kingly.'

Duggan sat down at the table 'Oh,' she said, without interest, and crossed her leg casually. 'They said this was something about my pension.'

'Ah, I'm afraid that was not entirely accurate. In fact it's a security interview. We don't like people to be unnecessarily alarmed, which is why you were told it was about pensions. I'm from the Security Service. As I'm sure you know, from time to time we interview people with access to particularly sensitive material.'

'What, you mean this is a vetting review?' asked Duggan. There was a hint of caution in her voice.

'Not exactly. Your vetting doesn't come up for review until next year. But it is connected. I wanted to ask you a few questions about your current security.'

'My security? I see,' she said in a bored voice. 'At least it's not Health and Safety.' Her face took on an expression of amusement, mixed with a trace of contempt.

What an arrogant, patronising woman, thought Peggy. She doesn't give a damn what I think.

Duggan was wearing a short black wrapover skirt, which had opened as she sat down to show a good stretch of thigh. She was forty-five and the skirt would have been daring on a woman half her age. Peggy herself was twenty years younger and would have hesitated before buying such a garment. If she had bought it, she would never have dreamed of wearing it to the office – perhaps to a party, and not just any party. But Belinda Duggan looked as though she did exactly as she pleased, with no hesitation or doubts.

'I'd like to start with the job you're doing now,' said Peggy, with a new note of authority in her voice. 'Just tell me what you are currently working on. Don't worry. I am cleared for codeword material.'

Belinda Duggan plunged into an elaborate description of her current job, which involved overseeing half a dozen teams of programmers, working on software projects. Most of the applications they were developing had to do with logistics – moving men and equipment and arms as efficiently as possible – and as far as Peggy could tell none involved any kind of encryption. When Duggan came to a natural pause, Peggy broke in.

'Thank you. You know, I was interested to see on looking at your CV – it's very impressive, by the way – that your work now doesn't seem related to your earlier interests. Your D. Phil. thesis, for example, was about decryption.'

'Interests change, Ms Kingly,' said Duggan. 'At least, mine did.'

'So you don't miss encryption, decryption, that sort of thing?'

'Not one bit. And it's moved on. Everything mathematical does, you know. Just as fast as all sciences. I couldn't go back into it if I wanted to.'

Peggy enquired about the management side of her job. Duggan explained that as a Project Director, she managed a team of project leaders.

'Do you keep in contact with the other Project Directors in the Department?' asked Peggy.

'Oh. There are a lot of firewalls,' she said. 'Codeword work, you know.'

Peggy was beginning to get fed up with Ms Duggan. She was just too breezy and pleased with herself. It was time to stop beating about the bush.

'Do you meet Charlie Fielding and his team?'

Duggan looked at her and paused for thought. This had gone home but Peggy didn't know why. 'Charlie's away at the moment – he's been seconded to a project outside London. It's very sensitive.'

'Do you know much about that project?'

Duggan shook her head. The trace of an amused smile was back on her lips. 'Very hush-hush. That's all I know. Is that a test question, Ms Kingly?'

'Yes, it is,' said Peggy firmly. This woman had a veneer as hard as varnish – there was only one chance to get through it, and she was going to take it. She'd go straight in and shock her. So she picked up a file from the table, made a show of flicking through it, tossed it down and asked, 'When was the last time you saw Hugo Cowdray?'

Duggan started, but quickly reasserted control. You had to hand it to her, thought Peggy. 'Hugo Cowdray?' Duggan asked, with bewilderment in her tone of voice. 'What about him? What's he got to do with security?'

'I asked, when was the last time you saw him?'

Duggan shrugged. 'I don't know. Weeks ago – he hasn't been in the office lately. Why?'

'Do you know where he's been?'

'I assume he's with Charlie. There's a whole team gone with him. Somewhere in Norfolk, I think they are. It's an open secret – there's a safe house up there. I don't know where it is. You'll have to use your own access to find that out.'

'Have you seen Hugo since he went there?'

'I've seen Charlie – he's often down for meetings with the finance chaps. But not Hugo.'

'And you haven't heard from him?'

Duggan began to look incredulous. 'What are you implying? Why this obsession with Hugo? He's a colleague but a distant one – we've never worked together. I know his name; presumably he knows mine. But that's the end of it.'

'Why did he send you an email then?'

'What email? When is he supposed to have sent that?'

'Recently.' Peggy said nothing more.

'I haven't had an email from him. Though the filters here are so ferocious that half the time you'd never know who has sent what.' She gave a little laugh.

'You're quite sure about that?'

'Yes. If you are suggesting otherwise, then I'd like to see this email.'

She knows quite well I can't show it to her, thought Peggy. But the way Duggan had moved so quickly on to the defensive made Peggy feel certain that she had been the recipient of Hugo Cowdray's message.

Duggan was shifting in her seat as she said, 'Is there anything else you want to discuss, Miss Kingly? I'll have to leave in a second as I have a briefing for Directors. Three-line whip for me, I'm afraid – even the Security Service has to make way.'

Peggy resisted the urge to say, 'No, we don't. So just stay where you are, Ms Duggan.' Instead she replied, 'That's all, Ms Duggan. For now.'

25

Bern, a quietly pretty city, determined not to
draw attention to itself, was a fitting home for the
country's Security Service. In the nondescript, modern
building, Doctor Otto Bech's office was no larger than her
own, but through the window Liz had a view that could
not be matched anywhere in Thames House. In a park, a
line of poplars bent like bows in the breeze, and further off,
across the wide river valley, a range of snow-capped moun-
tains glittered in the morning sun.

Otto Bech's appearance matched his low-key office.
With his tweed jacket and flannels, ruffled grey hair and
thick spectacles, he could have been an academic. Indeed
before he joined the police he had spent several years at
Lausanne University, his doctorate awarded for a disserta-
tion on the historical development of international finan-
cial protocols. Russell White had asked for Bech's help in
identifying the person Sorsky had referred to as 'a colleague'
– the man who had told him of the third-country penetra-
tion of the British Ministry of Defence. The previous day
Bech had responded, saying the Swiss had some informa-
tion which might be useful. Liz had come in person to
hear what it was, with White accompanying her.

In Bech's office a dour-looking youngish man, standing by a small conference table, was introduced as Henri Leplan. Bech explained that Leplan had been at the airport when the stretchered Russian had been flown out of Geneva. He motioned for the younger man to continue.

'We have made some progress,' Leplan announced as he pushed across the table a pile of photographic stills for Liz and White to look at. The top one showed a small private jet parked near a terminal building. It had Russian markings. In the second, the door of the plane was open and a short ladder had been dropped down. In the third an ambulance had drawn up beside the plane. As Liz and Russell White leafed through the sheaf of photographs the drama unfolded: two attendants were carrying a stretcher up the steps into the plane; then they had disappeared. The only other figure in the photo was a man in a dark suit, medium height and broad-shouldered, watching from the tarmac, his back to the camera. In the final photograph he had turned towards the terminal and his face was clearly visible.

Seen full on, the man had dark short hair, fleshy, slab-like cheeks covered with a five o'clock shadow, and a wide jutting chin. His eyes were so deep-set that in the photograph they looked black.

Leplan continued: 'The man in the suit is Anatole Kubiak. Officially he's a Commercial Counsellor in the Russian Trade Delegation in Geneva.'

White said, 'But he's actually the senior SVR officer here – Head of Security for the whole Russian mission.'

Bech smiled grimly. 'An unpleasant character, we gather.'

'Then he would have had the authority to send Sorsky back to Moscow,' said Liz.

Bech nodded. 'Kubiak must have given Moscow enough evidence to justify forcibly repatriating the man, though what happens to Sorsky now will be out of Kubiak's hands. He'll probably be recalled to give evidence if there's a trial, but I expect the outcome is already fixed. Even in these "democratic days", the Russian Special Services don't tolerate traitors.'

Liz stifled a shudder. She was wondering how Sorsky had been detected. She felt confident it had not been through any slip on her part. She'd followed his instructions to the letter. But what about Russell White's team – or the Swiss themselves? She glanced at White, who looked on edge, probably because he was having similar thoughts. Dr Bech's face betrayed no emotion at all.

She said, 'What I really need to know is who Sorsky worked closely with at the Russian Residency, so we can identify the colleague he called Boris.'

'Russell White has explained that, and I think we can help you,' said Bech, and nodded at Le Plan who leaned forward to put more photographs on the table. These were hazier than the first lot, having been taken off a CCTV camera – the date and time were digitally marked in a lower corner of each photograph.

The pictures showed a small stretch of a street at night-time, etched by a contrasting mix of shadows and pale light from the street lamps. The lens was focused on a building across the street, which had an awning in front that was adorned by white letters in italic script. Peering at the photograph, Liz could just make out the words *PussKat Club*. The place where Sorsky and his colleagues had gone after their celebration dinner.

'Since we didn't know exactly which night we were looking for, it took us some time,' Leplan explained. 'But eventually we found this.'

He picked up one of the photographs and handed it to Liz. Russell White looked over her shoulder. It showed two men coming out of the club, with a uniformed doorman just behind them. One of the men was Sorsky – Liz recognised the receding hairline, and his sharp features. He was supporting the other man, who was slightly shorter, but much broader. His face was half in shadow.

'Who is it?' asked Liz, though she thought she knew.

'That's Kubiak,' Leplan replied. 'The man at the airport. Head of Security.'

Liz's head was already spinning with the implications. 'You mean, he told Sorsky of the infiltration plot and then shipped him back to Moscow? Perhaps Sorsky's contact with me wasn't blown. Maybe Kubiak just realised that, having given the information to Sorsky, he had put himself at risk. So he set him up.'

'That's possible,' said Russell White, looking relieved. Turning to Leplan, he asked, 'Do you know where Kubiak is now?'

Bech replied. 'He's in the Trade Delegation. That's where his office is, the Security Department must be housed there. He went in at nine this morning and he's still there. We've had a static observation post on the office and on Kubiak's flat. He lives in the business district of Geneva. You see, we have our own interest in Kubiak. One of our officers was killed last month in an accident some distance from Geneva. We have reason to believe that Kubiak was involved. Until we can prove it, we want to know where he is.' He sighed. 'Though even if we can prove it, we won't be able to arrest him – he's got diplomatic immunity. But at least we'll be able to expel him. Until then I'm not going to let him out of our sight.'

'Good,' said Liz. 'Sorsky said that Boris or rather Kubiak has been making regular trips to Marseilles. Could you liaise with the French if he crosses the border? It would be very helpful to have him followed there.'

'Yes, we'll certainly do that. I don't want this fellow to slip out of the back door. If he was involved in the death of Steinmetz, I want to pin it on him.'

Liz turned to Russell White. 'Would you ask your Service for a Look Up on Kubiak, and I'll do the same with mine? We need to know if he's crossed our radar anywhere else.'

White nodded. 'Will do.'

26

OFFICERS SILLON AND MERGAS had been on the European Cross Border surveillance course so they were the obvious choices to follow the target thought to be travelling into France from Switzerland. The driver, they had been told, was a Russian intelligence officer, suspected of involvement in a fatal accident in Switzerland. If he did come into France, it was thought he'd be heading for Marseilles.

They had just pulled into a layby on the A41 in their dirty Peugeot when the call came on the radio. 'Target has just reached the border. He's alone and driving the car we notified, dark Mercedes 500 with Swiss diplomatic plates. He'll be with you in four minutes. Good luck.'

Mergas adjusted the radio as Sillon turned on the ignition. 'That was a close one,' said Mergas. 'We nearly missed him. Pity they didn't give us a bit more notice.'

'And a pity we haven't got any back-up,' replied Sillon. 'But it should be pretty straightforward till we get to Marseilles – if that's where he's going.' He sat, tapping his fingers on the wheel, checking his side mirror for the target car. He was always happiest when the chase was on; it was the waiting he hated.

Suddenly he stiffened. 'Here we go,' he said, and the Peugeot started to move forward. The Mercedes flashed by, going at speed; by the time Sillon had manoeuvred the Peugeot on to the motorway the big dark saloon was receding fast ahead of them. Sillon accelerated, cursing under his breath. They should have had at least two cars to do this job properly, more ideally – but there was a big job on in Marseilles, monitoring a bunch of suspected North African terrorists who'd arrived at the weekend.

Sillon wondered why this Russian was going to Marseilles. No one had said to them anything about suspected espionage, and there seemed to be no plan for a foot-follow if he left his car. It all seemed a bit half-baked to him. If their boss knew any more about it, he hadn't told them, but then Inspector Fézard was always tight-lipped, a believer in telling people only what they needed to know. They'd just been told to follow this guy and report back. If he went into Marseilles, as was expected, one of the cars on the North African operation would be pulled off to help follow him in the city.

Sure enough the Mercedes seemed to be heading that way, taking the clever route, avoiding Lyons and its snarled build-up of traffic, cutting down around Nîmes, then west to the A7 after skirting Chambéry. Traffic was light and the Mercedes was doing over 150 kilometres per hour, though the driver seemed to know the route well enough to slow down for the speed cameras. Sillon stayed back, closing the gap near exits in case the Mercedes left the motorway, and pulling closer when the black saloon slowed down to pay tolls at the *péage* stations. At Avignon the road split, and the Mercedes took the road marked Marseilles; it did it again before Aix-en-Provence. There didn't seem much doubt about the driver's destination, and mercifully he seemed entirely unaware that he was being followed.

They were thirty kilometres from the city when Mergas alerted control. Fifteen minutes later, as they passed a slip road, a familiar car joined the motorway at speed and, pulling ahead of Sillon, closed on the Mercedes, sitting between it and the Peugeot. The Mercedes took the second exit for the city, and the two surveillance cars followed. They moved slowly through an outlying industrial zone, heading towards the Vieux Port.

'*Merde*,' said Sillon; the harbour area was a den of small tortuous streets, where it would be easy to lose any target.

And when the A7 ended, the Mercedes drifted past the Porte d'Aix, standing isolated, like a smaller version of the Arc de Triomphe, down the Rue St Barbe with its modern concrete blocks and on to the wide Quai des Belges and the horseshoe-shaped harbour, the view studded by the unrigged masts of the hundreds of berthed sailing boats. Sillon could see the other surveillance car close behind the Mercedes, which now turned by the Air France office and swung eastwards on to La Canebière. It worked its way through the streets for five minutes, turning left and right, until it suddenly and inexplicably slowed down almost to a crawl. Sillon couldn't understand why unless it was looking for a place to park. They'd have to follow him on foot, he guessed. But suddenly the Mercedes pulled a dramatic U-turn, right in front of the following surveillance car, which was completely unable to copy without showing its hand. And by the time Sillon managed the turn, the Mercedes had disappeared.

Sillon cursed. The uneventful 300 kilometres they had travelled had lulled him into thinking the Mercedes's driver was completely unconscious of even the possibility of surveillance – then in the blink of an eye he was gone. As Mergas reached for the radio, Sillon said, 'This guy's a pro.'

'Well, we were told. He's a Russian intelligence officer,' replied Mergas ruefully.

27

H UGO COWDRAY HAD NONE of Belinda Duggan's arrogance, but Peggy worried that he'd be an equally tough nut to crack. When she'd last seen him at Brigham Hall he'd been wearing the uniform of the place – shabby sweater and jeans. Now, in a dark suit and tie, his tall figure seemed to dominate the little cubicle office. He looked distinguished but bewildered as he sat down.

Peggy had decided that with Cowdray she would come straight to the point. She didn't know whether Belinda Duggan would have already had the opportunity to contact him and warn him, but either way there was no advantage to be gained from beating about the bush.

'Good afternoon, Dr Cowdray. We met at Brigham Hall the other day when I came up to see Charlie Fielding,' she began. He nodded. 'I'm from the Security Service and I'm investigating a breach of security at Brigham Hall.'

'Really? What sort of breach?' His surprise and alarm seemed entirely genuine.

'An unauthorised email was sent from the house intranet to the MOD network.' Peggy looked at the file on the desk and told him the date and time when the email had been sent. She watched a flush rise like a stain on his cheeks, and she hoped that Cowdray wasn't going to be able to hold out for long.

Yet his voice, when he spoke, was calm. 'I'm not sure if there's a question behind this, but I did not commit this breach.'

Pressed by Peggy, he continued to deny point blank ever sending any emails to the MOD from Brigham Hall. His denials were emphatic – too emphatic, thought Peggy, who saw it as telling that he didn't ask who the email had been sent to. So she asked, seemingly out of the blue, 'What is your connection to Belinda Duggan?'

Cowdray made a great show of surprise. 'Belinda Duggan? What do you mean, "connection"? We're colleagues, but distant ones – we've never worked together. I'd say we were passing acquaintances, no more.'

This firm denial, which matched that of Belinda Duggan, rather threw Peggy. In the absence of any evidence to confront him with, she was contemplating what tack to take next when there was a tap on the office door. Annoyed, she looked up, expecting to see some member of the MOD HR Department trying to reclaim the use of the office. The battle axe who had installed her there in the first place put her head round the door and said, 'There's an urgent telephone call for you.'

'All right,' said Peggy slowly, wondering what was going on. 'Excuse me a moment, Dr Cowdray.' And she left the office, taking with her the file.

Charlie Fielding was on the phone. 'Sorry to disturb you but I thought you'd want to know that I've managed to retrieve some of the email Hugo Cowdray sent.'

'I'm just talking to him now. What does it say?' Her mind was racing with possibilities.

'Well, I wasn't able to retrieve much of it. But what I can see reads as follows:

'*N* . . . blank . . . blank . . . *o* . . . *t* . . . *e* . . . blank. And *six p.m.* I can't get anything else.'

Peggy wrote the letters down and looked at them hard. She liked crosswords and, sure enough, an answer came to her. 'That's a big help,' she said. 'I may have more luck with Dr Cowdray now. Many thanks.'

She walked back into the interview room and sat down again. She said abruptly, 'Just to recap, you say you barely know Belinda Duggan?'

'That's right.'

'Then why did you meet her in the Novotel?'

It was only a hunch, backed by the bare bones of an email, but it seemed worth the gamble.

At first it didn't seem to work. 'Who says I did?' Cowdray demanded.

He stared at her defiantly, but Peggy's hunch wouldn't go away – and suddenly she saw what this was about. She had no evidence, but Cowdray didn't know that, and if it didn't work she wouldn't have lost anything – she hadn't got anywhere as it was. She said, 'The French call it *cinq à sept*, I believe. You know, a quick rendezvous at the end of the day, then on home as if you've come straight from work. In your case, straight from Norfolk where you'd had a busy week.'

'I don't know what you're talking about.' But Peggy saw that his right hand was trembling.

'I think you do. The Novotel is very convenient – a stone's throw from King's Cross, where the train from Downham Market comes in. We've checked the register,' she said, her imagination in full flight. 'You must have used a different name to sign in. But hotels have CCTV – what doesn't these days? That's what the interruption just now was about; they've been going through the tapes and they've found you on one of them. And on the right day of the week . . .'

Peggy was slightly alarmed at how easily she'd invented all this, but Cowdray looked stunned. He tried to speak, licking his lips and opening his mouth, but nothing came out. He swallowed, then swallowed again. At last he said haltingly, 'How did you find out?'

'Your email.'

'But I—' And he stopped, realising what he had admitted.

'Yes, you deleted it, and Belinda deleted it – twice in fact, once on her laptop and once on the server.'

'Then how did you read it?'

'We couldn't at first,' Peggy admitted. 'But finally we salvaged just enough. Why don't you tell me what you two were up to?'

Cowdray lowered his head and pushed his fingertips against his eyebrows. When he looked up his eyes were red, slightly teary, but he gave Peggy a sheepish smile. 'Well, I'm not going to say "it isn't what it looks like".'

Peggy nodded. 'I wouldn't believe you if you did. But your personal life is your own business, Dr Cowdray. I don't want to know the details. It's only the security aspect I'm concerned about.'

He shook his head. 'You don't have to worry about that. The one thing we never talked about was work.'

'No pillow talk about encryption?'

Cowdray looked horrified. 'Absolutely not. I wouldn't talk about my work with anyone.'

She believed him, though his indignation was a little hard to take, given the alarm he'd caused. 'Why did you send an email? You know better than I do what the risks of doing that are. I understand it could help an outsider get into the system. That's why security is so strict – you helped set the parameters.'

'I know. What can I say? It was a fit of madness.' He shook his head in disbelief. 'We'd had a row. Belinda threatened to stop seeing me and I ... I suppose I must have been desperate.'

'Had you ever sent an email to her by that route before?'

'Never,' said Cowdray, so quickly and firmly that Peggy was left wondering if he was telling the truth.

What would your wife think about it? Peggy wondered, but she said nothing. She knew that Cowdray had five children. He had a lot to lose on a personal level, as well as jeopardising his career. What on earth did he see in that cold, arrogant woman to make it worth risking all that?

As Hugo Cowdray left the office, he looked smaller than he had when he'd come in. He'd asked what would happen next but Peggy had told him that would be decided by the MOD. Her job with him was done.

Later that evening she met Charlie Fielding again in the Angler's Arms.

When she told him what Cowdray had admitted, he was dismayed at first, then angry. 'We'll have to suspend him at once. There'll be a disciplinary board, and I know what their verdict will be. It's such a waste. Hugo's immensely talented, and he's gone and thrown it all away for the sake of a fling. As for Belinda Duggan, she'll be suspended too, though she may keep her job. After all, she didn't initiate the security violation, Hugo did.'

'But she lied to me,' said Peggy. 'If you hadn't cracked that email, Cowdray wouldn't have admitted anything, and

I don't think we'd have got to the bottom of it. Duggan's as unreliable as Hugo Cowdray, and that affects her vetting status. I'd like to be confident that she's put somewhere where she doesn't have access to highly classified information – at least for a time.'

'I suppose your Service will be making that demand formally.'

'I would think so. As for Cowdray, we have a bit of a dilemma. If I understand what you told me, the one possible way into the Brigham Hall system would be through the MOD intranet – which is why you were at such pains to keep the two systems separate?'

'That's right. I never thought anyone would breach that firewall – everyone knew it was absolutely forbidden.'

Peggy nodded, but she wasn't interested in Cowdray's behaviour any more; she had something more important on her mind. 'I also understand that even if the communication between MOD and Brigham were innocent, the danger is that someone – a mole in particular – could latch on to this link and somehow get into your system.'

'It's possible if you know how to do it. We call it "hitching" – like hitching a lift. It's a very remote possibility, as I think I told you, but theoretically a mole could use the email as a vehicle to get in.'

'But does it have to hitch in via Cowdray's machine? Because if that's the case, then if we immediately shut that down there won't be any way in. The gateway will be locked.'

'Yes. That's exactly right.' said Fielding with relief. 'Unless we're too late, of course.'

'But that's exactly what we don't want,' Peggy said. Fielding looked baffled, and she explained: 'Don't you see? This is our best bet for catching the mole, if there is one. If he tries to get into Brigham Hall through Cowdray's machine then we can spot him.'

'I suppose so ...' said Fielding warily. 'But I'd need to think about that – and what the risks are that he'll get in and we won't see he's there.'

'If we can't do something like that, we'll be right where we are now in looking for this mole – which is nowhere. And he might already have got into the system.'

'Oh, my God,' said Fielding, scratching his head. 'I'll have to work out the implications of all this. I can't help thinking how weird it will be to tell Hugo that he's screwed up so badly we want him to keep working.'

Peggy smiled at him. 'Well, not as weird as to find that everything you're working on was being monitored by some foreign state. Don't take too long to work it out,' she said. 'I don't think we've got much time.'

28

'WHAT DID YOU SAY?' asked Liz, looking up from her plate.

Martin said with a smile, 'I was asking if you'd like some cheese.'

'I'm sorry. I was thinking about something else.'

'I can see that. Do you want to talk about it?'

Normally conversation flowed easily when they were together but tonight Liz couldn't prevent her mind from drifting back to Switzerland. She'd come straight on from there to Paris to spend the weekend with Martin but she was finding it impossible to relax. She was disappointed that the French had lost Kubiak in Marseilles, when it had seemed that they were so near to finding out what business he had there.

And underneath that worry was a continuous mixture of guilt and anxiety about what might be happening to Alexander Sorsky. Liz couldn't help going over her meetings with the Russian, replaying everything he'd said.

She didn't want to explain all this to Martin. He would have understood, of course, being in the same business himself, but they normally avoided talking shop, unless, as occasionally happened, they found themselves working on two ends of the same case.

He laughed. 'I can see you *don't* want to talk about it, so let me tell you my news. My old friend Milraud has been spotted back in France with his wife. I'm going down to Toulon this week to see if they've shown up at the shop there or their house in Bandol. Milraud's too clever to do something so obvious, so I'm not very hopeful, but I need to check it out.' Liz nodded. She knew Martin would never rest until he had caught his former colleague from the DGSE, who had resigned and set himself up as an arms dealer. A crooked arms dealer, in fact, who now had an Interpol warrant over his head.

'That's not all,' Martin continued. 'I spoke to Isobel Florian about the anarchists Edward's daughter has got herself mixed up with. Isobel already knows about them – they've been involved in various anti-Capitalist protests. There's concern they'll try and disrupt a G20 meeting in Avignon next month; Isobel says they've got some violent people in their midst, so she's taking the threat seriously. The DCRI office in the South has managed to put an agent in, and Isobel is going down to Cahors this week to meet him and his handler. If I'm finished at Toulon in time, I'm going to drive up and join them.'

'That's really kind of you. I hope it's not a waste of your time.'

'Don't worry. It's never a waste of time to keep in touch with the DCRI. I'll need their help if I'm ever to catch Milraud.'

'Talking about the DCRI in the South, are they a good outfit? Their surveillance lost a target in Marseilles I wanted followed.'

'Is that what's been bothering you?'

'Partly.' And she explained about the contact with Sorsky, and how Kubiak, the Russian Head of Security in

Geneva, had been identified as the source of the information Sorsky had given her. 'Apparently he visits Marseilles quite regularly, and we need to know what he's doing there. I think it could be important. But the surveillance lost him, so we're none the wiser.'

Martin thought for a moment. 'Well, as I said, I'll be in Toulon this week and Marseilles is only a few miles up the coast. If you think it would be useful, I could go and have a word with them and find out what happened. I'd want to ask Isobel first, but I don't think she'd object.'

'Could you? I got the impression that they weren't taking it too seriously. If you could lean on them a bit, to find out what Kubiak's doing down there, it would be a huge help. Whatever he's up to, I can't imagine it's in France's interests any more than ours.'

'Of course. I'll make that very clear to the DCRI in Marseilles.'

He walked over to the windows and started drawing the curtains. Outside dusk had turned to dark, the *boules* players in the square across the road had gone home, and lights were now turned on in the houses further down the street. He said, 'Is there any other business to discuss?'

'I hope not. As far as I'm concerned I'd rather talk about anything else for the rest of the weekend.'

'I'll hold you to that. I don't think all this shop talk is good for either of us. Tomorrow I thought we might do something different for a change.' There was a glint in his eyes.

'Oh?'

'Yes. The races are on at Longchamp.'

'You mean, the horses?'

'I don't mean Formula One.' He made a noise like a buzzing fly, and Liz laughed. Martin said, 'I can think of nothing more boring than watching cars go round and round a track at three hundred kilometres an hour. Not when you have animals as beautiful as thoroughbreds to watch.'

'I didn't know you liked horses.'

'I do, provided I don't have to ride one. Though I imagine as a native of the countryside, you like that sort of thing,' he said teasingly.

'Pony Club for seven years.'

'And rosettes?'

'One or two,' she said.

'Modest as always – I've seen dozens of them in your room at Susan's house. Anyway, would you like to go tomorrow? It's in the Bois de Boulogne – and very pretty.'

'Absolutely. My father used to take me to the races at Newbury every year. Shall we have a flutter?'

'That goes without saying. You are looking at one of France's leading handicappers.'

'Really?' Liz asked with a smile.

'No, not really,' Martin said with mock sadness. 'If I ever have to make a living another way, betting on horses would not be an intelligent choice. I might as well throw money up in the air.'

'Ah, but tomorrow will be different. I'm feeling lucky.'

'Good. Now, you'd better join me in an Armagnac.'

29

THE WAVES OF IRRITATION emanating from Liz
were washing over Peggy, who was sitting next to her
in the MOD entrance hall, as they waited to be escorted
up to Sy3A. Liz had hoped to see Charlie Fielding alone,
without involving Henry Pennington any further, but she'd
been told firmly that protocol required that he be kept in
the loop. So here she was, about to subject herself to
another hour of Pennington patronising her and flapping.

Up in the Clarity suite, true to form, he was sitting behind
his desk, busying himself with some important-looking
papers, while Charlie Fielding sat at the conference table
with a laptop open in front of him. Liz had expected a
geeky-looking boffin, but this was a rather attractive man,
bespectacled and thoughtful-looking, with curly brown hair
and a broad smile. Peggy introduced Charlie to Liz and they
all sat down while Pennington continued his reading.

Finally, he got up from the desk and joined them, taking
his place at the head of the table.

Pennington looked accusingly at Liz. 'I gather this is all
going from bad to worse.'

She replied as calmly as she could, 'I believe we are
making progress. I wanted to see Dr Fielding because I

need to understand more about the project he and his colleagues are working on.'

Henry Pennington started to rub his hands together – the inevitable sign of agitation. Liz went on hastily: 'As you know, Peggy and I are now cleared to Clarity Purple, so you don't need to worry about security for this conversation.'

The hand-washing speeded up and Pennington said, 'I made it clear that I didn't approve of Miss Kinsolving being cleared to Purple. It seemed to me to be broadening the knowledge unnecessarily.'

Peggy flushed and Liz said determinedly, 'Take my word for it, Henry, it was necessary or we wouldn't have asked.'

She turned to Charlie Fielding. 'We've had the Clarity briefing, but it would be helpful if you would describe what you're actually doing at Brigham Hall.'

Fielding put his hands on the table as he gathered his thoughts. 'How much do you know about drones?'

Peggy said, 'Invisible planes in the sky?'

Fielding laughed. 'That's a start anyway, though they're perfectly visible. I'm sure you've at least heard about the remotely piloted drones – the ones flown by an airman sitting in an air force base in Nevada, chewing on a Hershey bar and looking at a picture of a scene 7,000 miles away; he presses a button and thirty people are blown up outside a Pakistani village. Some of them may even have been terrorists,' he added, raising an eyebrow. Henry Pennington tutted.

'Then there are simpler kinds of drone, unarmed ones that fly very high and take pictures and send them back, or at the most basic level actually bring the pictures back. Practically all these drones – except the very simplest, which can be pre-programmed – depend on continuous communication, either from the ground nearby or from a huge distance away via satellite.

'Cyber-espionage can be very sophisticated: it's not just hacking into someone else's computer and stealing the contents, it can also involve the continuous feeding of data to the attacker, or even the attacker controlling the computer and making it obey external commands.

'The media assume any attack that's detected these days is coming from China, but everyone is developing the capability – and trying to defend themselves against it. The French, the Americans, the Russians and us of course. Cyber-espionage – both conducting it and defending against it – is GCHQ's top priority nowadays.

'Back to drones. The cleverer the drone, the more sophisticated the communication system it needs to have. And the next generation is going to be very clever. They'll be able to control their own family of mini-drones, making decisions for themselves according to what they find on the ground.'

'They sound terrifying,' said Peggy.

'Well, yes, but it's still a very new science,' Fielding went on. 'As you know, Clarity is a joint programme with the Americans. The idea is that in a limited way the drone should be able to think for itself. For example, the controller could say something like, "Go down three hundred feet, but go up again if you see a gun emplacement on the ground." Or, "Fire your missile when the car looks as if it's stopping, but if it speeds up hold fire." Imagine how much more effective that would be than just being able to make it go left or go right.

'If the programme is successful, and it's early days yet, we'll have an expert system on board the drone that will let it make decisions as subtle as that for itself. But for now, it has to let someone else tell it exactly what to do and when.

'So Clarity is concerned with the communication systems and commands sent to drones. We've developed protocols that let us send instruction to these new drones in natural language.'

'Natural?' asked Liz.

'As opposed to artificial – which is what computer languages are. Look.' And he flipped open the top of his laptop and tapped a key. The screen was filled with row after row of numbers and symbols. 'That's raw ASCII, the bits and bytes that tell this machine what to do.'

'Looks like Chinese to me,' said Peggy. Then realising what she'd said, blushed and added, 'Oh, sorry. Let's hope it's not.'

'So where does Operation Clarity fit into all this?' Liz was anxious to move things on now. She could see Henry Pennington shuffling in his chair, ready to make an unhelpful remark.

'It encrypts the natural language commands in real time – which means they are protected by codes as soon as they're spoken. If any of the communications were intercepted, the interceptor wouldn't be able to make head nor tail of them – so they're hidden, if you like.'

Liz sat back, trying to take in his mini-lecture. 'Then if we look at Bravado's information, why would anyone want to infiltrate the programme?'

'To encrypt their own counter-commands, which would be accepted because they'd be similarly encoded.'

'How would you go about stealing the encryption code?'

'Well, first you'd need to get into our working system at Brigham Hall.'

'So this is where Bravado's mole in MOD comes in? If he exists.'

'There is no mole in the Clarity project,' said Henry Pennington, suddenly coming to life at the end of the table. 'I've told you that our vetting system in Clarity is totally reliable.'

Ignoring him, Liz went on addressing Fielding. 'I know Peggy's briefed you about her interviews with Cowdray and Duggan, and that you've agreed to keep them in play.'

'That's right. We've kept Hugo Cowdray's machine operating as normal. I have it on my desk at Brigham Hall and I take it back to my digs at night. It's set up as a dummy machine, so that anyone trying to get into the Brigham Hall system via the email footprint which Duggan and Hugo left, would find Hugo's PC alive and well. But if they tried to look further at the network – and to get into the encryption work – they'd hit a dead end. I've put an alert on the machine, so I'll know the minute anyone tries.'

Liz said, 'But wouldn't they know that, and realise they'd been sussed?'

'Not necessarily. Hopefully, they'll just think they've hit a brick wall. Even the most segregated systems have internal checks, so in theory at least, anyone coming in will feel they just haven't cracked the internal codes.'

'By which time,' said Peggy cheerfully, 'we should have nabbed the culprit.'

Fielding gave a fleeting smile. 'Only if we're quick enough. Or they're not quick enough to get out before we identify them.'

'Is there any evidence that anyone has used the Duggan footprint to try to get in?'

'That's the sixty-four-thousand-dollar question. As I said, we've set a trap for them, but it's a question of whether we closed the stable door in time.'

'I was talking to my colleague in the US Embassy the other day and he said there had been some technical hitches in the trials. Do you know what they were?'

'Yes, I do. The most interesting was when the drone seemed to ignore the ground controller's natural language command and do something different. Fortunately, it got back on course in the end.'

'Could that mean external interference?'

'Too early to say. The assumption at the moment is that it was some sort of technical failure. It's not impossible it was something external, but if it was interference it would indicate a very advanced infiltration of the system.'

Henry Pennington looked as if he were about to faint. 'Why don't I know about this?' he asked. 'Why wasn't I told?'

'Oh, you will be, Henry,' said Liz. 'If it turns out to be anything serious.'

30

O N TUESDAY, MARTIN SEURAT left Toulon feeling disappointed but unsurprised to have found no trace of his former colleague Antoine Milraud. When he'd first known him he had rather admired Milraud, thinking him clever and resourceful. But those qualities had eventually turned to shiftiness and cunning, driven by the relentless greed that had finally made him into a crook. Martin felt glad to leave Toulon and its neighbourhood and was looking forward to visiting Marseilles again.

He hadn't been there for ten years, but he remembered its notorious traffic jams. They were even worse now that the town had become the second largest city in France. He left his rental car in a car park in an area of the city where multinational corporations occupied grimly modern office blocks, surrounded by the even grimmer towers of public housing built for the large immigrant population.

A short taxi ride took him to the old quarter of the town, with its narrow slanting streets, small neighbourhood bars full of tough-looking North Africans, and alleyways festooned with clothes lines and smelly overflowing gutters. He walked through Le Panier, then joined the crowds shopping on La

Canebière, the city's main commercial thoroughfare, where every shop seemed to be holding a sale, and nothing was undiscounted.

Tough times, but these were tough people, as he knew to his cost. During his six-month secondment here, tracking an Algerian extremist cell, he had been shot at twice, and once had his car run off the road. Unlike the Parisians, the Marseillais didn't make the slightest effort to look sophisticated or chic; their clothes said you took them or left them as they were. But they were friendly, unreserved people, and when Martin stopped and asked directions from a kebab stall, the vendor, noting both his accent and the street he was enquiring for, asked cheerfully what a cop from the North was doing this far south.

The office of the Police Nationale, which contained the DCRI office, turned out to be a handsome old stone building with shuttered windows. The nail-studded wooden door was still in place at the top of the steps, but at the bottom access was gained via a metal barrier manned by an armed policeman in a flak jacket. Martin's documents passed scrutiny and he made his way up the steps into the building where a desk sergeant in the reception area sent him upstairs with a jerk of his head.

At the top of the stairs he entered a large, open-plan room, crammed with desks and tables and unmatched chairs, most of them unoccupied. A young uniformed policeman who was busy on the phone raised an inquisitive eyebrow, and Martin mouthed the name of the person he had come to see. The man gestured with a finger at the room's far end, where an office had been carved out in the corner. On the door a wooden sign read *DCRI*.

He knocked and a voice called out, '*Entrez.*' As Martin stepped inside he was struck by the contrast with the shambles of the open-plan exterior. This office was tidy and well decorated, with a new thick carpet, a modern desk, two matching chairs and a small conference table.

Its occupant, Maurice Fézard, was equally well turned out: tall, well dressed in a dark blue suit and tie, and polite, standing up to shake hands with him. Fézard had been notified of his visit by a call from Isobel in Paris, and judging by his helpful manner Martin guessed that a small bomb had been put under him. He lost no time in pleasantries, saying only, 'Monsieur, it is a pleasure to meet you,' before continuing, 'I may have some news to report. I assure you that we have been most thorough.'

'Of course,' said Martin. 'I hear you are known for your diligence.'

Fézard waved the *politesse* away. 'As I told Isobel Florian, we felt badly about losing this Russian, though mobile surveillance in this city is very difficult and to find him again after losing him was never going to be easy. Unfortunately the Swiss gave us very little notice and it was a particularly busy day. So I hope you will understand. Since Madame Florian phoned me, however, we have had some success.'

'I'm most grateful. Tell me what you've found – or what you haven't found.' Martin was pleased to find the local man had not taken offence at the pressure that had been applied from Paris.

Fézard lit a Gitane, after offering one to Martin who turned it down. He was pretty sure smoking was not allowed in the office, which suggested someone confident of his senior status. Blowing out a long plume of smoke, Fézard said, 'Marseilles is a big town, as I'm sure you know.'

'I was stationed here for six months in the nineties.'

Fézard nodded. 'Ah, then, you understand. Let us take a little stroll, Monsieur; I have something to show you.'

Martin was beginning to grow impatient with how long it was taking Fézard to reveal what he had learned, but felt he had no choice but to go along. They left Police Headquarters and walked into the nearby area of the Old Port, crossing La Canebière, which was warming up under the noon sun. Fézard led the way through a maze of small interconnected streets, alleys and entries little wider than a Vespa scooter – which seemed to be the favoured mode of transport in this part of the city.

Suddenly, ahead of them Martin could see the aquamarine of the Mediterranean, behind the walls that encircled the harbour. When they were still a street away, Fézard stopped. He pointed. 'Do you see the *tabac* up there?'

Looking ahead, Martin spotted the shop's sign. Fézard said, 'Yesterday one of my men spoke to the proprietor. I have had four teams on the case ever since Madame Florian rang. We have been combing every inch of the neighbourhood.' Knowing Isobel Florian was tough as nails with anyone not adhering to the highest professional standards, Seurat could well believe this was the case.

Fézard continued: 'He thought he recognised the photo the Swiss sent us of this man Kubiak. He said the man came in every now and then to buy Russian cigarettes. This is a neighbourhood of very mixed nationalities, so the shop owner stocks all sorts of tobacco. He said there wasn't any particular pattern to the man's purchases – though he saw him at least every month or so. Sometimes he'd come in for a few days in a row; sometimes just once.'

And? thought Martin impatiently. A stakeout of the shop might take weeks to get results.

Fézard said, 'You are wondering why we haven't put men to watch the shop, Monsieur. We have – and we've also had a lucky break. The proprietor mentioned that he happened to see this Kubiak somewhere else one morning. The owner had left his shop in the care of his assistant while he went to meet a friend in a café round the corner. They were sitting at a table on the pavement when the Russian walked past and went into a building just opposite the café. Come.'

He led Martin down the street to a corner with another road. Fézard said quietly, 'It's the second building on the right across the street.'

Looking around casually, Martin noted the building, a large brick edifice that had once been a warehouse – with thick external pillars, wide sash windows, and a protruding hook on its top fifth floor that must have been used in earlier centuries to pulley goods up and down. The ground floor now had a plate-glass entrance, giving on to a foyer with two lifts at the back.

'It's been done up,' said Fézard, 'like a lot of the old buildings here. Inside there are twelve companies renting space – the building's bigger than it looks. But let's move on and I'll tell you what we know about it.'

They walked around the corner and headed back towards headquarters. Martin asked, 'Do you know which company Kubiak was visiting?'

'No, I'm afraid we only know that he went into the building. We've checked out all the companies. None is Russian, and most of them are local, well-established companies trading in fairly unexciting things – olive oil, a shipping company, a wine middleman, that sort of thing. There's one Parisian company who have taken space – they sell specialised insurance for corporations. The firm's fifteen years old and privately owned by Frenchmen, and it seems completely reputable. Then there's a Serbian company, who interest us – but not for reasons that will interest you.'

'Oh?'

'At first we thought they might fit the bill – except for not being Russian. A new office, cash down for the lease.'

'But . . .?'

'They don't seem to have any clients, at least not in the normal meaning of business. Their staff turnover in the last six months has been extraordinary – all women, who come from Serbia to work and then . . . disappear.'

'Not a straight enterprise?'

'No – they're crooks all right. But not spies. It's pretty clear they're trafficking in women. Distasteful, but more our problem than yours.'

Fézard continued: 'We also found two hi-tech new arrivals. One is a database specialist company with three employees – a Belgian, a German, and a Frenchman. They have money from Oracle behind them and are doing R&D which our own boffins say is legitimate.' He shrugged.

'And the other?' asked Martin, more out of politeness than real interest. It was Russians he was looking for.

'Some South Koreans. Not surprising – there are substantial Far Eastern interests here.'

'What do they do?'

'It's a consultancy. They're advising Far Eastern enterprises on business opportunities in France and other parts of Europe. It seems quite above board. There's a South Korean Trade Office here and they had references from them when they took the offices.'

Martin sighed. He knew Liz would be disappointed, and having spent time on the case, he felt deflated himself. But there must be something going on that they hadn't yet discovered. Kubiak was not coming repeatedly to Marseilles for the benefit of his health.

Fézard said apologetically, 'I am sorry if your trip has been a waste of time, Monsieur.'

Martin shrugged and smiled wanly. 'Well, it is good to see Marseilles again,' he said, wondering if it would be another ten years before he returned.

31

I T WAS A LONG drive to Cahors but Martin's spirits rose as he drove, and by the time he reached the ancient town, sitting as it did in a hollow with the River Lot surrounding it on three sides, he was feeling cheerful. He knew the town well – he and his ex-wife had once owned a small *gîte* about fifteen kilometres away, where they spent the occasional weekend (occasional because it was a long way from Paris) and their longer holidays. On Saturdays they would come to shop in the outdoor market here, though in later years Martin usually found himself going there alone, since his wife had seemed less and less interested in his company. Later he discovered it was because she preferred the company of someone else.

He walked up one of the narrow side streets to Boulevard Léon Gambetta, a tree-lined street full of chemists and *parfumeries* and expensive clothes shops. Even in late morning it was crowded, with shoppers on the pavements and cars moving at a snail's pace up the steep slope. A few hundred yards along he came to a large open square on the side of which was a café with tables set outside, their umbrellas up against the sun. This far south, it was warm even in early spring.

Isobel was sitting at a table inside, sipping a cappuccino and reading a paper. She was dressed for the part in jeans and a fisherman's sweater, with sturdy hiking boots. Though she had a handsome face and a good figure, unusually for a Parisienne she seemed never to give a fig about her clothes.

'*Bonjour*,' he said, sitting down beside her and beckoning the waiter. Martin ordered his coffee and sat back comfortably.

'Any luck in Toulon?' asked Isobel, aware of his ongoing search for Antoine Milraud.

'Nothing doing,' he said with a shrug. 'Not that I expected to find him. But there is a bit to report from Marseilles.'

'So old Fézard has pulled his finger out.' But before Martin could go on, a young man approached their table.

'Ah, here's Philippe,' she said. Martin stood up and shook hands, as Isobel explained that Philippe was a DCRI officer stationed in Toulouse, an hour's drive away. It was he who had been looking into the anarchist *communards*, and had managed to plant an informant in their ranks.

'Tell Martin about your source,' she said.

'Well, it's a couple actually. I recruited them about a year or so ago when they were picked up on a minor drugs charge in Paris. I intervened and pointed them at the commune. We were getting increasingly concerned about the activities of this bunch. My two were accepted quite easily – they had the right background to make them convincing. They've worked their way in now. Done very well.'

'Yes,' Isobel broke in, 'you've done a good job with them.'

Philippe smiled at the compliment but then more soberly said, 'Only one of them is coming today; his girl-friend's staying at the commune. He may be quite nerv-ous, though I've warned him that a couple of colleagues are coming to this meeting. He's desperately afraid of their cover being blown. He thinks the commune members would hurt them badly if they found out he was working for us. Now, before we go to see him, is there anything in particular you want to know? If you don't mind, I think I'd better ask the questions. He'll be anxious enough as it is.'

Martin said, 'There's an English woman who left the commune recently and went back to Britain. Her name is Cathy – she has a little boy, though the father disappeared some years ago. Someone from the commune has been to see her – we know his name, René, though I haven't got a surname. Apparently, he tried to get money from her. I'd like you to ask Marcel about this René.'

'I know about René. He's become the leader of the commune, even though their anarchist principles mean they shouldn't have a leader – so much for ideological consistency. He's a veteran of left-wing movements; I bet he knew more about Marxist dogma when he was twelve than the average French boy knows about football.'

'A lifer,' said Isobel.

'That's right, and it's in the family. His father's a politics lecturer with Maoist tendencies.'

'That sounds very dated,' observed Martin.

'That's because it is. The father was involved in the Paris student protests in '68, and got caught up in a demo in the Latin Quarter. He was hit by a CRS van and has been in a wheelchair ever since.' Philippe shrugged. 'It seems that he lived his politics after that only vicariously – through his son René.' Philippe looked at his watch. 'We'd better be going. I've arranged to meet Marcel in a safe house near the cathedral. There's a market today in the square, so no one's going to notice us.'

They paid and left the café, then crossed the boulevard and walked down a cobbled side street towards the cathedral square. A child straddled a bicycle in front of them, and overhead a woman leaned out of a window, shaking out a tablecloth. Reaching the square, they found the market at the height of its activity. Long trestle tables laid with coloured cloths displayed the wares of the region: cheeses, cured meats, olives, breads, *patisserie*, and bottles of the local ink-black wine. The aisles were packed with customers – local housewives with their woven willow baskets, tourists holding cameras – all of them tasting, haggling, paying, then moving on to the next row of stalls.

In a corner of the square a pizzeria was open for early lunch business. Martin and Isobel followed Philippe across the market throng and through the restaurant's open door. The owner stood behind a zinc bar, wearing a white shirt and apron and polishing a wine glass with a tea towel. Seeing Philippe, he gave a nod, and raised his head almost imperceptibly towards the upper floors of the building.

The staircase was at the back of the restaurant next to the toilets. At the top, across the landing, was a closed door. Without knocking, Philippe opened the door and went in, Martin and Isobel right behind. A young man in corduroys and a blue denim jacket was standing by the window on the far side of the room, which was dominated by a round table in the centre. Turning around as he heard them come in, he looked alarmed.

'These are the colleagues I mentioned,' said Philippe. 'It's all right. They are friends. It's quite safe.'

He motioned Martin and Isobel to sit down. The young man, Marcel, hesitated then joined them, though he kept his chair back from the table – as if he wanted to be able to escape at any moment.

'So,' said Philippe, 'you said last time that things were stirring at the commune. What's happened?'

Marcel breathed out noisily. 'It's all quite tense. The G20 are meeting next month in Avignon, and we had made plans to protest. Half of Europe should be there,' he added, with a mixture of defiance and pride. 'But we've been having arguments about what exactly we should do.'

'Do?'

Marcel shrugged. 'René is not content with merely demonstrating. He wants some action.'

'What kind of action?' asked Philippe.

'He wants something more *explosive*,' said Marcel, and grinned at his little joke until he saw the stony expression on Isobel's face. He said hastily, 'René has been trying to buy guns in Marseilles, and I think explosives too.'

'Why Marseilles?' asked Philippe.

Marcel raised an eyebrow. 'Are you serious? You can buy anything in Marseilles – from a kilo of coke to a Vietnamese girl with one leg.'

Philippe asked, 'Are the others happy about this?'

'Of course not. Marguerite told me all the girls are worried sick and I know that many of the men have doubts. But they're keeping their doubts to themselves.'

'Why?'

'They're scared.'

Philippe scoffed. 'Of René? You told me he's no bigger than a flea.'

'But Antoine is,' said Marcel, and it was obvious that he was scared too.

'Tell us about this Antoine. Who is he?'

'That's a good question. From things he's said, I'm sure he's done time in prison. His politics are positively primeval – but he's not there to discuss Bakunin with the rest of us.' Marcel shook his head. 'He's violent. One of the girls criticised something he said, and he gave her a slap. When Jean – that's one of the older guys – objected, Antoine punched him in the gut so hard he couldn't breathe for over a minute. Jean's face was blue.'

Martin caught Philippe's eye, and he gave a tiny nod. He said to Marcel, 'Was there a woman called Cathy living in the commune when you arrived? An English woman.'

Marcel gave a knowing smile. 'Funny you should ask. She left before I came, but René and Antoine are going to see her next week.'

'Why?'

Marcel gave his little smile again. He didn't say anything, but rubbed his first two fingers against his thumb meaningfully, in the universal sign for money.

'Why would this woman give them any money?'

This time there was nothing small about Marcel's smile, and he laughed out loud. 'For the same reason we do what René tells us to do. Because if she doesn't, Antoine will knock her teeth out.'

32

'Your favourite Englishman has just rung, Andy. He's coming over.'

'Oh, hell. What does he want?' growled Andy Bokus. It was a wet, windy Thursday morning. Just the kind of day that made him resent all the more being stuck in London for another year.

'Said it's urgent,' Bokus's assistant replied. 'I think it's about those traces you sent to Langley. The guys on secondment to the MOD. And he's bringing Liz Carlyle.'

'Oh, make my day, why don't you? Her I can stand – just. But not when she hunts with Geoffrey Fane.'

'Well, they're on their way. I've put the files down in the Bubble.'

He'd already told Liz Carlyle on the phone that Langley had chased up the vetting and found nothing out of the ordinary. They'd also been looking closely at their end of the Clarity programme, but without more information about what they were looking for, they hadn't unearthed anything suspicious. So what was this new flap about? Maybe the Brits had discovered something else.

Twenty minutes later, with the courtesies over (which always took time with Geoffrey Fane), they repaired to the

Bubble in the basement of the Embassy. Bokus sat down across the table from Liz Carlyle, with Fane at the end. Carlyle had said nothing during the initial banter between the two men, and Bokus thought she looked tired, which also made her look younger and more vulnerable. He might have found her attractive if she hadn't been such a pain in the ass.

'Well, what can I do for you two this time?' he asked.

Carlyle replied, 'It's about the Clarity programme and my Russian source Bravado.'

'I've had the vetting checked like you asked,' Bokus cut in, 'and Langley are happy with it. I've got the files here; you're welcome to look at them. There was a high-level briefing for the Joint Chiefs of Staff last week about the progress of the Clarity programme. It's going pretty well – there's been the odd technical hitch but I suppose that's not surprising with an experimental system. Your information got a mention too, and believe me, it was taken very seriously. But without more detail there's not much that can be done at our end, since your source said the mole was in the British MOD. Can't he be more specific?'

Bokus saw Fane give a small sigh and the Carlyle woman was looking uncomfortable as she shook her head. It looked like their source must have dried up.

'Has something happened to Bravado then?' he demanded.

Fane pursed his lips. 'You could say that.'

Carlyle said, 'It seems that he's gone back to Moscow. But not voluntarily.'

'So he's blown.' This was not a question.

'Seemingly,' said Fane. 'But it doesn't alter the situation. If the mole is working for another country, then I can't see the Russians tipping them off, even if they know that Bravado has told us about it.'

'They'll know all right, if they've uncovered him. I wouldn't give Bravado any chance of keeping *schtum* where he'll be now.'

Liz frowned and shook her head, as if to get rid of an unpleasant thought.

'Anyway, you know my views,' went on Bokus. 'If anyone's planted a mole in the MOD, it'll be the Russians themselves; I never did buy this third-country story. It probably just means the mole's an illegal – with third-country documents.'

'That's possible,' Carlyle conceded. 'But it seems unlikely. I was the one who talked to Bravado, and I was convinced. He only learned about this mole by accident.'

'That's what he told you,' said Bokus caustically.

The woman looked unruffled. 'If you're suggesting that Bravado wasn't telling the truth – that he was part of some disinformation plot – I think you're wrong. Why on earth would the Russians do that? Why alert us to the existence of a mole in the MOD if they've really got one in place? It makes no sense.'

She was right of course and Bokus didn't have an answer. But he wasn't big on retractions.

'So what do you want me to do?' he finally asked. Meeting with the Brits, Bokus always felt he had to have everything spelled out. They had called the meeting; they presumably wanted something from him; yet here he was, having to tease it out of them. No wonder the Empire had gone down the tubes – their colonial subjects had probably had enough of English ambiguity.

Liz said, 'We're focusing on the list of foreign nationals seconded to the MOD . . .'

Bokus interrupted, 'I told you, I've checked with Langley and they said all the ones who've been in the States were thoroughly vetted.' He lifted a hand and let his palm come down hard on the folders on the table. 'Have a look if you want.' He turned to Fane, who was watching them spar with amusement.

Liz said, 'Hang on, Andy. Let me bring you up to date first with our investigation. Thanks to the Swiss, we are pretty confident that the source of Bravado's information was a guy named Anatole Kubiak, the Head of Security in the Russian Mission in Geneva. He's SVR of course. We know a bit about Kubiak already and he's not a very pleasant type, as Geoffrey can explain.'

Fane, who'd been lounging back with his long legs crossed, sat up and leaned forward.

'It turns out that we have quite a file on our friend Kubiak,' he began. 'We first came across him in Delhi in the mid-1980s. He was working the Scientific and Technical area, getting alongside Western businessmen for what he could pick up and who he could recruit. He was quite young then, in his late twenties, and it was his first posting abroad. He seemed to be on a very loose rein and we wondered whether he had some protection – a father in a high position or something. He spent a lot of time drinking in private clubs with his Western contacts – drinking far too much. Because of his behaviour, our Station spotted him as a possible recruit. We had a couple of trusted business contacts get to know him, and they reported that he was very loose-tongued – especially for those days. He was quite prepared to criticise the Communist system and praise the West, and our contacts didn't think it was a come-on to win their confidence – they thought he meant it. It was as though he was asking to be recruited.

'But there was something else too. He frequented a brothel, the same one each time. It specialised in girls

– and I mean *girls*, twelve- and thirteen-year-olds, tiny little things. We thought this made him pretty vulnerable, so we put one of our young officers alongside him to line him up for a recruitment pitch. We'd worked out quite a good scenario; it was going to be a combination of ideology and his own compromising behaviour. But just as we were ready to go with it, Kubiak was suddenly posted – he left Delhi almost overnight and soon reappeared in Poland. We couldn't get at him there in those days, and he didn't come out again, so we lost interest.' Fane looked at Bokus. 'I'd be very surprised if your Station in India hadn't noticed him too, Andy. It's worth getting Langley to do a trace.'

Bokus grunted. 'We had a big Station in Delhi in those days,' he said. 'Sounds like they wouldn't have missed that guy unless they were asleep.'

'Maybe you kept up the pursuit longer than Geoffrey's colleagues,' said Liz. 'It would be interesting to know, because there is definitely something strange about the man.' She explained that the Swiss had discovered that Kubiak was making regular trips to Marseilles, and had visited a particular office block there. 'One of the firms in that building is a South Korean hi-tech consultancy which no one seems to know much about. It may just be coincidence, but I think we should look at the South Korean working in the MOD.' Seeing a sceptical look on Bokus's face, she said, 'I know it sounds like a long shot, but we have nothing else to go on.'

'That guy's as clean as a whistle. I told you,' said Bokus, scrabbling through his files and producing one. 'Park Woo-jin. Thirty-one years old, a programmer in object-oriented languages. Whatever that means,' he said with a grimace at Liz.

He returned to the dossier. 'He's been vetted very thoroughly by us. Born in a suburb of Seoul. Father was a clerk in an insurance company, mother a kindergarten teacher – though I'm not sure how you say "kindergarten" in Korean. Park was spotted when he was just twelve, for his mathematical aptitude. He won a scholarship to Seoul University when he was sixteen years old, and studied high-level math before switching to computer science for his Master's degree. During his National Service, he was moved into software development for their anti-missile systems. After that he joined Korean Intelligence, though his work remained military rather than intelligence-oriented. Unmarried, no known hobbies except for an addiction to computer video games – surprise, surprise.' He closed the file. 'Sounds like your average geek, only a Far Eastern variety. He worked for six months in the Pentagon – and, believe me, you don't get through the outer corridor there until they've turned you inside out.'

He looked at Liz. 'Anyway, how do you know this Kubiak guy is visiting the Korean firm? You said there were others in the building. He might be visiting one of them.'

'It is possible, Elizabeth,' said Geoffrey, stirring himself again. 'Don't forget that, according to the French, one of the companies there is trafficking women. In Delhi Kubiak was very fond of whores; no reason to think that's changed.'

'There you are,' said Bokus, leaping in. 'I'll bet it's nothing to do with the Koreans. There are Koreans all over Europe. They're big traders.'

Liz shook her head. 'I still think Langley should have another look at Park Woo-jin.'

Bokus was annoyed by her insistence. He was sure she'd got the wrong end of the stick, and he strongly suspected that Geoffrey Fane thought so too. But he wasn't going to argue, not at this stage anyway. There was just the smallest chance she might be right, so he gave her his warmest phoney smile. 'I'll get on to Langley right away. Anything else I can do for you?' he asked.

'Not for now,' replied Liz Carlyle, with a smile he felt was equally bogus.

When they'd gone, Bokus went back to his office on the fourth floor. Looking out of the window he could see Fane down in the square, striding ahead of Carlyle, waving his umbrella to hail a taxi. Bokus turned around when his assistant came in.

'Did it go well, Andy?'

'No,' he said, and started to reach for the phone on his desk, which was his secure direct line to Langley. Then he had another thought. 'Hang on a sec. Get me the Korean Embassy, will ya? And after that, I'll want to speak with our Paris Chief.'

33

PEGGY WAS IN THE A4 control room, sitting on the old leather sofa that was kept there for anxious case officers while a surveillance operation was in progress. Wally Woods, the A4 controller, set strict rules in the control room: case officers could be present provided they didn't speak except to answer questions. Yet he did find it useful to have them there, as surveillance operations rarely went entirely as predicted and it was helpful to be able to involve the case officer in the quick decisions that often needed to be made.

This was the third day of surveillance on Park Woo-jin. It was a miserable morning, unseasonably cold and spitting with rain. It was 8.30 when Reggie Purvis bought a coffee in the old-fashioned coffee bar on Broadway and stood by the window sipping it. Unusually for him, he was wearing a suit and tie under a raincoat. They made him indistinguishable from the civil servants and office workers who stood around him, having a quick shot of caffeine before starting work. Like many of them, Purvis had iPod plugs in both ears, and his face bore the vacant expression of someone listening to an interior orchestra the outside world couldn't hear.

Ten minutes later as another wave of passengers emerged from the subterranean bowels of the District line on to the pavement in front of St James's Park Underground Station, Purvis spotted his target: a young man in a new-looking leather jacket. He was short, five foot six at a stretch, with cropped black hair and Far Eastern features. He paused briefly outside the station entrance and bought a paper, which he tucked under his arm, then he stood for a moment, putting his change away and looking around. But there was nothing particularly vigilant about his gaze, and he seemed completely unaware of Stephen Sachs, who had been in the same carriage all the way in on the train from Ealing Broadway, and who now passed him without a glance.

The young man walked to the corner and Purvis quickly swallowed the dregs of his coffee and went out into the street. It was raining harder now, and Purvis turned up the collar of his coat, walking quickly, following the man in the leather jacket as he crossed Broadway on to Queen Anne's Gate, heading for St James's Park. This was the same route the man had taken on each of the previous days, and it was clearly his standard morning routine.

But why did he get off the tube at St James's? One further stop would have brought him to Westminster, much nearer the MOD building where he worked. Getting off here gave him a ten-minute walk. Fair enough, if the day were fine – perhaps he liked the exercise – but today nobody in their right mind would want a longer walk to work. Not in this rain.

The iPod sitting in Purvis's jacket pocket was a two-way radio, and the plugs in his ears weren't bringing him the dulcet notes of Coldplay or Adele. 'Tonto's heading to the park. Same route as usual,' he said, lowering his chin, so the mini-mic that doubled as a tiepin would pick up his words.

'Got it,' said a voice in his ears. Duff Wells, in tracksuit and trainers, was jogging slowly around the lake in St James's Park. Further along by Horse Guards, Maureen Hughes, dressed in a smart black mac and black tights, was holding an umbrella with one hand and a small Schnauzer on a lead with the other. His name was Buster, and he belonged to one of the doormen at Thames House. In the foyer of the MOD itself, Marcus Washington sat like someone waiting for an appointment, but in fact making sure that the man in the leather jacket made it to work.

According to the A4 team, on the last three mornings Park Woo-jin's walk had followed the same pattern: down through Queen Anne's Gate and into the park, across Horse Guards Parade and then through the Arch into Whitehall and the MOD. It was like the performance of a play with a constantly changing cast, though the lead character remained the same.

They were all wondering how long they would keep following the Korean, who so far had gone innocently to work and back each day, returning home alone to his flat in an MOD-owned house in Ealing, never venturing further afield than the Thai restaurant at the end of his street and the DVD shop a hundred yards further along, where he had up to now rented *Toy Story 2* and a Kung Fu film.

Purvis slowed down as he neared the park. Along Birdcage Walk the buds on the trees were turning into tiny leaves, still too small to give shelter from the steady downpour. Rain was beginning to soak through his coat as he stood waiting at the lights while taxis chugged by, sloshing more water into the gutters at the side of the road. Duff

Wells had certainly drawn the short straw today. He must be drenched jogging out there in the park.

Then through his earphones Purvis heard Wells's voice come to life. 'Tonto has sat down on a bench. Halfway along the side of Birdcage Walk. He's reading a paper.'

'In the rain?' It was Wally Woods in the control room.

'Yep. Hang on a minute ... he's up. Walking again, approaching Horse Guards. Towards you, Maureen.'

'Got him,' came Maureen's voice.

'Why'd he stop?' Wally Woods enquired.

'Dunno. Looks odd. And he's left his paper in the bin.'

In the control room Wally looked at Peggy. 'Do you want that paper?'

Her eyes were shining. Something was happening at last. She thought for a split second. 'No. Tell them to leave it and wait. Prepare to follow if someone collects it.'

The instruction was relayed to the watchers. There was a pause. Purvis crossed Birdcage Walk and went into the park. He could see the bench in front of him. Several office workers were hurrying along the path, their heads down against the rain. As he approached the bench, he saw a man coming towards him, walking more slowly than the office workers, his hands in his pockets, seemingly oblivious to the rain.

'I think we may have contact,' said Purvis into his tiepin. He pressed a button in his pocket and a concealed camera started to take pictures of a heavy-set man in a dark overcoat. 'I reckon he's Chinese. Definitely not a Westerner.'

Wally looked at Peggy with raised eyebrows. But before she could speak Purvis's voice came over the speaker again. 'He's stopped right by the bench. He's looking around.' There was a pause, and the tension in the control room was building when, 'Bingo!' Purvis exclaimed. 'He's taken the paper out of the bin.'

'Ask them to follow him. We need to know where he goes,' said Peggy.

'I have Tonto,' said Marcus Washington from the MOD. 'He's gone inside.'

'Unknown target heading north across the park now, towards The Mall and Waterloo Place.' That was Maureen on Horseguards Parade.

Some fast deployment by Wally Woods meant that by the time the target emerged on to Pall Mall, where he turned left heading for St James's Street, he was being trailed by a black taxi containing two men and a woman. When finally he turned into the door of the Stafford Hotel, he was still apparently unaware that his progress from St James's Park had been logged and photographed all the way.

34

THE DIGS CHARLIE FIELDING shared with Hugo Cowdray were three rooms in a Norfolk farmhouse otherwise occupied by the owner – a widow who made up for the deficiencies in her late husband's pension by renting out her top floor. She had initially seemed suspicious of the two prospective tenants put forward by the letting agency in King's Lynn, but Fielding's cheerful manner had won her over in the end – along with a hefty deposit and a guaranteed rental of six months. She didn't know exactly what had brought them there, and Fielding hadn't told her, though the man with the badge who'd come to inspect the flat before they moved in had made it clear it was something hush-hush. She had hoped Fielding would fill her in on the secret, but in answer to her veiled enquiries, he had merely smiled.

Tonight he had the flat to himself – Cowdray had gone down to London for a long weekend, to spend time with his wife Cynthia and their children. He probably needed to; Fielding didn't know what Cowdray would have told his wife about his adventures with Belinda Duggan, if anything at all. But Cynthia was a clever woman, and she would have sensed that something was up.

Here in the flat, he and Cowdray each had their own bedroom, but shared the large low-eaved sitting-cum-dining room, and the adjoining makeshift kitchen. Fielding was working this evening on his laptop at the dining-room table; across the room, on a small pine side table, Cowdray's laptop was also open, powered up, ready and waiting.

Waiting for what? Fielding wondered. He was certain Cowdray had no involvement in leaking information about the work going on at Brigham Hall. His had been a personal failing, not a conscious betrayal of his country, though God knows what was going to happen to him when all this was over. Fielding felt upset about the whole business, still stunned that such a close friend and colleague had let down the side so badly. At least Cowdray was cooperating fully now, though Fielding had been strictly limited in what he could tell him about the ... what precisely? Operation? Wasn't that what these intelligence people called it? Yes, though intelligence had been the last thing Hugo Cowdray had shown.

It was just as he was feeling lowest about the situation that a red light blinked and flickered in the corner of his screen. He stood up at once, and went over to Cowdray's machine. Conventional anti-virus programs traditionally worked behind the scenes, but the detection program he'd installed on Cowdray's machine was not an off-the-shelf item. He watched as the screen cleared and a pop-up window appeared in the centre. **External Invasion** it declared, and then began to list the sectors under attack, every five seconds pausing to write the cached information to disk. Whatever was out there, Fielding realised, it was moving through Cowdray's machine at extraordinary speed, jumping seemingly at random through his FAT files and directories, but covering so much ground that it would soon have canvassed the entire local permanent storage of the machine – all 500 gigabytes.

And then suddenly it was gone, and the pop-up window closed and the screensaver – a colour photograph from the Colorado Rockies that Cowdray had snapped during a summer holiday there – reappeared. Fielding realised his heart was beating like a metronome on speed.

He took a deep breath and pulled up a chair, then went to work on Cowdray's machine. The tool he used was called, ironically in the circumstances, The Mole, since it burrowed like the little velvet mammal deep beneath the surface of the transactions between Cowdray's laptop and the unknown intruder, working back along the trace left by the foreign URL, moving in nano-seconds to isolate the particular machine that had been busy snooping here. It sped unimpeded into the generic network of the MOD, then effectively turned down a side lane, emerging into the collective LAN of the unit – how could he fail to recognise the tag? – run by Cowdray himself back in less stressful times when he had been just a boffin, if a senior one, at the MOD's HQ.

But there it stopped. No specific URLs came up on screen, nor any of the bespoke identifiers used by the MOD. Damn, it hadn't got back to machine level; the intruder had been even cleverer than Fielding had feared. There was nothing of value now for it to steal, but what Fielding didn't know was what it might have managed to extract before today's invasion.

He picked up the phone and rang Peggy Kinsolving.

35

CATHY TREGLOWN OPENED THE door cautiously. She was relieved to find only René standing on her doorstep. He was wearing a blue denim jacket and rough peasant trousers. He smiled at her, sweeping a wave of brown hair off his forehead, and reflexively she smiled back.

Then she remembered her father's warning phone call. *These are not your friends,* he'd insisted, and for once part of her agreed. After all, her last meeting with René had been pretty unpleasant. When he had asked her for money for the commune, she had hesitated, and he had immediately grown angry. He didn't seem to realise that though she remained committed to the cause, she had other things – in particular her little boy – to spend her money on.

But now as he came in he exuded charm and *bonhomie*, handing her a bottle of Cahors red he had brought with him from France. Cathy led the way into the sitting room and René sat down on the sofa while she went into the kitchen and put the kettle on. Through the window she could see Teddy pretending to drive the toy truck her father had brought him on his last visit. He did spoil the boy, she thought crossly, then her mood lightened at the sight of her son enjoying himself. Her plan had been to send Teddy round to play with his friend Richard this afternoon, since she didn't want him around when the French were visiting, but she'd forgotten to arrange it in time. So it was a relief that Antoine hadn't accompanied René; it must mean they were no longer angry with her.

When the kettle boiled she filled the two waiting mugs and carried them into the sitting room where she gave one to René. She sat down in the armchair while he sniffed the steaming mug suspiciously. 'It's tea,' she said, and he shrugged, as if he expected nothing better from the English.

They chatted for a while about the commune, with René answering her questions about the many friends she'd left behind. She missed the old farm near Cahors, and the camaraderie there'd been among the commune's members, at least when she first went there. René seemed happy to answer her questions and give her news about the place. He told her that the vegetable garden she had started was thriving, but that they'd had to replace the bird feeder she'd put up when it had fallen apart in a recent storm.

She was beginning to think that Edward had been wrong about René. Her old French comrade was being the soul of affability, but then, he had always been a charmer. Half the girls in the commune had slept with him at one time or another; not just because he was their *de facto* leader, but because he had charisma – the charisma that had made him leader. He wasn't a big man, he wasn't handsome, and sometimes he talked too much (she remembered the dreary political lectures he'd insisted on giving), but there was an appealing intensity about him which, coupled with the charm he could turn on when he wanted to, could sway even the most sceptical.

'You know, Cathy,' he said, 'you are much missed at the commune. You could come back any time.'

'Thank you. But you see—' she began to explain.

René waved one hand dismissively, and suddenly his relaxed mood seemed to have changed. 'But that's not what I'm here for. I told you last time, we're feeling the pinch a bit. And we have plans – the G20 is meeting next month in Avignon. We aim to be there.' He spoke as if he were planning a holiday. 'But plans only get you so far if you don't have the money to carry them out.'

'What sort of plans need money?' she asked. 'We've been at G20 protests often enough in the past. They didn't cost anything.'

'And they had no impact whatsoever. We need to escalate our protest.'

'What do you mean?'

'The bankers and the politicians are happy to use force to keep us down, so we're more than justified in using violence ourselves. But taking up arms is expensive.'

'Arms? You mean you want to buy guns?' she asked, trying to sound comradely, though inwardly she was shocked. This was not something they had ever envisaged at the commune when she was there. Surely the others would also be appalled. Had things changed so much since she had left France? Maybe it was even worse than she feared. 'Or is it explosives you mean? Are you planning to blow something up?' Her voice quavered slightly, but she couldn't help herself. This was truly frightening.

René just looked at her, unwilling to answer. Then he said, 'Never mind the exact objectives. The point is, you can help us realise them.' His expression was half-seductive, half-intimidating.

Cathy thought of what Edward had said. *That friend of mine you met – you know, the one who came down to Brighton with me that day? As you might have suspected, she has good contacts with the police and . . . security people in general. I asked her to look into your friends in Cahors.*

Cathy had started to protest, angry he had brought someone to her house under such false pretences. But Edward had gone on: *Now hear me out, Cathy, if only for Teddy's sake. I'm afraid Liz didn't discover much that was good about these people. This chap Antoine in particular is nothing but a thug. Please be careful if you have to see them again.*

She said carefully, 'It's a bit difficult for me right now. I've lost my job.' A lie. 'The benefits system is hopeless here, and I've got a son to raise.'

'Ah, Teddy,' said René with a smile that was only fleeting. 'The *petit garçon*. He too is missed at the commune. Such a sweet boy.'

'He is,' she said, wanting to change the subject.

'You know, it would be truly awful if anything ever happened to him.'

She couldn't bring herself to reply.

'*Tu m'écoutes*, Cathy?' he asked, and his smile was now rigid and unfriendly.

'I hear you,' she replied.

'You know, Antoine doesn't like children. It's quite unusual – I mean, there are many people who don't want children, and aren't particularly keen on them. But Antoine actively dislikes them. I would never want a child of mine to spend time alone with that man. You know his temper . . .'

Cathy felt fear wash through her veins like iced water; her arms ached and her legs suddenly seemed heavy and leaden. She struggled to stand up. She needed this man to leave, needed him to get out of here right away. At last, she made it to her feet.

But René remained seated on the sofa. He smiled. 'You're meant to ask me a question now, Cathy.'

'What question?' she said, trying not to stutter the words.

'How much money we need from you.' He stared up at her, and there was nothing friendly in his unwavering gaze. 'The answer is ten thousand pounds.'

She started in surprise, but he said smoothly, 'Come, come. It's not all you have. You were very indiscreet the last time we met. It will still leave you enough to feed the boy – enough indeed to keep you off the dreaded benefits.' He gave a dry laugh.

'It's very difficult.'

'I know it is, Cathy,' he said in a voice so soothing that it frightened her even more. 'But it's hard for all of us.' He leaned forward and whispered, 'Remember the cause. It's bigger than us all. That's why I know you'll make the sacrifice.'

She nodded dumbly – anything to get the man out of her house. And she saw to her relief that he was finally getting up. She followed him out into the hall. He opened the front door, then paused in the doorway. 'I will come in about ten days' time, Cathy. I'll ring to let you know precisely when. Have the money ready for me, all right?'

She nodded, wanting only for him to go. As René started to pull the front door shut, he said quietly, 'Don't even think of going to the police. Not if you love your little boy. You wouldn't want Antoine to pay you a visit, now would you?'

36

THE PHONE WAS RINGING as Liz came into her flat. She fumbled for the light switch, dropped her bag and briefcase on the floor and made it across the sitting room just in time. 'Hello,' she said.

'Liz, it's Edward here. Have you got a minute?'

'Of course,' she said. She looked around the room, which was messy even by her standards. She'd planned to tidy up this evening, so any diversion was welcome.

'Cathy rang me from Brighton. She was in quite a state.'

Liz remembered that the French anarchists were due to visit. 'Is she all right?'

'Yes – I mean, she hasn't been hurt or anything like that. René came as planned, but on his own. Though that was bad enough; she's very shaken up.'

'What happened?'

'He asked her again for money. They want ten thousand pounds – a contribution to the cause, he called it. Apparently, they're planning to disrupt the G20 conference next month in Avignon. Cathy thinks they're trying to buy guns, and maybe explosives.'

'Does she know any more – what kind of explosive, or

where they're getting it from?' This was no longer just a family problem; now it was a professional matter.

'No, she didn't get much out of him. But for once Cathy saw sense and said no when he asked for money. She told him she'd lost her job.'

'Good for her.' Anything to get that creep off her back. 'How did René take it?'

'Pretty badly, I gather. But it's what he suggested could happen next that upset her. He was threatening that Teddy might be harmed if she didn't give them the money.'

'What? Where is he now? Has he gone?'

'Yes. He's gone for the moment. But apparently there's a violent sidekick. A thug called Antoine.'

'I know – my French colleagues told me about him. Did René say Antoine would hurt Teddy?'

'More or less.'

'The police will take a dim view of that.'

'I know, but the problem is, we've only got Cathy's word against this chap René's. And he's probably buggered off by now, back to France. I don't see what the police here can do.' Edward paused, and breathed out noisily. 'That's why I rang you. I'm awfully sorry, Liz, and I certainly understand if you can't help. It's just—'

I know, she thought, it's just Teddy. But that and the mention of explosives were more than enough reason for her to get involved. She said, 'Leave it to me, Edward. I think I can help.'

Liz called Isobel Florian as soon as she arrived at the office the next day. She explained what had happened to Cathy, and what else René had told her.

Isobel said, 'That's the first firm evidence we have received. We know he has been making trips to Marseilles, but we didn't know exactly what for – Marcel, our source inside the commune, thought it was probably weapons, but now it sounds even worse.'

Liz said, 'Obviously the G20 summit has to be our priority, but I am worried about Cathy and her little boy. René threatened that if she didn't help finance their plans, he would come back – along with this fellow Antoine.'

'You certainly don't want that. We've checked, and this Antoine has a criminal record a mile long. He's very violent. But it seems to me that we could easily kill two birds with one stone. If we can find out when those two are going to England, I would arrange a raid on their commune. I'm sure we'll find plenty there. That would allow us to issue an Interpol warrant for René and Antoine. The moment they set foot in the UK, they'll be arrested. Until they're extradited to France, the only part of Britain they'll see is through bars.'

37

AT THIS TIME OF the evening Queensway was crowded with after-work shoppers. The cold wind and rain which had lingered all week, a reminder that winter wasn't long over, had now given way to a warm southerly breeze and clear skies. As dusk fell traces of pink mingled in the sky with the yellow of the streetlights.

Andy Bokus found Ujin Wong waiting for him at a table in the back of the dim sum restaurant. Bokus had come straight from Grosvenor Square and wore a suit, but Wong was dressed trendily in a cotton jacket and black turtleneck – he could have been a film director, designer or the owner of an art gallery. To Bokus, as they shook hands, Wong was practically unrecognisable from the timid youth he had first known.

'It's been a long time,' said Bokus, thinking of their last meeting in Washington. Wong had been seconded to the Agency as part of the exchange programme with close allies, and Bokus had been his mentor for a month. At that time the Korean had spoken poor English and had been very shy; it was difficult to know just what the hell to do with him. After a week, Bokus had been counting the days until he was shot of the guy.

Bokus was also tasked with looking after his visitor outside work. He was damned if he was going to take him to the theatre, or lead him, uncomprehending, through the halls of a museum. Instead, almost out of desperation, he took him along to FedExField in Maryland to watch a Redskins football game – Bokus had season tickets.

To his complete surprise, Wong had taken to American football at once, hollering for the Skins with the best of them, and cheering like mad each time they scored a touchdown. Most important, he had matched Bokus beer for beer, which for Bokus was always a good sign in anyone.

After that, he took a belated look at Wong's file, and discovered that the Korean had already experienced more misery in his life than Bokus was ever likely to. Both his parents had been killed by a North Korean incursion when he was little more than a baby; his childhood had been spent in an orphanage. But he was a plucky little guy, who was working hard to improve his English and was willing to pitch in with anything Bokus threw his way. By the time Wong's secondment had ended, he and Bokus had become firm friends.

'We must mark this occasion,' Wong said now, motioning to a waiter. 'Two Tsingtao,' he ordered.

'I heard you were coming here,' said Bokus. 'When did you arrive?'

'Last month. They asked me to take things slowly – we're pretty low-profile in this country. I was going to call you though.'

They reminisced for a while and exchanged news of their respective families. Then Bokus said, 'You'll have to come out to the house for dinner one night. But I wanted to see you alone this time. I've got a little business I could use your help on. Strictly unofficial, if you don't mind.'

'Okay. Tell me about it.'

The waiter arrived with their Chinese beers and a trolley loaded with dim sum, and Bokus waited while they were each served. Then, after taking a large gulp of beer, he said, 'There's a guy from your agency seconded to the MOD here. He was vetted by us two years ago for a secondment to Langley. He was clean then . . .'

Wong raised an eyebrow. 'But now?'

'Let's just say we're not sure. The Brits are convinced he's up to something but they don't know what or who with.'

Wong nodded, pursing his lips. 'You said he'd been vetted two years ago?'

'Yeah. But our vetting has to depend a lot on the information you guys supply.'

'Meaning?' asked Wong, bristling.

'Ujin, relax. You guys are as good as we are at this sort of thing. Which means occasionally both of us slip up. I'm not saying that's happened here – in fact, I'd put money on this guy being clean. But the Brits are on my case, and I need to know for sure, if I'm going to tell them they're wrong. You can understand.'

Wong nodded, a little reluctantly. 'So what do you want me to do?'

Bokus poked awkwardly with his chopsticks at a dumpling, held it up slowly, then snapped at it before it could escape and started chewing. Between chomps he said, 'I want you to get your people to take another look. I could do it through my channels, go to Langley, have them request it officially, then sit over here on my fat ass and wait. But I haven't got time for that. Like I say, the Brits are pressing me. I have my own ideas about their problem, but they're not going to listen to me until I erase their own suspicions.'

Wong signalled the waiter for two more beers. 'So who is it you want to know about?'

Bokus reached inside his suit jacket and took out a small envelope which he put down on the table and pushed across to Wong. 'His name's Park Woo-jin. There's a mug shot and enough personal details in there to find him in your database.'

Wong ignored the envelope. 'Is this a very senior guy?'

'Not at all. He's just a computer gnome working in the MOD's systems division. He's good – they wouldn't have sent him here otherwise – but not a big cheese.'

Wong laughed. 'I never understood that expression, you know. But then, we Koreans don't eat much cheese. Anyway, I'll talk to some people back in Seoul. Is there anything else I should know about this guy?'

'Don't think so.' Bokus added, more casually than he felt, 'The one thing you might want to look for is some Russian connection. Like I say, I doubt our friend here – ' and he gestured at the envelope which lay untouched near Wong's plate ' – is the guy the Brits are looking for. But if he is, I'd give you odds he's got some SVR tie-up.'

Wong looked at him inscrutably. Bokus realised that the guy had grown up; there was nothing kid-like or unconfident about the Korean now. He said, 'That's twice you've offered to put money on this guy being clean, Andy. But I guess you're not that sure yourself.'

Bokus frowned, and Wong went on cheerfully, 'Anyway, how did the Skins do this year?'

38

MARCEL WAS IN THE garden planting beans, taking advantage of the late-evening light. When he completed the last row he stood up, brushed the soil from his hands and inspected his handiwork. Ever since Cathy, the English woman, had left, Pascale and he had been in charge of the kitchen garden; Marcel reckoned he had planted enough to keep the whole household in fresh vegetables right through to the early autumn. There were bushes of soft fruits as well – raspberries, currants and gooseberries – and cherries, apricots and plums in the old orchard.

He was about to pick a few lettuces for supper when a shadow crossed the ground in front of him. He turned and jumped at the sight of René, just two feet behind him. 'Christ, you startled me.'

'Did I?' René seemed amused.

'I didn't realise you were back.'

René's mouth set in a hard line. 'Well, I am, and I need you to come with me.'

'Where are we going?'

'You'll see.'

He did, but not for three hours, the time it took them to drive south to Toulouse, then east past Carcassonne and along the Mediterranean coast to Marseilles. René drove the VW camper with Marcel sitting in the passenger seat beside him. To Marcel's alarm Antoine accompanied them, lounging on the cushioned platform seat they'd installed at the back of the van to use as a bed. On the floor beside him was a two-foot length of steel pipe, wrapped at one end with thick black tape, presumably to serve as a grip. The sight of it made Marcel nervous, and added to his feeling that there was something very dodgy about this trip.

'Is there a spare coat back there?' he asked Antoine. René had been so insistent on leaving straight away that he hadn't even had time to grab a jacket.

'Nope,' came the curt reply.

When Marcel tried to break the tension by asking René how his trip to England had gone, he only received a grunt in reply. So he gave up, and sat in silence, wondering why they wanted him along on this expedition and what on earth it was about.

When the lights of night-time Marseilles could be seen in the distance, René seemed to grow more alert and Antoine sat up on his bench in the back. Several miles short of the city boundary they turned off the main road and drove through a suburb of modern apartment blocks and shopping malls. A few miles further on René turned the van sharply down a narrow road with no streetlights or traffic and suddenly they were out in the countryside, with dark fields on either side and no sign of houses.

René drove slowly, peering through the windscreen, looking for something. After a few miles a small building, no bigger than a caravan, showed up in the lights and they swung off the road into a large empty gravel yard with an aluminium barn at the back. It could have been the premises of an agricultural merchant, but in the dark

Marcel could not be sure. Whatever it was, he knew he'd never be able to find the place again.

René drove the van to a far corner of the yard, reversed it so that it faced the barn, and parked under the branches of the tall trees that lined the border of the property. He turned off the engine and extinguished the lights.

'Now,' he said to Marcel, 'I'll tell you what's going to happen. In a few minutes two men will arrive. We'll get out and talk to them, then they're going to give us some goods. If these goods are okay I'll pay them some money, and then we'll all go home. Got it?'

'What do you want me to do?'

'Not a lot. When I get out, you get out too and come with me. You don't need to say a word – in fact, make sure you don't open your mouth.'

'What about …?' he began, wondering what Antoine was going to do.

'I said, don't open your mouth. Starting now.'

They sat in silence after that. A few minutes passed, and then Marcel heard the low rumble of an approaching vehicle. Lights flickered from the road, then suddenly swept across the gravel yard. The vehicle pulled in and stopped by the barn. After a moment they heard two doors open then slam shut.

René suddenly turned on the camper's lights full beam, and Marcel saw two men standing in front of a Range Rover, shielding their eyes from the lights until René turned them off again.

'Come on,' he said, and they both got out.

René had a torch in his hand and he turned it on as they walked towards the Range Rover. One of the two waiting figures did the same, and as they approached each other all four were bathed in a honey glow of light. The two visitors wore military-style gilets and combat trousers with heavy boots. They looked to be North African, probably Algerian, Marcel thought. The taller of the two had a ragged beard, and smiled now, revealing prominent teeth. '*Bonsoir*,' he said cheerfully. He pointed at Marcel. 'This is not the same colleague you had last time.'

'No. The other man is unwell. Anyway, let's get down to business,' said René. 'Have you brought the goods?'

'Of course.'

'We need to see them.'

'Ah, and we need to see the money.'

'Goods first,' said René.

The Algerian hesitated, looking at René and Marcel. Then he shrugged. 'As you wish.'

He led them to the back of the Range Rover, opened the rear door and shone his torch on to a long flat cardboard carton that lay wedged carefully between two bricks. The Algerian turned to René. 'Before I open this, I need to see the money.'

René reached into his jacket and brought out an envelope. 'Four thousand Euros. It's all there.'

'Of course.' The North African pointed to the back of the Range Rover and, when René had put the envelope down next to the cardboard box, reached into one of the pockets of his gilet and produced a Stanley knife. He grabbed the end of the box and slit it down the side in one quick movement. Using his other hand to hold the box in place, he ripped it open and flipped the lid back.

All four of them stood there, looking at the contents – two Uzi machine-guns, parts highly oiled, their charcoal metal buffed to a sheen. They were clearly brand new.

René broke the spell. 'Beautiful, but there's something missing.'

'Missing?' asked the North African, the smile gone from his face.

'We are paying for four. I don't see four guns there.'

'Perhaps you have misunderstood, Monsieur.'

'I don't think so,' said René, and when he took a step backwards, Marcel did likewise.

But it was too late. With one quick lunge the North African had pressed the Stanley knife against René's chest. Before Marcel could move, the other African had pulled his own knife – a bigger weapon, the size and shape of a Bowie knife – and pointed it menacingly at Marcel.

'What do you want?' asked René.

The North African laughed. 'Nothing. You've paid your money, and you can take the merchandise. We're all done here.'

'I don't think so,' said René. Marcel wondered what he meant; there didn't seem to be much chance of a refund.

The North African was starting to smile again when something moved through the air and struck him hard in the face. A bunch of splintered teeth flew out of the man's mouth, followed by a spray of blood. The North African fell back, hitting his head against the Range Rover's boot, and shrieking in pain.

Suddenly Antoine was standing beside Marcel, holding the metal pipe. The other North African waved his knife, and Antoine gave a harsh laugh. 'Try me,' he said tauntingly, and stepped forward. The North African's courage suddenly failed, and he ran for the safety of the trees.

The man with the beard was half-lying, half-leaning against the Range Rover, holding his mouth with both hands. Ignoring him, René reached in and retrieved the envelope full of cash, tucking it into his jacket pocket. He nodded at Antoine, who pushed the wounded man brusquely aside, lifted the cardboard box on to his shoulder and walked with it towards the camper van.

Marcel and René followed him, leaving the Algerian still moaning in pain. There was no sign of his colleague. They got into the camper van and drove off quickly, retracing their route. René drove carefully now; Marcel knew that, with Uzi machine-guns in the back of the van, the last thing they wanted was to be stopped by the police.

As they joined the motorway again, heading west, René said, 'You were right, Antoine. They weren't straight, those guys.'

'I didn't like the look of them when we first met. But you know, two guns are not enough.'

'Don't worry, we'll get more.' René laughed. 'And at least these two were free.'

39

THE BANK DIFAULT-LÉGÈRE WAS family-owned
and famed for its discretion. In recent years, new
privacy laws introduced by the Swiss government had
forced Swiss banks to cooperate with both their own and
other countries' tax authorities, and reveal a previously
undreamed-of amount of information about their clients'
transactions. Inevitably, many banks had suffered, losing
clients to the still secrecy-enshrouded environs of
Lichtenstein, Andorra, or other countries willing to sacri-
fice respectability to serve their deep-pocketed depositors.

Difault-Légère had suffered less than most Swiss
banks, for though it had not openly resisted the new
measures, it had done its best to ignore them. Behind its
imposing nineteenth-century façade on Zurich's fabled
Banhoffstrasse, the banking hall continued to operate
much as it had always done, safeguarding the interests of
its rich international clientele. The bank's attitude was
clear: governments and their regulations come and go, but
Difault-Légère and the wealth of its private clients were
permanencies.

With this in mind, Otto Bech climbed the short flight
of steps to the bank's grand entrance, feeling wary. He

glanced at the two stone figures of Cerberus guarding the door, and remembered that in classical mythology it was the task of these three-headed dogs to keep people in the Underworld once they'd crossed the River Styx. He hoped the Difault-Légère dogs would prove more flexible, as he had a dinner engagement back in Bern with the Justice Minister.

Bech's appointment now was with the bank's President, Herman Kessler, whom he knew from years back. When he was running the National Fraud Squad, Bech had dealt with all the senior bankers in Switzerland. A cautious man, with a sharp tongue when displeased, Kessler had never been particularly cooperative, and even now, after Bech had stressed that national security issues were involved, the banker had not been forthcoming when asked for CCTV footage of the mysterious Nikolai Bakowski.

Over the phone Kessler had said, 'Before we go much further, I have to say that I am somewhat reluctant to help. Herr Bakowski, after all, is a client of ours; he might have something to say about this invasion of his privacy.'

'It's hardly an invasion. The image you sent us was not at all clear. We need a good look at the man.'

'Perhaps. But I need to feel confident that you have good reason to do so. Herr Bakowski, as I say, is a valued client.'

'Doubtless. But, Herr Kessler, what do you know about your client?'

'Know?' Kessler sounded affronted. 'What should I know? The man had references that entirely satisfied me.' The inference was clear: if Herr Kessler was satisfied, no more needed to be said.

'I assume you would want to be sure that this client of yours actually exists. So far as we can tell, Herr Bakowski does not. We can find no trace of him anywhere in the cantons, and Immigration could find no record of his entering the country. Which points to this man being an impostor, who established his account with Bank Difault-Légère under a false name, using a false passport.'

'Can you prove that? Many people lead very private lives, and know how to protect themselves against intrusive enquiries.'

'Come now, Herr Kessler. I hardly think you mean to imply that I am being particularly intrusive. If you will let me look at the CCTV images, I think I should be able to resolve any doubts.'

'And if that is not possible?'

'Then,' said Herr Bech, his patience suddenly snapping, 'you will be having a different conversation, with my successor at the National Fraud Squad. You can explain to him why you allowed a foreign national to hold an account with you, knowing that he was not who he said he was. You would not, I am sure, wish the Bank Difault-Légère to be investigated for financing the drugs trade or international terrorism. So I will call on you at two-thirty this afternoon and will expect to see the CCTV pictures.' And with that parting shot, Bech had put the phone down.

Now a doorman in a tail coat opened the tall mahogany door, and ushered him across the marble floor of the banking hall into a waiting room furnished with antique side tables and a Louis XV sofa and chair. Bech sat and thumbed unseeingly through the pages of *Connoisseur* magazine for the twenty minutes Kessler kept him waiting.

At last another tail-coated flunkey came in and led him out into the hall and up the sweeping staircase to the first floor and Kessler's palatial office at the front of the mansion house. The banker, a pale, silver-haired, slightly stooping figure in black jacket and striped trousers, rose stiffly from behind his desk at the far end of the room and watched in silence as Bech walked across the carpet towards him. 'Good afternoon, Herr Bech,' he said, making no apology for keeping his visitor waiting. 'Do sit down. Would you care for coffee?'

'Yes, please,' said Bech, and watched as Kessler reached under his desk and pressed a buzzer. They made stiff small talk for a moment without alluding to the matter at hand until the coffee was brought in and poured by yet another flunkey in tails. As he left the room, Bech hoped that at last they could get down to business.

Kessler reached into the top drawer of his desk and brought out a manila envelope. Without a word, he pushed it to a point halfway across the desk. Bech took his time reaching for it, then slowly withdrew a series of photographs. These were much clearer pictures than the one he'd seen before, and there was no doubt about the identity of the man caught, variously, at the teller's cage, turning around after his transaction, then leaving the banking hall.

Bech put the pictures into the envelope, which he slid back across the desk to Kessler. He sat silent for a moment until, unable to contain his curiosity, Kessler asked, 'Is that helpful, Herr Bech?'

'Very,' he replied, thinking he'd let Kessler sweat. But he relented, not wanting to act as churlishly as the banker, and added, 'Herr Bakowski is in fact a man called Kubiak. He is one of the most senior Russian intelligence officers operating in our country.'

Kessler's eyes widened. 'I see,' he said.

'You told me last month that the money going into the Bakowski account has been coming from a variety of sources – all of them former republics of the Soviet Union.'

'That's correct.'

'Were you able to find out anything more?'

'As a matter of fact, I have. Not that it was easy. Most of these new countries are entirely unregulated when it comes to finance,' Kessler said disdainfully, clearly unaware of any irony in his remark. 'They are disinclined to cooperate with their counterparts in the West, fancying themselves competitors, not colleagues.'

It was clear what Kessler thought of these upstarts, though to Bech the arrogance of the old patrician banker seemed entirely hypocritical. As his behaviour over the Bakowski account showed, Kessler himself was not choosy about the sources of the money his own bank was willing to handle.

'However,' he went on, 'we do have contacts among the banks in these countries, and in two cases – Belarus and Kazakhstan – I managed to discover where the money being sent to Herr Bakowski's account originated.'

He paused, perhaps to heighten the drama of his discovery, and Bech sat expressionless, forcing himself to wait patiently.

'The money sent from these two countries came originally from Switzerland.'

'*Switzerland?*' Bech could not contain his astonishment. This meant the money was going in a loop, starting here in the cantons, heading east to the rough-and-ready commercial world of the ex-Soviet republics, then winging back west all over again.

'It does seem rather strange,' Kessler said. This, coming from a banker who had probably seen most financial wheezes, was a significant acknowledgement. 'I hope the information means something to you.'

'It does, Herr Kessler, it does.' But, in truth, Bech was damned if he knew what.

40

I T WAS GOOD TO be able to work alone at his terminal
again. For the first few days after the drone briefly went
AWOL in the desert of Oman, Dick Cottinger had had
company – lots of company. You didn't have to be Einstein to
figure out that this was the result of something going wrong
with the new communications system. Which explained the
presence of coders, cryptanalysts, plain analysts, the base
commanding officer, big shots from the Pentagon, and a host
of outsiders from the NSA and CIA and damn near every
other Federal agency Cottinger had ever heard of.

But as the trials of the drone continued, entirely unevent-
fully, gradually all the fuss and seemingly most of the
suspicion had faded away. Even his superior officer Colonel
Galsworthy had started to leave him alone to get on with
the remaining trials. Cottinger had been all nerves after
the initial incident, but now his confidence was coming
back. He looked around him, and since it was a weekday
the desks were almost all occupied. Galsworthy was on the
far side of the room, with a coffee cup in his hand, chatting
to one of the prettier female clerks.

Now the drone was moving slowly, no more than 100
m.p.h., south towards the Arabian Sea. In the far distance

the flat landscape rose sharply to a high escarpment, but much closer – probably less than five miles away – a tall tower-like construction was visible in the flat desert.

Cottinger checked the sequence of instructions on his clipboard and looked at the digital clock on the wall. Ten seconds to go. He counted down, cleared his throat, and leaning slightly forward said, in the clearest tones he could muster: 'Descend to five hundred feet. Target is ahead of you. Look for anti-air weapons, and take evasive action if you see them. Otherwise, proceed towards the target.'

He watched as the drone began to descend and the features of the drab terrain became distinct – he could see individual outcroppings of rock now. The tower was clearly visible: it must have been fifty feet high, though it looked taller, looming out of the flat sea of sandy gravel bed. It had been put up by a squad of US marines the month before.

'How's it going, Lieutenant?'

Cottinger turned to find Galsworthy standing behind his chair. 'Okay, sir. We'll be simulating firing in about two minutes.'

'Okey-dokey,' he said, and walked away. Galsworthy was pretty relaxed today, thought Cottinger, but then they'd now had days of these exercises without a hitch.

He noticed that the drone had speeded up slightly, and the tower was getting alarmingly big on the screen. It was a simple affair of steel piping, put up purely for the purposes of the exercise.

'Reduce speed to eighty miles per hour.'

To his surprise the drone accelerated instead, surging to 150 m.p.h. according to his console. 'Reduce speed to eighty miles per hour,' Cottinger repeated, his voice rising. He looked at the altimeter dial on the console and saw the drone was also too low – it had descended to three hundred feet and falling. On the screen below the ground was whiz-zing past in a blur.

'What's the matter, Lieutenant?' Colonel Galsworthy was suddenly back behind him.

Cottinger pointed to the screen. 'It's going way too fast.'

'Well, tell it to slow down,' Galsworthy said, sounding edgy.

'I have, sir.' He leaned forward towards the microphone on the panel at the front of his desk. 'Reduce speed. Eighty miles per hour.'

By now the drone was flying at close to 200 m.p.h., and the tower loomed less than a mile away. Looking at the altimeter, Cottinger saw the drone was down to fifty feet; on the screen its nose looked to be level with the top of the tower.

'Jesus Christ!' Galsworthy exclaimed. 'What is it doing?'

'Ascend to five hundred feet,' Cottinger shouted. Then, forgetting his carefully learned commands, 'Get up, get up, get up!' he shouted. He'd left his chair now and was stand-ing up, staring at the monitor, sweat standing out on his brow as the drone hurtled towards the tower. Would it clear it? 'Ascend to five hundred feet,' he tried again, but there was no response.

He clenched both fists and waited tensely as the drone narrowed in on the tower. Closer and closer – he closed his eyes for a second. And then suddenly, as the screen filled with an image of steel piping tied together like metal latticework, his terminal screen went blank.

'What the hell!' shouted Galsworthy.

Cottinger ignored him and, grabbing his keyboard, typed in a series of commands. The terminal screen refreshed, and a satellite view of Oman filled the screen – nothing came from the drone. The satellite camera zoomed, gradually magnifying. A dark smear appeared in the centre of the screen and grew in size as the camera zeroed in. The smear was an ascending trail of wispy smoke and through it, as the magnification increased, Cottinger could glimpse a tangled mess of steel on the ground where seconds before the tower had stood. Nearby a fire was blazing; he could make out the skeletal remains of the drone burning on the desert floor.

Galsworthy cursed loudly. 'What happened?' he demanded.

Cottinger stared at the smouldering wreckage on his screen. He knew the drone was expected to take charge of itself one day, but this had come a lot earlier than expected.

'Well, sir, how can I put it?' he said at last. 'It looks as if our drone just committed suicide.'

41

THIS TIME BOKUS CALLED on Fane, who must have alerted Liz Carlyle as she was there when the American arrived, standing by the window, looking down at the Thames at high tide. Though Bokus hadn't asked for her to be there, he was glad she was; he could get the bad news over in one fell swoop.

'Thanks for seeing me,' he said as they sat down in the corner, round a table which Fane claimed had belonged to his great-grandfather. Trust him to bring his family heir-looms to work, thought Bokus sourly. Fane's office was much smaller than his at Grosvenor Square, yet there was something undeniably impressive about it. Its elegant furniture and expensive curtains seemed to say that you didn't need an office the size of a tennis court to show your status. It made Bokus wonder grudgingly if there wasn't something to the British liking for understatement.

'You said it was important,' said Fane, going straight to the point without the usual small talk.

Bokus was sweating, slightly nervous about the news he was about to break.

He took a deep breath. 'Operation Clarity has had a bit of a setback and it's been temporarily suspended.'

'What setback?' asked Liz Carlyle. 'We've heard nothing.'

'It was in Oman. That's where they've been running trials on the new control system. We've lost one.'

'Lost one?' she asked incredulously.

Bokus nodded.

'What happened?' Fane said, uncrossing his legs and leaning forward in his chair.

'Nobody knows for sure. It seems one minute the test drone was flying along just fine, being directed by the voice commands, then all of a sudden it went nose down into a target it was meant to photograph. Like a dog deciding to ignore its master's voice.' Bokus smiled weakly, but neither Liz nor Fane smiled back. 'So it seems you two were right to think we have a problem.'

'Are they sure it was external interference?' asked Fane. 'You know, Andy, these technological marvels are so beyond the ken of us mere mortals that we sometimes forget they can foul up in the same way people do. "To err is human" and all that sort of thing, but the worst mistakes in my view are technical.'

Bokus shook his head regretfully. 'It would be nice to think so, but Langley's told me there was unauthorised intervention in the commands sent to the drone. Don't ask me for the technical detail, but they think the Air Force commands were somehow overlaid with contradictory ones. The drone didn't know which set to believe, so it pretty much said "what the hell", and looked for the nearest exit sign. It's made them look back at another glitch which they'd previously put down to a technical malfunction.'

Fane asked, 'Could this sabotage have come from some other source? I mean, how do you know it's connected to Operation Clarity?'

'Unfortunately, Clarity's the only place it could have come from. To overlay the legitimate orders, the bogus ones would have to unravel their encryption, and then duplicate it themselves. To do that they'd have to go to the source of the encryption code. That's your MOD project.'

'Bugger,' said Fane, and sat further forward in his chair, crossing his arms.

'So we need to find this mole right away,' said Liz. 'Has Langley come back to you about Park Woo-jin?'

'Yes,' said Bokus, wondering if he should mention his source Ujin Wong. Better not, he decided. They'd met again briefly in a pub near Victoria, and Wong had told him he could find nothing at all suspicious about the programmer Park Woo-jin. 'But I'm sure it's not Park. They've gone through the original vetting, and checked with the Koreans as well. Both are certain he's clean.'

'Well, that's obviously not true,' said Liz, a split second before Fane angrily said, 'Balls.'

'What makes you so sure?' asked Bokus crossly.

Liz snapped, 'We've had surveillance on Park Woo-jin for the last ten days. He made a drop in St James's Park on his way to work. It was crystal clear. Either your people aren't looking hard enough, or the Koreans are pulling the wool.'

'Meaning what exactly?' asked Bokus. He was surprised by the news about Park Woo-jin. The Korean intelligence people were usually very good. They might have made a mistake the first time round, but if they'd had another look, when Ujin Wong asked for it, they should have spotted anything wrong with Park. What was going on?

'Meaning Park Woo-jin is reporting back to Korean intelligence. That's the only thing that makes sense.'

'But why would he do that?' asked Fane. He had picked up a pencil and was rocking it fast between his thumb and forefinger. 'I mean, we all know our allies like to know what's going on, even the genuinely friendly ones. But honestly, would the KCIA really go to the trouble of planting an agent in the project of two close allies? Think of the risk. And the information they might get couldn't do them an iota of conceivable good, while,' he continued, warming to his theme, 'risking God knows what ructions with their largest benefactor if it were discovered.'

'It doesn't make any sense, I agree,' said Bokus. 'Unless,' and he paused until he felt their eyes upon him, 'Park is working for someone else. Like the Russians. Langley's view is that this is a sabotage operation, and increasingly they feel Moscow is behind it. The people at State are talking about calling in the Russian Ambassador and making a formal protest.'

'That would be ridiculous,' said Liz. 'What do they expect the Russians to say?'

'Of course they'd just deny it,' Fane chipped in. 'So all that would do is raise the level of international tension quite unnecessarily.'

'And anyway, how does Langley explain Bravado's information, if the Russians are behind this?' asked Liz.

'They think it was some kind of double bluff. The theory back home is that Bravado didn't want to go the whole road to betraying his country, so he wrapped the information up by saying the attack was being carried out by a third country.'

'But what about Kubiak? Where does he fit in according to your theory? Did you do a trace with Langley?'

'Yes. There's a big file. They did have him in their sights in Delhi, same as your lot did. They did a background study then and apparently his father was a senior General in the Defence Department. So he had brilliant access, as well as the prospect of rising high in the KGB. Our Station had him surrounded with access agents, including the madam at the whorehouse. They were planning to offer a big salary but keep him in place. He'd be able to indulge his passions, knowing a golden handshake and easy retirement awaited him in the States.

'But in the end they didn't go ahead. Langley didn't like his profile; our shrinks assessed him as borderline psychopathic. I think the feeling was he'd be too difficult to control. The madam told us a lot about his personal habits – one of them was that he was violent, almost casually so. Apparently he'd nearly killed one of her girls when she did something he didn't like, or maybe she wouldn't do something he did like. There was also an incident when we had him under surveillance, and he assaulted a taxi driver – beat him up really badly, then walked off as though nothing had happened. He was drunk at the time. It had to be hushed up by his Embassy – they paid off the driver before he could complain to the police.'

'From what Bravado said, it sounds as though he hasn't changed a lot,' said Carlyle.

'No, though his career doesn't seem to have taken off as expected,' Fane chipped in. 'Head of Security in Switzerland isn't where he would have hoped to end up. But at least he survived the changes at the end of the Cold War, probably with the help of his father. '

'Well, that's all very interesting.' Liz was looking impatient. 'But I still can't believe there's any Russian connection to Park Woo-jin. He's obviously up to something, and I'm not at all sure Korean intelligence is telling us all they know. I think our best bet is to concentrate on the man who picked up Park Woo-jin's drop. According to the hotel where he stays when he's in London, his name is Dong Shin-soo, but so far we have no trace of him entering the country under that name. We don't know where he is the rest of the time; we don't even know for sure that he's Korean.'

'Okay,' said Bokus, thinking that he was the one getting the worst news. He knew Fane and Carlyle weren't happy to find out that the MOD leak was real – Bokus himself was dismayed by the discovery. But from what he was hearing now, the situation was even more complicated than he'd thought. He'd still put his money on the Russians being involved, though the evidence was going Korea's way. Which not only meant that one of America's staunchest allies was doing the dirty, it also meant his old pal Ujin Wong hadn't been telling him the truth.

'But don't take your eye off Kubiak,' he said, as a parting shot. 'Take my word for it. The Russians are in this somewhere.'

42

AT FIRST IT SEEMED like just another routine surveillance job. Follow target codename Tonto from the MOD to his residence in Ealing. Same every night, thought Duff Wells. Leaves MOD dead on five, walks across St James's Park, through Queen Anne's Gate to the tube station, and takes the District line to Ealing Broadway. A short walk home. Job done.

This evening Duff Wells was covering the tube journey. Stephen Sachs had come in on the tube from Ealing with the target this morning, so this evening he'd just kept a weather eye on him from a distance as he crossed the park. He was probably still there, waiting for the 'stand down' from Wally Woods in the control room. Maureen Hayes had watched Tonto leave the MOD building in Whitehall and would get on the train at Westminster Station, in case Wells needed back-up. Not likely, he thought. This was one of the most predictable targets he'd had for a long time.

Meanwhile, out in Ealing, Marcus Washington was waiting in a white builder's van a hundred yards down the street from the MOD house where Tonto was staying, just to make sure that he went home and stayed there. Unusually, Washington was on his own tonight, as an urgent operation in Tottenham had come in late in the afternoon, and Wally Woods had taken the risk that solo cover would be enough – it seemed more than likely Tonto would conform to his usual pattern and stay put for the evening.

Wells was standing at the front end of the carriage behind Tonto's. He could see him, sitting comfortably reading the *Evening Standard*, ignoring a white-haired lady with a large bag who was standing in front of him. Wells had heard through his headphones that Hayes was safely on board the train, two carriages further back. Wells was thinking about his daughter's birthday in two weeks' time and whether they could afford to buy her the Smartphone she wanted. It wasn't the cost of the phone itself that was the worry but the two-year contract you had to take out with the phone company. Then there was the problem of monitoring who she was texting and emailing, to say nothing of the wider world of the internet. And she was only thirteen.

Tonto stood up and Wells's daughter was forgotten. Was Tonto offering his seat to the old lady? No, he was getting off at the next stop, Chiswick Park, three stops before his usual one. Wells sent a quick alert to Maureen Hayes and the control room and prepared to get off too. This was a bit more like it.

He stood on the platform watching Hayes walking briskly up the steps to the exit, in the midst of a few dozen commuters, followed a few yards behind by Tonto. Wells waited till they'd both gone through the exit barriers then followed on behind.

In Ealing Marcus Washington suddenly sat up behind the steering wheel of his van and turned on the ignition. With a squeal from his tyres, kicking up a little fountain of gravel, he accelerated out of his parking space. Unlike ordinary builder's vans, his was equipped with a three-litre engine, but it didn't do him much good in the local rush-hour traffic and it still took him fifteen minutes to get to Chiswick Park. There he saw Wells casually strolling down the pavement that ran along the north side of a little park. Responding to the voice in his ear, he drove straight past then, fifty yards further on, pulled over and sat, with engine running, waiting for his colleague to reach him.

'What kept you, sunshine?' asked Wells with a grin.

Woods and his team in the control room were receiving the pictures that Maureen Hayes was taking now as she strolled through the park. They showed the target sitting at one end of a bench, at the other a Far Eastern-looking man; they seemed to be talking.

Woods picked up his phone and dialled. 'Peggy? I need you up here straight away. We've got choices to make.'

Two minutes later Peggy Kinsolving was standing next to him, listening to transmissions from the team on the ground.

Wells: 'Tonto and the new arrival are still talking. It's the same guy who picked up the drop in St James's Park.'

Hayes: 'I can see the car that brought the new target. It's a minicab – got the sticker on the back window – looks as if it's been told to wait. Here you go.' And a photograph of a blue Peugeot saloon, its registration clearly visible, came up on the screen in the control room.

Woods turned to Peggy. 'What do you want us to do? There's not enough resource to take on both targets. Who shall we go with?'

Peggy thought for a split second then said, 'Stick with the new target. Let's try and house him. I'll trace that minicab back to its firm and see what I can find out from them about their customer.'

'OK,' replied Woods. 'We'll do our best. But we've only got the one van on the job, so no guarantees.'

While Woods relayed the new instructions to the team, Peggy went back to her desk to set about identifying the minicab company and driver.

Ten minutes later the new arrival stood up, leaving Park Woo-jin sitting on the bench, and walked back to the waiting minicab. The Peugeot saloon drove away from the park, unaware that the innocuous builder's van a hundred yards behind, which now contained all three of the surveillance team, was following it. The minicab made its way to the Hogarth roundabout where it joined the A4 heading west.

Traffic was heavy, but Marcus Washington managed to stay close, though he had to cut up a dawdling commuter near Hounslow and drew a horn blast from an irate lorry driver as he speeded past him just as he was about to overtake. When the Peugeot turned off at the Heathrow exit, Washington was two cars behind it and he managed to stay in that position all the way in through the tunnel. But as they emerged into the airport proper, he was caught by a red light, which he wasn't able to jump. He could see the Peugeot ahead as it moved into the left lane for Terminal Two. He waited impatiently until the light turned green then shot ahead, but suddenly had to jam on his brakes for a little saloon car that had stalled at the very beginning of the entrance road to the terminal.

The air in the van turned blue as the three occupants cursed in unison. Duff Wells leaped out and ran to the car where he found a near-hysterical young woman at the wheel. She seemed to have run out of petrol. With the help of a policeman, who had come to investigate, he pushed the little car over to one side. Leaving them to sort out the problem, Wells leaped back into the van, which was now blocking a long line of hooting cars.

Washington drove fast along the drop-off lane, hoping to catch a glimpse of the man getting out of the minicab. But there was no sign of him or the blue Peugeot, which must have dropped him and driven straight off. There was little chance of finding the man in the crowded terminal, especially as they had no idea what flight he was catching.

Just as they were preparing to admit defeat and sign off the job, a further instruction came through from Wally Woods. Peggy had traced the owner of the Peugeot and found out that he was employed by a minicab company based in Chiswick.

Trees Taxis occupied a small basement underneath a hairdresser's shop in Chiswick High Road. A hand-painted sign hung on the railings outside. Maureen Hayes climbed out of the van a hundred yards past the premises and walked back. Down a short flight of concrete steps she found an open door and a very small room with a counter barring the entrance. A fat Sikh in a blue turban was leaning his elbows on an open appointments book on the counter, while behind him a much younger counterpart, sitting at a switchboard, was talking into a microphone.

'Yes?' said the Sikh.

'I'm from the Home Office,' announced Hayes, waving a pass. 'I would like to speak to the owner.'

'That's me,' said the Sikh, 'and him,' he added, indicating the young man behind him. 'He's my son.'

'Are you Mr Tree?' asked Hayes doubtfully.

'No, ma'am. I bought the business off Mr Tree five years ago when he retired. How can I help the Home Office?

You'll find all our drivers are fully registered and licensed to drive public carriage vehicles. We are all British citizens. No illegal immigrants here.' He laughed at the very idea.

'Do you have an office where we could talk privately, Mr . . .?'

'Gurpal Singh. No, I don't. This is our entire premises. But I have no secrets from my son.'

'One of your drivers, in a blue Peugeot, took a fare to Acton Green about two hours ago. He waited for him and then drove him to Heathrow. Terminal Two, I believe.'

'Yes, that's right. It was Charlie did that job. For the Chinese bloke. What's he call himself, Mo?' He threw the question over his shoulder to his son.

'Mr Dong,' replied Mo. 'He rang last night. Same as before. Pick up at Heathrow, drive to his hotel in town, maybe drive here and there. Then, after a day or so, drive him back to Heathrow.'

'How long has he been a customer?' asked Maureen.

'He first booked us about six months ago. Could be a bit longer. Comes every now and then. Is there something wrong with him?'

'I'm not sure yet. One of my colleagues may want to come and talk to you further. Perhaps ask you to let us know next time he rings – and please don't tell him we've been asking about him. We'll be in touch. Thanks for your help.'

'It's always a pleasure to help the Home Office,' replied Gurpal Singh with a grin.

Hayes turned to climb back up the steps. Then something occurred to her.

'When you pick him up at the airport, does he give you the flight number?'

'Yes – in case the flight's delayed.'

'So where's he fly in from?'

Mo answered, 'It's always the same. Air France from Marseilles.'

43

M RS MILNER LIKED TO rise early and walk her dog before too many people were about. She lived in a mansion flat off Victoria Street, and had done so for more than three decades – so long that she could ignore the new owner's edict against pets. Milly wasn't any trouble anyway. Her barking could be insistent, but except for Wednesdays when the rubbish collection men were just below Mrs Milner's window, Milly confined her yaps to her daily walks outside.

Most of which were in nearby St James's Park, which she loved – Milly that was, since Mrs Milner had always thought it slightly overrated. Too many tourists and flowerbeds and not enough open space; to her way of thinking the park was too neat. It was really just an adjunct to Buckingham Palace at one end, and all those Government Departments in Whitehall at the other. She often recognised well-known people on its paths, but this did not impress Mrs Milner. As she and Clemency Robinson, her oldest friend, often remarked to each other, they had been brought up in an era when to appear in the newspapers – except on the occasion of one's birth, marriage, and death – was not a desirable state of affairs.

This morning Mrs Milner had set out with Milly for their daily constitutional slightly later than their normal time – it was ten-past eight, she'd noted as she left her flat. Crossing Birdcage Walk she had seen nothing unusual, and as she slowly made her way towards Horse Guards there was the usual collection of MPs and civil servants on the paths. Not many tourists around yet, though she noticed a diminutive Chinese-looking man.

At the east side of the park she carefully crossed Horse Guards Road, but only after first stopping furtively to allow Milly to do her business. Not for Mrs Milner the new practice of bringing a plastic bag along for collection purposes – Heaven forbid – but at least she was selective about where Milly was allowed to go. And who would think seriously of fining a woman in her mid-eighties for the indiscretion of her dog?

It was as she entered the Horse Guards parade ground that she saw the unusual event ahead of her. The small Chinese-looking gentleman she'd noted earlier was twenty yards in front. It was funny seeing him striding through the park – not like a tourist, more like a civil servant on his way to work. Not that Mrs Milner thought there was anything wrong with that. She liked people from the Far East, having lived for five years in Hong Kong with Mr Milner. There was a courtesy about them she approved of. Call it old-fashioned, but Mrs Milner liked it just the same.

Nearing the arch at the far end of Horse Guards Parade, the man quickened his pace slightly – and it was then that Mrs Milner saw the two other men appear, as if from nowhere. Neither of them looked as though they belonged in this part of London – they were both wearing weather-proof jackets and to Mrs Milner's mind looked like toughs.

They seemed to be working in tandem, making a beeline for their target from either side of him.

What were they going to do to him? Maybe they were part of one of the pick-pocketing gangs she was always reading about. In any case, the Chinese-looking fellow seemed utterly unaware of their approach. Or of the woman dawdling by the arch – Mrs Milner had seen her before, walking her dog, which Mrs Milner had avoided since Milly had never got on with Schnauzers. This woman was looking at the little man as well. Surely the two toughs weren't going to harm the fellow here in broad daylight. Though in London these days, who could be sure? Maybe she should call out to warn him.

Then the little man seemed to sense the presence of the other two. He turned around, and when he saw them he started visibly. He tried to make a break for it, sprinting off back across the parade ground, but they were too quick for him – far too quick. In seconds each of them had grabbed an arm, and they held the little fellow between them. One of them was speaking as they began leading him across the parade ground towards a car parked, quite illegally, on the roadside.

The odd trio passed within spitting distance of Mrs Milner, and in the eyes of the Chinese gentleman all she could see was fear. She wanted to stop them all, ask the men just what they thought they were doing, perhaps threaten to call the police. But there was something in their eyes that said no one should interfere with them. Least of all an old lady walking her dog.

44

THE *MAS* WHERE THE *communards* lived, twenty kilometres south-west of Cahors, must originally have been the residence of a minor aristocrat. There was still an ancient orchard in the walled garden next to the residence, and the house itself, though almost derelict when they had first taken it over, would once have bordered on the grand.

Marcel and Pascale, as a couple, had been allocated one of the large rooms on the first floor. It might once have been a grand salon, with its high ceiling and two tall shuttered windows that faced south towards the kitchen garden and the pretty meadow beyond. But like the rest of the house, it had suffered from years of neglect: the ornate cornice that ran around the ceiling was cracked and bits were missing where the damp had come through; the parquet floor had lost some of its pieces and the upright metal rods that held the shutters in place were brown with rust. But young and in love, Marcel and Pascale saw the beauty not the rot. They ignored the missing bits of cornice, they'd covered the holes in the floor with cardboard, and Marcel had put enough oil on the shutter bolts to mute all but the mildest squeaks.

Even this late in spring the evenings in the Quercy could be very cool, and with only one blanket for their rusty bedstead, the couple had made a ritual of jumping into bed together, huddling under the solitary blanket, and cuddling each other for warmth. But tonight when Pascale was ready to get into bed, Marcel remained standing, looking moodily out of the window, smoking a hand-rolled cigarette.

'What is it?' she asked, shivering in the bed.

'We have a problem, I fear.'

'We do indeed,' said Pascale. 'I'm freezing! And standing out there, you must be, too.'

Marcel took a last drag on his cigarette and chucked it out of the open window. It was not something one would do in August, when the grass lay parched and white under the scorching sun, but the spring had been unusually wet. He turned and looked at Pascale. 'I'm afraid it's not a joking matter,' he said soberly. 'I'm worried.'

'Why?'

He looked at her. 'Why do you think?'

Both were well trained enough not to speak carelessly, even though the chances of being bugged in this huge relic of a room seemed remote. So Pascale just nodded, indicating that she understood. Both of them had been on edge since Marcel had returned from Marseilles. He had told her all about the meeting with the North Africans, Antoine's violence, and how they had brought back two Uzis.

Marcel came over to the bed and climbed in under the blanket. When he spoke it was in a whisper in Pascale's ear. 'I was in the walled garden, sharpening the blades on the mower. René and Antoine were talking by the garden shed. They knew I was there; that's what I found odd. Because René was saying that delivery of "the package" had been advanced – it would happen tomorrow instead of next week.'

'What package?'

'I think it must be the explosives he was hoping to get from another source.'

'Christ!' Pascale exclaimed. 'But why talk like this in front of you if they suspected you? And I still don't know why they took you to Marseilles.'

Marcel laid his hand on her thigh and squeezed gently. 'It was a test – like this business in the garden.'

'How are they testing you?'

'René knows that if I'm an informant, I'll want to communicate the news of the package's early arrival. Can't you see – it's the perfect trap? If I don't try and contact Philippe then the explosives will go undetected once they're here. But if I do make a move to contact him, René will know I'm a traitor.'

'So what are you going to do?'

Marcel gave a wry smile. 'It's more what I *have* done, my darling. Or tried to do. I didn't think I had a choice. Philippe warned us, as you know, never to use the mobile phone to contact him. But I decided it was worth the risk, and I could also tell him about the two machine-guns we got in Marseilles. When I came up here, though, I couldn't find my phone. It was there –' He pointed to the small pine cabinet on the far side of the bed. 'But it was gone when I came up to look for it after lunch. I am sure someone has taken it.'

'René?'

'Perhaps. Or someone else under his orders.'

'So you couldn't alert Philippe. But why should René be suspicious now? It's not as if you actually did phone Philippe; you didn't have a phone.'

'Yes, but I didn't stop there.'

Pascale looked alarmed, and Marcel explained, 'You remember how Philippe said that in an emergency we should leave a chalk mark on the big boulder by the main road?'

'Yes. He said he would drive by at least once every twenty-four hours. If we left a mark he'd know the DCRI should move in at once.'

'*Exactement.* So that's what I planned to do. Late this afternoon I thought I would take a walk – and quite by chance it would take me by the main road . . .'

'So did you?' asked Pascale anxiously.

'I was not allowed to.'

'René stopped you?'

Marcel shook his head. 'It was subtler than that. I started to take my walk, thinking I'd go through the woods and cross to the road under cover of them. Then little Fabrice came running out. "*Come back*," he shouted, and when I turned round he said René needed me right away. When I got back here, René said he wanted me to clear space in the cellar for the delivery the day after tomorrow. So I went downstairs and moved all of two empty suitcases and a small box of books – it hardly required me to do that. Yet he'd sent Fabrice to make sure I came back to do the job. Why?'

'All right, so he may suspect you. But he has no proof of anything.'

'No, he doesn't. So tomorrow I plan—'

Pascale was already shaking her head. 'Forget it. Tomorrow you mustn't do anything. René will be hyper-alert. Let's wait until the package arrives, then we can try and contact Philippe again.'

'It may be too late by then,' he protested.

But Pascale was adamant. 'We'll just have to take that chance.'

45

THE MESSAGE FROM TOULON was the last thing
Martin Seurat needed. Frantically busy with a terror-
ist case involving an Algerian cell in the Paris suburbs, he
simply didn't believe what it said – that his former colleague
Antoine Milraud had been sighted at an antiques fair in a
small town in the hills north of Toulon. It seemed most
unlikely that he would revisit his old base of operations
where he was well known. But the antiques business had
been the cover for his less savoury operations and, Seurat
supposed, given Milraud's arrogance, it was just possible.
And there had been an earlier sighting . . .

Six months ago, he would have been down to Toulon
like a shot. He couldn't have explained his fixation with
Milraud, except that the man's betrayal had hit him hard
personally. He had once been such a good and honest
officer, as well as Seurat's closest friend in the ranks of the
French Secret Service. Martin Seurat was usually able to
keep emotion out of his work; he had only scorn for most
of the people he found himself pitted against, though it
was a professional aversion he felt rather than a personal
one. But Milraud was different. Milraud had been trusted
by the people he worked with. Milraud had been 'one of

us'. And he had taken the trust of his colleagues and smashed it as if it were worthless.

Yet Martin realised that his own fixation with nailing his ex-friend was beginning to subside – otherwise he would already be looking at airline schedules for the short hop south to Toulon. What accounted for this slackening of his fervour? Was it Liz's influence? She seemed to understand his desire to catch his nemesis, but she didn't encourage it. He admired the way she could feel intensely about her own work, without ever letting her emotions interfere with her professional judgement. He'd like to think that he was equally dispassionate, but knew that, for a time at least, he had been almost obsessed with catching Milraud.

When his phone rang he was still trying to decide if he should perhaps go down to Toulon, just to make sure this was another false lead. He was still in two minds about it when he said hello.

'*Bonjour*, Martin, it's Isobel. Something seems to be developing with these *communards* down at Cahors.'

'Has something happened?'

'No. But Philippe rang me to say that he was supposed to hear from his source Marcel, but he hasn't. He says it's the first time Marcel has missed a fixed contact.'

'Could he be away?'

'No, he's there all right. So's his partner. Philippe walked the boundary of the place, and with his binoculars he saw both Marcel and Pascale outside the *mas*. But he can't contact them. It's not safe to ring or text in case someone else has access to the phone. But Philippe's worried, and he's not the worrying type. He thinks we should go in sooner rather than later.'

'And you agree?'

'I do. We know they were trying to acquire firearms and possibly explosives. They seem to have succeeded: the shipment was supposed to arrive next week, but there's some indication from our people in Marseilles that it's showing up sooner. I'm worried that once they've got the stuff they may move it somewhere, ready for the G20 in Avignon. It starts in two weeks, but the Minister is very anxious that we try to close off any threats now. Just shut things down, he says, and worry about evidence later.

'So, I'm proposing to go in with local police tomorrow at first light. Do you want to come along? I'm also going to alert Liz Carlyle – we should find René and Antoine at the commune, but in case we don't she needs to alert her immigration colleagues.'

'Good idea.' If Martin remembered correctly, René would be visiting Edward's daughter Cathy in three days' time. Hopefully, this meant that he would not have left for England yet.

Isobel was still talking. 'I'm flying to Toulouse after lunch tomorrow. Seat 13A,' she said with a laugh.

'I'm on,' he said. 'I'll see if 13B is still free.'

46

PADDINGTON GREEN POLICE STATION – one of the places that God forgot, thought Liz as she walked up the steps of the hideous 1960s concrete block. She had been there before: the police station had been converted in the 1970s to hold high-security suspects, mainly terrorists, in a suite of below-ground cells and interview rooms. She was heading there now, accompanied by Charlie Fielding, to interview the man who had been arrested by Special Branch officers earlier in the day.

They went down two flights of stairs, then along a narrow corridor, painted battleship grey, which had steel-reinforced cell doors to either side. At the counter at one end of the corridor they were joined by one of the arresting officers. 'Has he said anything?' asked Liz.

'Nothing much, ma'am. He asked why he was being held. When I told him he'd find out soon enough, he stopped talking.'

'Has he asked for anyone?'

'No. I said he could make a phone call, but he didn't want to.'

'So he hasn't asked for anyone from his Embassy?'

'No.'

The officer accompanied them into the interrogation room, which was bleak and bare, lit only by an unshaded overhead light bulb. The effect was grim – a grey-and-white world, like a still from the film of *The Spy Who Came in From the Cold*. Except that Park Woo-jin was no Richard Burton, thought Liz, as the door opened again and the prisoner was brought in by an armed police officer, who stood guard by the door.

Not that Park Woo-jin seemed to present any sort of physical threat. The short, rather fragile Korean, whom Liz recognised from the surveillance photographs, seemed to have shrunk. In his nondescript grey office suit, white shirt and unremarkable tie, he looked pathetic rather than menacing.

He nodded politely to Liz and Fielding as he took his seat on the opposite side of the table, putting his hands together neatly on top.

The Special Branch officer said: 'Mr Park, I am an officer of the Metropolitan Police and these are two government officials who are here to interview you about a matter relating to national security. I have offered you the opportunity to contact someone but you have refused. This interview is being recorded and I should warn you that . . .' He continued giving Park Woo-jin the standard warnings. Then he sat back in his chair, duty done, and let Liz take over the questioning.

'My name is Jane Falconer and this is Mr Fielding.'

'What is this about?' asked Park, coming to life suddenly. 'Your people would not say when they stopped me. I was on my way to work. They will be wondering where I am.' His flawless English had a slight American inflection, but there was not the slightest hint of the sing-song cadence that characterised so many Far Eastern speakers of English.

Park gave a weak smile. 'I don't want them to think I am neglecting my duty.'

'Mr Park, we became aware several weeks ago of a serious security breach affecting work being done under MOD auspices. It involved the department's computer systems and was without doubt some kind of cyber-attack – highly classified areas were hacked into by someone who did not have any permission to be there.'

'That is most alarming,' said Park with a look of concern.

'It is, Mr Park, but fortunately we think we have discovered the identity of the individual who did this.'

'I am glad,' he said.

'Yes. We believe it was you.'

Park frowned. 'That is a serious charge.'

'Yes, it is. That's why we are giving you an opportunity to tell us what you were doing, and who you were acting for. What you say now could affect what happens to you next.'

'What exactly are you accusing me of? I am sure this is a misunderstanding.'

Liz could see that he was rapidly trying to gather his thoughts. Fielding spoke for the first time. 'You intruded into a protected cyber-area where outside entry was strictly forbidden. No one could have got there by mistake.'

'I don't understand what you mean. You see, in my job it is often necessary to explore a bit. They say curiosity kills the cat, but not a programmer.' He smiled, inviting them to smile back. When that didn't happen he pursed his lips. 'Possibly I am sometimes a bit too curious. It is an occupational hazard.'

Fielding shook his head. 'There's curious, Mr Park, and then there's intrusive, and then there's spying. We're here about spying.'

Park opened his eyes wide. 'No, no,' he insisted. 'I am not a spy.'

Fielding had taken notes out of his jacket pocket. 'There isn't much doubt. You entered a codeword-protected network within the last two weeks. It could not have been done accidentally or casually; it required a sustained campaign to find a way in. You found an opening – by chance, I think – and then you hitchhiked past the firewall. We've traced the intrusion to you, without any doubt.'

Liz knew the last assertion wasn't true, but Fielding said it with confidence. She watched Park Woo-jin carefully and could see he was uncertain. 'It could have been someone else on my computer,' he said at last.

'Let's not waste each other's time,' said Fielding, and Liz saw that he was angry. She wondered which bothered him more – the embarrassment of having his 'secure' network hacked, or the treachery of Park Woo-jin.

The prisoner didn't say anything for a moment; he closed his eyes and they all sat in silence. It was important to keep him talking, but paradoxically the best way of doing that seemed to be to let him think. After almost a minute, he opened his eyes and looked at Fielding.

'Okay, so maybe I went somewhere I shouldn't. But it wasn't with bad motives. You could say I have the soul of a hacker while I wear the uniform of the authorities. I have to admit, my curiosity has sometimes got me into trouble. Back in Korea, and once even at Langley – if you don't believe me, you can consult them there. I've always been interested in seeing how secure these "secure" sites are. I like a battle of wits with the gate-keepers. When I see a "no trespassing" sign, it is like a red flag to a bull.'

He looked beseechingly at Fielding, as if a fellow boffin would understand this. But the other man shook his head in annoyance. 'Come off it,' he said sharply. 'It wasn't like that and you know it. For one thing, there weren't any "entry forbidden" signs; there weren't any signs at all. This wasn't forbidden territory, it was unknown territory. You went looking for it, Park. The question is, why?'

'Curiosity. Like I said.'

'Rubbish. There wasn't anything to be curious about. You went to enormous lengths to find an opening to a project you couldn't even be sure existed. That's not cyber-travel; that can only be espionage.'

'Not true.' Park Woo-jin seemed unperturbed by Fielding's assertions. 'I was only browsing.'

'Then why did you copy code you found in the network when you cracked into it? Your crawler was sticky, Park. We know it picked up code along the way and retreated with it, like a honey bee loaded with pollen.'

Was Fielding guessing this? Liz wondered. Could he be sure Park Woo-jin had downloaded encryption systems he'd found? The evidence pointed that way emphatically, yet could he prove it if Park Woo-jin insisted it wasn't true?

But Park Woo-jin didn't deny it. 'I just took a sample. The bot was told to do that.'

'Why? What were you going to do with it?'

'Nothing – when I looked at it, I couldn't make head nor tail of the code.' He shrugged. 'Curiosity again; and I wanted a memento. The bot's designed to bring back evidence of where it's been.'

Fielding exhaled in exasperation. Looking at the young Korean, Liz realised that not only had he had kept his composure so far, but that he was actually *enjoying* this questioning; he was treating it like a computer game. This was bad news. Sometimes, overconfidence in a suspect was helpful, since they could grow arrogant and slip up. But not Park Woo-jin: while the conversation remained largely technical, he felt completely at home. He and Charlie Fielding would lock horns for ever, and so far Park Woo-jin had learned more than he had given away.

'We'll take a break now,' she announced, and the Korean looked at her with a curious expression, almost of disappointment. She motioned to Fielding and they both stood up. The Special Branch officer said, 'Interview suspended at 16.15,' and switched off the tape recorder.

Fielding followed Liz out into the corridor, looking puzzled, as the armed guard closed the door behind them. 'I hope you don't believe a word he's saying,' he said.

'I don't. You've done very well,' she added. There was no point in sharing her frustration with Fielding; he'd done the best he could. Bringing him along had probably been a mistake, but it was her mistake not his. It was time to go on the attack, and Fielding would only be in the way.

'I'm going to go back in before he's had time to think things through and invent more excuses. I'll do it by myself, Charlie.'

'You sure?' Fielding looked surprised and rather hurt.

'You've been a big help, and I'm grateful. You've set him up for me; now I've got to make him fall over.' She turned towards the Special Branch officer, who was waiting discreetly along the corridor. 'Let's go back in. I'm ready now.'

47

Park Woo-jin looked relaxed when Liz and the Special Branch officer came back into the room. Without looking at him, Liz said, 'Park Woo-jin, you admitted to Mr Fielding in our earlier session that you had made an unauthorised intrusion into a secret programme and stolen some of the contents. You said that you were motivated purely by intellectual curiosity. So perhaps you would tell me, who is Mr Dong?' As she spoke the name she looked at him and noticed his expression change. There was a brief silence, then he said, 'I don't know a Mr Dong. Are you sure you have the right name?'

Not at all sure, thought Liz to herself, but without replying she took out of an envelope a surveillance photograph of the unknown man walking by himself in St James's Park and pushed it across the table. 'Who is this?'

'I don't know him,' replied Park Woo-jin after studying the picture for a moment.

'Think again,' said Liz, and produced a photograph of Park Woo-jin and the same man sitting together on the bench on Acton Green.

There was an even longer pause. Then Park Woo-jin said, 'Oh, yes. I was confused for a moment. That is a cousin of my mother's. He came to visit me.'

'Where does he live?'

A longer pause. Then: 'In Seoul. He was on business in Europe and he came to visit me.'

'I assume from what you say that he is South Korean?' A nod. 'When did you last see him before that visit?'

'Several years ago.'

'Park Woo-jin, none of this is true, as you know. This man comes regularly into this country and I don't think he comes from Seoul. What was it that you left in the waste bin in St James's Park a week or so ago, for him to collect?'

On the table in front of him, Park Woo-jin's hands had clenched. Liz pushed a series of photographs across. They showed him walking towards the bin and dropping in the newspaper, the approach of Mr Dong, Mr Dong putting his hand in the bin and then withdrawing it clutching the newspaper. The pictures had time-codes on them from which it was clear that the actions were in sequence. 'Well?' said Liz.

Park Woo-jin said nothing. 'I should tell you,' she continued, 'that since you were picked up this morning, I have been in touch with your Embassy and have shown them these pictures. They do not know who Mr Dong is either and they very much doubt that he is one of their citizens. It is certain that he does not use a South Korean passport when he comes into this country. Having seen these photographs your Embassy people agree with me that you have some serious explaining to do.'

There was a silence. After a moment Liz resumed, 'The penalties in this country for espionage are serious and I have no doubt that in your own country they are just as serious – possibly more so. And then there is the United States to consider,' she added. 'They have a close interest in your activities, given your previous employment at Langley.'

Park Woo-jin was no longer replying. All the self-assurance he had shown when he was talking to Charlie Fielding had disappeared. His hands on the table in front of him were constantly moving, clutching at each other. But frightened though he undoubtedly was, he still showed no sign of caving in.

Liz had not finished. 'I don't know which judicial system would be the least unpleasant,' she mused. 'In this country we no longer hang or shoot spies but we do give long prison sentences for espionage. Our prisons are probably more humane than some of those in the United States,' she said thoughtfully, 'where I believe they do have the death penalty for spies. But I don't know how they are treated in your country. Perhaps you could tell me.'

She leaned forward, both hands on the table, and looked straight into his eyes. 'Five years in prison here or in the USA or even in Korea might be bearable; ten years just about. But we're talking about twenty minimum, and more likely close to thirty. Tell me, Mr Park, have you ever thought about what you'll look like in the year 2040? You'll emerge from prison, if you emerge at all, without parents, without a wife, and without children. And without a country happy to take you. Whoever you are working for has abandoned you, and now you haven't a friend in the world. Unless . . . you tell me the truth, all the truth, right now.'

She looked at her watch to show that she had other things to do, and that if he didn't make his move soon, she'd be on her way to do them.

Park Woo-jin still said nothing. He was obviously considering his options. Liz didn't know if he'd get even six months with the evidence she had, much less thirty years, but she could see she'd scared him, and so she left the next move to him.

She could hear Park's breathing as they sat in silence; he was inhaling deeply, as if trying to suck an answer out of the dead air of the underground room. When she looked at him she found his eyes staring at her questioningly, all certainty gone.

'What would happen if we had an honest conversation?' he asked. She was taken by surprise. What was he up to? He suddenly looked and sounded like a frightened student rather than a trained spy.

She said cautiously, 'I would of course share whatever information you gave me with our colleagues in the United States and in your Embassy. Then it would be checked. If it were truly honest, and we will know if it is not, it would certainly be taken into account when we were considering what to do with you.'

'How do I know that's true?'

'You don't. But you've been in England for a while now. You know what kind of people we are, and how we work. That should help you make your mind up.' She couldn't think of any other reason why he should trust her.

But Park nodded. 'One thing,' he said. 'You must promise that no harm will come to my parents.'

'Your parents?' Liz was amazed. He was sounding more and more like a frightened child. 'I assume the Korean authorities will want to talk to them, particularly if you don't tell me the truth. But if I think you're being honest with me, I'll ask them to leave your parents alone. I can't promise anything, though.'

He nodded. 'I understand. You will, too, when I tell you everything.'

He talked very softly and slowly, as if subdued by his own story. He said that his parents were simple but intelligent people – his father was a clerk in Seoul, and his mother taught in a primary school. But for all their relatively humble status, they had lived with a secret for many years. For they were *North* Koreans, who had been infiltrated into the South, via China, in the 1970s, shortly after they were married, with false identities as South Koreans. Their spy masters did not plan for them to relay secrets from their work; they had none. The plan was much more long-term. The real point of their infiltration was so that they would bear children who could be educated and encouraged to attain important positions in South Korean society. It was the children who would be the spies. The parents had to ensure that when the children were old enough to understand, they would reject the propaganda they would be fed officially about the North. The fact that Park was an only child had increased the pressure on his parents – and on Park himself. He smiled a sad smile, and in that sadness lay his acknowledgement that he had never had a choice.

'How old were you when you became aware of your parents' position?'

He shrugged. 'It's hard to say. By the time they fully told me, I knew most of the truth. You see, in South Korea there is much more indoctrination than people in a place like Britain realise. Here all you're ever told is how horrible North Korea is; the South is made out to be some sort of perfect society, though in some ways it is little more than an extension of America – there's very little true Korean culture left; everything, from television to things you buy in shops, seems to come from Disney. But from day one a South Korean child is taught to worship the state, and to hate the North Koreans. With my family, there was always a different perspective – my parents didn't want me to rebel, far from it, but they made it clear that what I was learning in school about North Korea was not the truth.'

'Did they have contact with their North Korean controllers?'

'They must have, but I was never aware of it. Except once, and that involved me. A man came to visit when I was ten years old; they said he was a distant cousin. We had supper together and then my parents left me alone with this man. He asked me lots of questions – about school, and what subjects I liked, and what sports I played. But he asked me another question that seemed odd at the time. If I had to choose to obey my government or my parents, which would I pick? Most South Korean children would have said their government – that's what I mean about indoctrination. But I said my parents. He seemed very pleased by this.'

After that Park knew he had been selected to play a role, but he didn't know what it was and his parents wouldn't tell him. Like all parents, they wanted him to do well, and the first step was to succeed in school; but behind their aspirations for him lay an unspoken agenda, which he associated with the 'cousin' who had asked him all the questions.

Fortunately, Park Woo-jin was a clever child, already three years ahead of his classmates in mathematics by the age of twelve. He had taken to computers like a fish to water, and graduated from university with highest honours.

'Did you know by then who your parents were working for?'

'Yes, and I knew that the torch had been passed on to me. After all, there wasn't much either of my parents could tell the North Koreans – it was made clear that this was to be my responsibility. The instruction came that I should try and find a post with the military.'

That proved easy enough – listening, Liz realised that the Korean military would have been delighted to have a programmer with this young man's skills, especially as many of the gifted young computer experts were flocking overseas in droves to make their fortunes in America's Silicon Valley.

Fearful he would do the same, and impressed by his talents and his diligence, the military had promoted Park Woo-jin rapidly, and he was cherry-picked after only five years' experience for a plum secondment to the Pentagon. He had passed the positive vetting process without a hitch, and passed it again when the Americans had had him checked. The North Koreans had done well with the false documentation of his parents. He did not know who his parents really were or what had happened to the people whose identity they had adopted. But the process must have been watertight as he passed all vetting with no problems.

He'd enjoyed his stay at the Pentagon, especially since the North Koreans had asked nothing from him, perhaps deciding there was no point in risking his exposure when he was operating at only mid-level in the Defense Department But when the opportunity for a second secondment had come his way – to the UK's Ministry of Defence – everything had changed. He'd been contacted and encouraged – no, told – to apply, and when he'd landed the post, had been given a controller who'd insisted on regular meetings. His contacts with North Korea's Intelligence Service had been very limited until then – in Washington he'd met an Embassy employee on only two occasions – but once in London there had been drops of information and sometimes weekly meets.

'With the man in the photographs?'

'Yes.'

'We know him as Dong Shin-soo. What's his real name?'

'I don't know. I didn't call him anything.'

'Where is he based?'

'I don't know but I think it must be somewhere nearer than Pyongyang. In Europe maybe.'

'How did he contact you?'

'He sent an encoded email, with a time and place embedded. Sometimes I did not meet him. When I had information, I would pass it by a drop, as you photographed me doing it in St James's Park.'

'What did he want you to do?'

'He wanted me to gain access to a project being run at a separate site.'

'Did you know what the project was?'

'No.'

'Or where it was located?'

'No. I only knew the prefix used as an identifier for its network. But access was forbidden, and for a while I thought it would be impossible to get in.'

'But you managed.'

Park Woo-jin gave a wry smile, recognising that his success was what had landed him here. 'I left what is known as a trailer. It lets all sorts of information flow through it, then when it sees what it wants, it grabs it. In this case the network identifier tipped it off.'

Liz imagined a fish waiting for food where the river narrows and the water funnels between two rocks. The fish was checking out the bits and bugs floating above its head until finally it saw the fly – Hugo Cowdray's email – it had been watching for and rose to grab it.

'Did you know what was in the code you managed to extract?'

'No. It was heavily encrypted. It would take more than one person to break that kind of code. That's not my speciality.'

'But you gave the code to your controller here in St James's Park?'

'Yes.'

'And what did he do with it?'

'How should I know?' Park Woo-jin protested, and Liz found his reaction too immediate to be contrived.

'It must have been very valuable to have you take such a risk. For years you were operating under heavy cover – you said yourself you rarely met anyone from the North Korean Intelligence Service. Suddenly you're meeting them frequently, and you're given a critical task. Didn't you wonder what it was all about?'

'Of course I wondered. But I assumed it was a weapons system of some sort, and besides, there was no point in me poking my nose into things that didn't concern me.' He realised the absurdity of what he had just said, and smiled sadly. 'I mean, it wasn't worth the risk.'

Liz felt a pang of sympathy for this young man who, if he was telling the truth, had never had much of a chance. *If* he was telling the truth . . . To be sure of that, his story would have to be assiduously checked in three countries.

Just to satisfy herself, she asked out of the blue, 'Have you ever been to Marseilles?'

He looked at her as if she were mad, and shook his head. She was sure that part of his story was true. Park Woo-jin was a pawn, not a king.

48

From Toulouse Martin and Isobel drove north on a near-empty motorway towards Cahors. Both of them were a little on edge, not sure what the raid the following day would bring.

They stayed the night in a village about four miles from the commune, in a bed and breakfast run by a gay English couple who said they'd settled in this part of France because the English had not invaded en masse.

At dinner, eaten at a long farmhouse table, another guest mentioned that her grandmother had once had friends who'd lived nearby. 'The place was called Le Barbot,' she said.

One of their hosts laughed. 'That must have been a long time ago. She wouldn't want to see it now. It's still there but it's falling to bits. It's been occupied for a few years now by a kind of commune. Apparently the owner's an old lady who lives in Paris. They rent it off her but she never comes down here.'

'How do they support themselves?' asked Martin, reaching for his wine glass.

'Nobody knows for sure; perhaps one of them is rich. They grow their own vegetables and keep chickens and a few cows, but beyond that, who knows?' He turned to the guest who had first mentioned the place. 'I wouldn't advise calling in there – they don't like visitors. There's a chain on the gate and the postman has to leave letters in a box at the top of the drive. For *communards* they don't seem particularly peaceful. The last time anyone tried to have a snoop around, they were run off the property.'

This time it would be different. By 6 a.m. the next morning Martin and Isobel had met up in a local schoolroom with her young colleague, Philippe, and an armed group of DCRI officers. In support were a team of gendarmes, under the command of Inspector Cambery from Cahors.

The estate had been recce'd by plain clothes officers the day before, and Isobel showed the team the pictures they'd taken as well as some Google aerial views of the nearly one hundred acres, with barns and stone outbuildings. She said that as far as was known there were about thirty people living there, including women and children. Concluding the briefing, she said, 'It is very hard to say what we will be encountering at Le Barbot. I hope there will be no violence but we think there are arms and possibly explosives hidden somewhere on the estate. Our purpose is to find and remove them. We need to identify everyone present; arrest anyone who resists. Our particular targets, who should be arrested on sight, are the ringleaders, René and Antoine.' She passed around photographs of the two men. Antoine's picture, Martin noted, was a police mug shot.

They drove in convoy, led by Inspector Cambery and his team in a police van. A bolt cutter soon disposed of the chain on the gate and the convoy drove along the rough track that led to the front of the house. The drive ended in a circle of mud and sparse gravel on which a VW camper van was parked next to a C2 Citroën. The police van came to a halt, blocking the exit route for any vehicle.

Cambery lifted the tarnished brass knocker on the front door and let it fall with a resounding bang. Silence from within. After thirty seconds, he banged the knocker down again. When he was about to lift it for a third time, the door began to open and they found themselves face to face with a small boy, not much taller than the handle he had managed to turn.

'*Bonjour,*' he said brightly. 'I am Fabrice.'

'Are your parents here, Fabrice?' asked Cambery and the boy nodded. 'Go and get them for me, will you? There's a good boy.' He turned and ran up the dilapidated staircase while Cambery stepped into the hall and motioned his men to follow. Meanwhile, Isobel, Philippe and the DCRI team fanned out to search the estate.

When they were all inside, Cambery issued orders. 'Mauriac,' he said, pointing at one of his men, 'stay here and guard the front door. No one is to leave the house.' Two more men were despatched to the rear to guard any other exits, and two were sent upstairs to check all the rooms. 'I want everyone down here in the hall. They can get dressed later; don't let them dawdle. Get their names and particulars.'

In less than ten minutes a motley collection had assembled, some in night clothes, some wrapped in blankets, and a few in hastily thrown-on clothes. There must have been twenty-five of them, thought Martin, watching as one of the policemen, now carrying a clipboard, went to each resident in turn, taking down their names and details. Half of them were women, and there were three or four small children as well as Fabrice. Seurat noticed Philippe's agent Marcel standing at the rear, along with a young woman who must have been his partner. But there was no sign of Antoine or René.

'Inspector,' he said to Cambery, who was supervising the small crowd. 'Their leader is not here. Nor his sidekick Antoine.'

Cambery raised an eyebrow. 'If they're hiding in the house we'll find them. My men are very thorough.'

But Martin was not satisfied. He walked down the hall and stopped in front of the man standing next to Marcel. 'What's your name?' he demanded.

The man started, his fright obvious. 'Aubisson, Monsieur.'

Martin nodded and turned to Marcel. 'And yours?' he barked.

'Jacob. Marcel Jacob, Monsieur.'

'Come and show me the rest of this floor.' And Martin opened a door that led into the drawing room off the corridor. Once inside he turned to Marcel who had followed him in. 'Where is René?' he asked quickly.

'I don't know. He was here last night.'

'And Antoine?'

'He left the day before yesterday on some errand.'

'Okay. You'd better go back and join the others.'

The drawing room faced the rear of the house, looking out on to what must once have been grand formal gardens. Martin opened the French doors, stepped out on to a paved terrace and walked along the rear of the house until he came to the back door, where he found one of the policemen on guard. 'Has anyone tried to come through this way?' he asked.

'No, Monsieur. There was a woman in the kitchen making breakfast, but she was told to join the others.'

'And you've seen no one else?'

The policeman shook his head. Martin was about to go inside again when the officer added, 'Except for the milkman. But that's all.'

'The milkman? When was that?'

'Just after we arrived. He was coming out of the kitchen.'

'How do you know he was a milkman?'

The policeman looked at him strangely. 'He was carrying the empty bottles, Monsieur. And he had a milkman's apron on.'

'Then where is the milk float?' demanded Martin, his voice rising.

The policeman pointed across the back gardens. 'He left it on the other side of those trees. He said the track this side's too overgrown to drive along it.'

'*Merde!*' said Martin, and ran across the lawn. Ahead of him he saw where the vestigial lines of a track went through the trees. He followed it until the wood ended at a large field of melons, small and unripe this early in the year. Peering across the field to the road, he wondered if René had made a run for it that way. Probably not: the little wood he had just come through was in fact a dense untended copse, full of brambles and bushy undergrowth – and full of hiding places he thought. They might search all day and never find the man.

He was looking around hopelessly when his eye caught a flash of white on the ground, underneath a bush about forty yards from where he was standing. As he drew closer, he saw that it was a piece of cloth – a bit of sheet, perhaps, or a scrap of torn shirt. He knelt down and tugged at it – it was a crumpled apron. Further inspection revealed a metal crate containing six empty milk bottles, one of them smashed.

He was standing up when a voice said, 'Put your hands in the air. Slowly . . . very slowly. Then turn around. If you do anything stupid – anything that even *looks* stupid – I will shoot you.'

Martin did as he was told. Turning, he found himself facing a thirty-ish man in a white T-shirt and khaki combat trousers. René. Martin recognised him from the photographs. He stood about five feet away, holding an automatic pistol.

'I'm no great marksman,' said René, 'but at this range even I won't miss.'

Martin nodded to show he had no intention of trying anything on. He only hoped the others would come soon. But would they? Isobel and her team might be anywhere on the estate, and Cambery and his policemen were occupied in the house.

'You won't get very far, you know,' said Martin, in his most assured tone.

'Perhaps, though I think they will be busy in the house for a while yet. There are quite a lot of us to count off.'

'But it's you they're most interested in.'

'Really?' René seemed pleased by this, but then his tone changed. 'What do they want anyway? We aren't doing any harm.'

'Not yet, you mean. And if you're so peaceful, what are you doing carrying that?' He nodded at the gun.

'It's a good thing I have it, or I'd be having this conversation with handcuffs on. As it is, your presence creates a bit of a problem.'

Realising that himself, Martin wondered if there were some way he could distract the other man or even persuade him to put his gun away and just go. But then René said, 'Put both your hands behind your neck.' When Martin hesitated, René took half a step back and pointed the gun at his head. He quickly clasped his hands behind his neck.

'Now turn around. And don't do anything with your hands.'

Martin had had close calls before; twice in his life he had thought it certain he would be killed. But to be killed by a scruffy *communard*, some sort of anti-capitalist, that he hadn't bargained for. It seemed so utterly . . . *banal.*

He could sense René behind him, and said as calmly as he could, 'Whatever you've done, René, is nothing in comparison to this. You might get five to seven for buying guns, ten if you're unlucky. But killing me will mean you'll never see trees like these again or a pretty girl on the street or eat a *plat du jour* with a carafe of wine. At least, not until you're too old to enjoy them.'

'I'll take my chances. By the time they find your body I'll be out of the country. Now, do you want to kneel down or remain standing up?'

The final moment was suddenly upon Martin. He wondered what to think with his last thoughts, and the only image that entered his head was of Liz – laughing, as they dined one night at the bistro near his flat. He said, 'I'll stay standing.'

He waited and in the little wood all was silent. He took a breath, then another. René was hesitating – Martin could sense that, and wondered if he should say something else.

But before he could speak another voice broke the silence. A female voice. 'Drop the gun or I will shoot you in the spine. You won't die that way, but you'll never walk again.' There was a slight pause, then the voice urged, 'Hurry up!'

Martin heard something fall to the ground. Praying it was René's pistol, he turned round. It was, thank God. Behind René stood Isobel, both arms extended, pointing her gun.

Martin quickly retrieved René's pistol. He felt relieved but shaky – and angry. It was hard to resist the temptation to hit the other man.

'Now let's head for the house,' said Isobel, motioning with her gun for René to lead the way.

'Just a minute,' said Martin, pointing the retrieved weapon at René. The man's eyes widened in fear, and Martin realised he must think it was his turn to die. 'There is something we need to know – believe me, it will make things easier for you if you tell us the truth. Where is Antoine?'

René took a deep breath. 'I sent him to Marseilles two days ago. He was taking a delivery. He's due back tonight.'

'Okay,' said Martin and lowered the gun; as René walked ahead of them, Isobel kept hers trained on his back.

As they reached the track Martin said to her, 'I'm not sure what to say, except thank you. No one's saved my life before.'

She gave a little laugh. 'Don't worry. I'll try not to make a habit of it.'

49

BECH WAS TIRED. IT had been a long week, full of meetings and business dinners – and his trip to Zurich. The discovery that Russian Intelligence was moving money out of Switzerland then circuitously bringing it back was still unexplained. Herr Kessler clearly thought he had done his bit and had come up with nothing more. What Kubiak was up to remained a mystery, and as the man himself seemed to have disappeared from Geneva, it was likely to stay that way

Bech was about to pack up and head home when there was a tap at his door. 'Yes,' he said.

Leplan stuck his head round the door.

'What is it?' Bech asked crossly, certain it could have waited until Monday. Leplan was good at his work but far too cautious – he checked in with Bech much more often than the other senior officers.

But now he came in without his usual hesitancy, and there was no apology for intruding this late on a Friday afternoon. 'I've got some news I think you will wish to hear,' he announced. He was clutching a folder of papers.

Bech knew what this would be about. Leplan had been non-stop in his pursuit of Kubiak in the past weeks, ever since he'd watched the Russian supervise the forced repatriation of Sorsky at Geneva airport. 'Have you found him?'

'No,' said Leplan, but it was clear from his face that he had found something. Bech motioned the younger officer to sit down. He was impatient now not to get home, but to hear what Leplan had to say.

'We've had the tests back from the forensic mechanics,' Leplan announced. 'They demonstrate irrefutably that the paint on Steinmetz's car came from a Mercedes that was sold to Kubiak six months ago.'

'Perhaps. But he may not have been driving it at the time,' Bech said mildly.

'It's his personal car. A special order he put in; it's not an official vehicle. It is very unlikely anyone else was driving.'

'Okay. But that's still not enough to connect him to the accident that killed Steinmetz. He could just say that he'd scraped the car on the street in Geneva.' Bech was becoming annoyed now – was this all the officer had to tell him?

But Leplan pressed ahead. 'He might have more trouble explaining this.' He opened the folder and pulled out a paperback book, which he put down on the desk.

Bech peered at it, mystified. It was in English – *To Kill a Mockingbird*. He hadn't read it himself, but his children had. It was a staple of English classes in the Swiss school system. And even Bech had seen the film; in black-and-white, with Gregory Peck defending a beleaguered black man facing a false charge of rape. But what did this have to do with Kubiak?'

Leplan laughed, a rarity in Bech's experience. 'Don't worry, Herr Bech, I haven't gone mad. You see, I had a visit today from Steinmetz's widow, Mireille.'

'How is she coping?' Bech asked automatically.

'As well as can be expected. I think she's OK financially. She has her widow's pension and a generous gratuity, but of course her life in future will be very different, especially when her daughter Anna goes to university. But that's not why she wanted to see me. She brought me this,' he said, pointing to the paperback. 'Apparently it was returned to her by the police along with Steinmetz's wallet and watch.'

'Was the book his?' It seemed unlikely.

Leplan shook his head. 'No, it belongs to his daughter. She'd left it in the car the day before he was killed, when Mireille picked her up from school. It's a set text apparently, and she had made lots of notes in it – so Mireille said her daughter was glad to get it back. But then she found this.'

He picked up the book and opened it, then handed it to Bech, open at a blank page at the back. On it was scrawled **GE 672931.**

'What's this?' asked Bech. And then he understood. 'A licence-plate number.'

'Exactly. It's the registration for the Mercedes saloon belonging to Anatole Kubiak. Steinmetz must have written it down when he was following the car.'

'Didn't you say he had been part of the surveillance on Kubiak once before? Maybe he wrote the number down then.'

'No. The book was only put in the glove compartment the day before the accident. Mireille told me that she stopped at the supermarket on the way home from school. Anna stayed in the car, and took the book out of her bag to read while her mother shopped. When Mireille came out of the shop with a trolley full of groceries, the girl got out to help her put the bags in the boot – only she didn't put the book back in her bag, she just stuffed it into the glove compartment and forgot about it. The next day Steinmetz took his wife to the airport, and for reasons I still don't understand, ended up following Kubiak towards Lausanne. At some point he wrote down the Mercedes's licence plate, probably in case he lost the tail; that way he could still trace the ownership of the car. Instead he was run off the road. Only now we have the number.'

'And the two match?'

'Of course.' Leplan looked annoyed by the question. 'Why else would I be bothering you, Herr Bech?'

Bech sat back in his chair, and breathed out noisily. 'You realise it would never stand up in court.'

'Yes, I know that. And even if it ever came to a charge, I know that the Russian would simply claim diplomatic immunity and skip home. But at least we now know he did it.'

50

LIZ HAD LEFT A message on his phone, but when Edward phoned her back on her mobile he only got her voicemail. But there had been nothing worrying about her message; she'd said that the Cahors commune had been raided and René had been arrested. Antoine had not been there, but Liz had sounded confident that he would soon be picked up. Apparently, after hours of searching, a cache of liquid explosive, half a dozen handguns and two Uzis had been found. Evidence enough to put René away for a long time.

What a relief. Now, Edward hoped, Cathy would sense what a close call she'd had, cut all ties with the *communards* and settle down to creating a secure life for herself and young Teddy. Maybe a suitable chap would turn up one day so she wouldn't have to be a single mother for ever – or maybe he wouldn't; the important thing, he felt, was to get Cathy and Teddy settled.

When his daughter opened the door Edward was relieved to find her smiling, and he was pleased when she gave him a big hug. She led him into the kitchen, from where he could see Teddy playing in the garden. When Cathy started to open the back door to call the boy, he stopped her. 'Hold on a moment. I've heard from Susan's daughter – you know, Liz, the woman you met here.' He was glad when she didn't frown. 'It seems René and his friends have been raided by the police down in Cahors. They found weapons and explosives at the commune.'

'I'm not surprised.'

'No, I'm sure you're not. But it means they won't be coming here and bothering you for money. From what Liz said, it sounds as if they'll be in jail for a long time.'

Cathy nodded. 'They're not all bad, you know,' she said. 'Some of them are my friends.'

But Edward could see she was relieved. It must have been the most tremendous strain for her. He said cheerfully, 'Why don't I go out and see my grandson?'

When the doorbell rang Edward was still in the back garden with Teddy. Reassured that she was no longer under threat, Cathy went and opened the front door, expecting to find the postman or a delivery from Amazon. Instead a familiar bulky figure was standing on the doorstep. As the door opened he lunged at her.

It was Antoine.

'Help—' she started to shout, but he clamped a hand over her mouth.

As Cathy found herself pushed back from the door, Antoine hissed, '*Tais-toi!*' He pressed his other hand on to the back of her neck, and pinched the tendons there until she nodded obediently. Anything to stop the pain.

He half-propelled, half-dragged her into the small sitting room, kicking the door closed behind him as they entered. 'I will take my hand off your mouth if you promise not to scream. If you do, I will hurt you. *Compris?*'

Cathy nodded, and he took his hand from her mouth, though the other one stayed gripping the back of her neck, keeping her close to him. His breath was a nauseating mix of cigarette smoke and hamburger. She turned her face to the side and breathed in, trying to calm her nerves.

'Now, first things first. Where is your boy?'

'He's not here,' she said, keeping her eyes averted. Just then a boyish yelp came from the garden. Antoine tightened his hand on the nape of her neck. 'Do not lie to me again. So, he is in the garden?'

Cathy nodded weakly.

'Good, then we both know what can happen if you do not cooperate. I am here for the money. Do you have it?'

Cathy was too terrified to say no, but saying yes would be equally dangerous – she had six pounds in her purse and that was all. 'I have to give you a cheque.'

Surprisingly, Antoine did not seem disconcerted by this. 'I did not expect you to have ten thousand in cash. So let's get your cheque book.'

'It's in my bedroom,' she lied, thinking that might give her an opportunity to shout to her father.

'No, it's not,' Antoine said firmly. 'René told me it's in the desk over there.' He pointed to a corner of the room where her mother's small bureau stood. Cathy kept the bills there, and her cheque book. René must have sniffed around during his last visit while she was making tea.

She tried again. 'It's not there now. I was paying bills last night.'

Antoine moved his hand upwards and suddenly gripped the loose ends of her hair. He pulled them hard and she flinched with sudden pain as her head jerked back. 'Do you think I am a fool?' he said angrily, then released his grip. She lowered her chin in relief, and the pain stopped.

He turned her around until she was facing him and suddenly slapped her hard across the cheek. Cathy struggled not to cry out in pain. 'If you don't write the cheque in the next thirty seconds,' Antoine threatened, 'I will do it again. And then I will fetch your boy.'

Outside Edward was doing his best to play football with Teddy. He'd bought him a junior-sized goal a month before, one with a string net so you didn't have to chase the ball each time a goal was scored. But Teddy couldn't decide if he wanted to be goalkeeper or striker, and finally they compromised on passing the ball back and forth. Each successful pass elicited a happy laugh from the little boy, and Edward was pleased to see him so carefree – recently Teddy had often seemed subdued, especially when relations between Edward and Cathy had been at their most tense.

It was when Teddy had kicked the ball towards the back door, and Edward had gone to retrieve it, that he heard the short sharp noise from inside. He paused, listening hard, but nothing followed. He stood there until Teddy cried impatiently, 'Get the ball, Grandpa. Get the ball.'

'Just a minute,' he said, still listening hard. Nothing. In two quick bounds he climbed the steps to the kitchen door and opened it. 'Cathy,' he called.

There was no reply.

Could she have gone out? It didn't seem likely – he'd only been in the garden for a few minutes with the boy. Perhaps she was talking on the phone. But then what had that noise been?

He walked through the kitchen, stopping for a second to look at the rack on the wall with its neat line of knives. Should he grab a weapon? It seemed needlessly melodramatic – Cathy was probably in the loo.

Nonetheless, he walked quietly down the corridor towards the front of the house. He didn't call out again.

The door to the sitting room was closed. He slowly opened it. 'Cathy?' he said.

Then he saw her, and the stranger in the room. The man was standing behind Cathy, with one arm drawn across her throat. He was shorter than Edward, a little under six foot tall, but heavily muscled, wearing a T-shirt that showed off biceps that could only have been created by hard work in a gym.

Cathy looked at Edward with fear in her eyes.

'Who the hell are you?' he demanded. 'And what are you doing to my daughter?'

Cathy tried to speak, but the man's arm tightened on her throat and her attempt spluttered into silence.

Then the man spoke. 'My name is not your concern. I have business with your daughter.' His accent was French, but his English was excellent. 'If you don't interfere, she won't get hurt. Neither will you or the boy.'

Edward had seen his share of trouble. He knew there was no point in cowering in front of this thug; that would only fuel his sense of physical superiority. He said, 'How dare you? Get out of this house at once.'

'I'd be quiet if I were you, old man.'

'Get out,' Edward said loudly.

Suddenly Antoine released his grip on Cathy's throat. Pushing her aside, he stepped forward. His right hand came swinging quickly through the air – too quickly for Edward to duck. It hit him hard on the side of his mouth. He felt a tooth crack as he stumbled and fell forward, landing on his knees just short of the fireplace. Blood filled his mouth and he spat it out, staining the beige carpet. He sensed Antoine standing over him and the Frenchman said, 'Don't get up, or there'll be more where that came from.'

Edward looked at the fireplace. He could see the set of fire irons – a bellows, a poker, tongs. He stayed on his knees, and heard the man turn back towards Cathy. 'Now write the cheque, and make it out to cash. If you try and cancel it, I promise I'll be back, and this time I'll get your little boy.'

Cathy walked to the desk, and fumbled in the drawer. She must have hesitated for the Frenchman grew angry. 'Write it, bitch, before I give your father a good kicking!'

Edward waited until he heard the scratching of pen on paper. He turned his head very slightly and saw that Antoine was now standing behind Cathy, watching her make out the cheque. Edward carefully reached out his hand until he could grab the poker, then in one quick movement heaved himself to his feet, blood still dripping from his mouth.

Antoine had turned around. Edward raised the poker. The Frenchman laughed. 'Who do you think you are, old man? If you swing that thing at me you might get lucky and break a bone or two, but then, I promise you, I'll take it off you and beat you to death.'

There was relish in his voice, and looking at his heavily muscled figure Edward realised that what he said was true. Edward himself was tall rather than heavy-set, and while thirty years ago it might have been an equal match, there wasn't much question of who would win a fight today. But he couldn't do nothing, not when his daughter was in danger, and little Teddy too.

He stepped forward, and raised the poker with both hands. Antoine waited with his hands ready and his legs akimbo in a karate stance. Behind him Cathy had turned and was staring at them, fear contorting her face.

Edward took another step and started to swing. As Antoine raised his arm to block the blow, Edward stopped swinging the poker. He brought it back, this time very low, and crouching down, swept it with all his strength against Antoine's leg. There was the cracking noise of breaking bone.

'Ahhhh!' the Frenchman shouted, and fell to the floor, clutching his knee. Agony spread across his face as he lay writhing on the carpet, but Edward was taking no chances. He moved until he stood near Antoine's prone head, and raised the poker again. 'If you even try to get up I will split your head in half,' he said, without taking his eyes off the fallen man. 'Cathy, go out and ring 999. Tell them you have an intruder in the house, and he's got your little boy.' He sensed she was in shock, and said as coolly as he could, 'Go on, girl, there's no time to waste. Make the call, then fetch Teddy and run to the neighbour's.'

He heard her go, but kept his eyes fixed on Antoine, who had both his hands on his injured knee and was sweating with pain. Edward took a step back; he didn't trust the Frenchman an inch. 'I repeat: if you so much as lift your hand, I will hit you again. But this time I'll hit your head. Nod if you understand, or I may hit you anyway.'

Slowly Antoine's head moved up and down.

'Well done,' said Edward, hoping the police wouldn't dawdle.

They didn't. The magic words 'he's got my little boy' did the trick, and within four minutes by Edward's watch two patrol cars screeched to a halt outside the house. Cathy had ignored the second of Edward's orders: she sent Teddy running to Mrs Wolfson next door, but stayed behind herself. She opened the door as the police ran up the steps, and explained rapidly that the older man in the room next door was her father, and that the intruder was the heavy-set man lying on the floor.

51

L IZ CAUGHT THE FIRST flight to Marseilles, still
shaken by Edward's phone call of the evening before.
His account of the fracas when Antoine arrived unexpect-
edly at Cathy's house had been chilling. He'd stressed that
both Teddy and Cathy were all right, but she could read
between the lines and knew he was minimising the danger
they had all faced. It had clearly been a close call with
Antoine, and could easily have ended in something
horrendous.

René had been clever. He'd sent Antoine to Brighton
three days earlier than he'd said he himself would show up
there. His claim when he was arrested at Le Barbot that
Antoine had gone to Marseilles had been a completely
plausible red herring.

Marseilles. The place seemed to be the key to everything
that had happened recently: to Cathy's problems with the
commune, to the efforts to subvert Operation Clarity; to
the meetings with Sorsky; and to the Russian intelligence
officer, Kubiak, who had supervised Sorsky's expatriation
and afterwards been seen in Marseilles. Liz gazed out of
the window of the plane as they began to descend over the
Massif Central towards the Mediterranean, and the pilot

announced that in twenty minutes they would be on the ground.

It was disappointing that her interview with Park Woo-jin hadn't provided more information. He had seemed to her, by the end, to be telling the truth, but the trouble was that he didn't know much beyond his own story.

Bokus had rung her the previous day about the man they knew as Mr Dong. South Korean Intelligence had identified him from the photographs as a senior North Korean intelligence officer, Dong Shin-soo, which made complete sense of Park Woo-jin's story. Searches of the flight manifests for the arrivals from Marseilles that the Singhs' taxi firm had met indicated that he travelled on a French passport. But why he was based in Marseilles remained a mystery, and her conviction that Kubiak's trips there were connected in some way to Park Woo-jin's spying at the MOD was still not backed by any hard evidence. Liz knew Marseilles was a cosmopolitan port, full of immigrants from North Africa and further afield, where no doubt the answers to many mysteries could be found. But would it provide the answers she was looking for?

She caught the airport train to the centre of the city. By now it was almost eleven o'clock in the morning and the streets around the port were buzzing with activity. She had rung Martin the night before to arrange a meeting place and to tell him the news about Antoine. Now an extradition request was being sent to the British authorities.

Martin was waiting for her at the bar of a café in the old port, halfway along a cul-de-sac of small shops.

'It's good to see you,' he said, kissing her on the cheek. 'Is Cathy really all right? And how is Edward now?'

'They're both OK, thanks. Though pretty shaken up. Edward was very brave – he's not exactly a spring chicken.'

'No, but once a soldier, always a soldier.'

Liz suppressed a smile. Edward and Martin not only shared a military background but a fierce pride in it as well.

Martin said, 'I feel very badly about Antoine.'

'You mean that he slipped through the net? You're not to blame. By the time René told you he'd sent him to Marseilles, Antoine was already at Cathy's. *We* were supposed to stop him at the border, but he used a false passport. It must have been stolen, they think. It's nobody's fault – there's not much Immigration can do when someone travels under a false name. Anyway,' she said, 'what are the plans for the Korean firm?'

'We'll go in first thing tomorrow morning. The local DCRI have had surveillance on the place for a few days now and they've got a pretty good idea of who goes in and out. They start work early – everyone should be in there by eight o'clock.'

'Have there been any more sightings of Kubiak?'

'None. So we considered waiting another day or so, to try and get him as well; he hasn't been seen in Geneva for almost a week. But if he's not here now, there's no reason to think he'll show up any time soon.'

'Okay. The mystery for me is what the link is between him and this man Dong Shin-soo. We don't know if Dong has anything to do with this office here – it's a *South* Korean company after all, so if he were connected, it wouldn't make much sense. And I still don't understand the Russian involvement with the place.' Martin looked down at his coffee. 'Too many unanswered questions,' he said. 'I have to agree: it doesn't make any sense.'

'If you set out all the pieces in this little puzzle, you're left with the choice of believing that there is a South Korean-North Korean-Russian plot, which is absurd, or . . .' And Liz paused as she thought about the unspoken alternative.

'Or?' Martin asked gently.

'One of the three isn't who or what we think they are. Or – don't say it isn't complicated – they *are* who they say they are, but they're also something else.'

Martin laughed. 'Well, let's hope we'll know a lot more after tomorrow.'

'What are you doing until then?' asked Liz

'I have to make some calls to Paris. Fézard has offered me the use of an office in the Préfecture. You're welcome to come with me, but otherwise I thought we could meet up in an hour or so for lunch. There's a bistro just down the street that I'm told is very good.'

Liz looked at Martin fondly, thinking how very French he was. In less than twenty-four hours they'd be going in with armed police to try and solve this mystery, but for now, his lunch was what mattered most. There was actually something very sensible in this approach, she reflected. What was the point of sitting around, tensely eating soggy sandwiches and drinking instant coffee – the usual refreshment when A4 and Special Branch were waiting for an operation to begin?

'Actually, I may leave you to it for now. I'd like to get a feel for the neighbourhood.'

He nodded. 'Of course. The South Korean office is very close by . . . just round the corner. You'll easily recognise it – an old warehouse that's been renovated. Be careful though, just in case Kubiak is around. We still don't know whether he saw you in Geneva meeting Sorsky, and we don't want to alert him.'

Martin signalled for the bill, and Liz waited while he paid. As they left the little cul-de-sac, he pointed down the street at the awning of the bistro. 'I'll see you there at one,' he said, and suddenly reached for her arm. 'I'm glad you're here, Liz. But keep your eyes open.'

'I will,' she said, surprised by his sudden solemnity. It wasn't like him to worry.

52

M<small>ARTIN</small> S<small>EURAT WAS ALWAYS</small> punctual. Through-
out his marriage he had endured (sometimes
patiently, towards the end mostly not) his wife's casual
indifference to time. Fortunately, Liz was a good time-
keeper, which meant her lateness for lunch was unusual.
And a little frustrating, since he had much to tell her.
When he'd got to the Préfecture he had expected to hole
up in the cubicle Fézard had commandeered for him, but
a young detective had found him and said the boss would
like to speak to him.

He'd found Fézard in high spirits, almost jubilant. 'Ah,
Monsieur Seurat,' he'd exclaimed as Martin walked into
his elegant office, 'I have some news. Good news, I'd say.
This man Dong whom MI5 have been following has made
an appearance here. Guess where?'

'I assume at the airport,' said Martin lightly.

Fézard began to frown, then stopped and laughed. 'Like
all Parisians, you employ a subtle humour, Monsieur. But
seriously, you should know that this man Dong has been
seen by my men this very morning, entering the same
office block as our South Korean friends. Not only that,
one of my men had a word with the building's receptionist,

and she says she has seen the man before. He takes the elevator to the fifth floor, moreover, which is where our Eastern friends work.'

Now Martin sat at the bistro table, thinking that Liz had been right: there were three parties to this odd drama. But confirmation of her hunch merely heightened the mystery, unless it turned out that this Dong character was working for the South Koreans – in that fraught peninsula, the two Koreas were constantly trying to turn the agents of the other side. But if Dong had been turned, why didn't the British and Americans know about it? Surely they would have been told by the KCIA.

His puzzlement persisted as he sat waiting for Liz. She was only twenty minutes late but it was making him nervous just the same. He told himself to calm down, and remembered when his daughter, fresh at college in Paris, had shown up an hour late for lunch, explaining that she had just been window shopping and had lost track of time. But Liz wasn't a young girl, and in Seurat's experience she was never late.

So after half an hour had passed he rang her mobile. It was switched off – another thing that was odd. She never turned it off when she was away from her office; she needed to be available for calls from Thames House in London. By now, his mild anxiety had turned to full-blown worry, and after another half-hour of fruitless waiting he called Fézard, explaining the situation. Fézard understood the gravity of her non-show at once, and immediately came to join him in the bistro to discuss what to do.

Martin said, 'I think I'd better call her office in London and see if they've heard from her. Isobel Florian is arriving any minute; I'll let her know as well. Maybe Liz called her for some reason.' Not that that seemed in the least likely.

'All right.' Fézard pointed to three men standing on the pavement outside the bistro. 'Those are my officers. They'll be combing the area – there's always a chance she's got lost. Easy to do in Marseilles. And I'll alert the local police as well – they'll check with all the hospitals in case she's had an accident.'

'Good,' said Martin. He hesitated momentarily, then said, 'I was thinking about the raid.'

Fézard nodded. 'Me too.'

'If something's happened to Liz, then it might be connected to the Korean office. She might have been seen and even taken there. Which means we should move in sooner rather than later.'

'I agree and I would be surprised if Madame Florian didn't agree too.' Fézard looked at his watch. 'If we've had no news of Ms Carlyle by four o'clock, then I would suggest we enter the offices at four-thirty. I have constant surveillance on the building, and they have seen nothing suspicious since the appearance of Dong. There's an entrance at the back – a loading bay for large items and furniture; I will make sure they are watching that as well. If she is in the building, then no one will be able to take her anywhere else without our seeing it.' He left unspoken what Martin feared most – that anyone taking Liz out of the building might be transporting a corpse.

Peggy Kinsolving usually ate lunch in the Thames House canteen, then took a short walk along the Embankment – usually only as far as Tate Britain – to stretch her legs and get some fresh air before starting work again. But today a persistent drizzle made the prospect of a stroll seem uninviting, and besides she had a lot on at the moment, so she was at her desk when the call came in from France. 'Hello,' she said tentatively.

'This is Martin Seurat of the French DGSE. I'm calling from Marseilles.'

Peggy had never actually met him, but they'd spoken on the phone before, since this was the second case that he and Liz had worked on together. And though Liz had never mentioned it, everyone knew that she and Martin Seurat had become an item. 'Hello, Martin. It's Peggy. How can I help?' she asked, slightly puzzled to find him on the phone.

'Have you heard from Liz?'

'Not today. I thought she'd be with you. She was catching a flight early this morning to Marseilles.'

'She was here this morning – we met for coffee. Then we were supposed to meet up at lunchtime, but she hasn't appeared. She's almost two hours late.'

'That's not like her.'

'I know, and I'm concerned. Her mobile is switched off – which isn't like her either.'

'Could she have got lost?'

'That was my first thought – the Old Port here is a bit of a rabbit warren. But in that case I'm sure she would have phoned me. I hate to say it,' he said, then paused before continuing, 'but I think something may have happened to her. Everyone's been alerted over here, and we've got people looking all over the city for her. But you had better tell your people that Liz is missing. They can call me direct if they need to speak to me. You should also tell them that we've brought forward the scheduled raid on the Korean office – instead of waiting until tomorrow, we're going to go in at four-thirty. Unless Liz shows up before then.'

He gave Peggy his mobile number, then rang off. She sat for a moment, thinking what to do next. There was no mistaking the urgency in his voice; he did not seem to believe that some small misunderstanding could have occurred to account for Liz's failure to show.

Their boss was on holiday, most of her colleagues were out at lunch or on business, so there was no one for Peggy to consult. There was only one thing for it. She might look silly if ten minutes from now Seurat rang her to say Liz had reappeared, though Peggy would far prefer that – any embarrassment was worth knowing Liz was safe. But in the meantime it would be irresponsible to delay. She picked up her phone and dialled DG's private office.

She was answered by the near-legendary Private Secretary, Anne Whitestone, who'd seen four Director Generals come and go. 'This is Peggy Kinsolving in Counter-Espionage. I have an emergency. I've just heard that Liz Carlyle is missing in France. Martin Seurat from the DGSE rang me from Marseilles. They are worried that something's happened to her.'

'Come up straight away, Peggy,' said Anne Whiteside calmly. 'DG is here and he'll want to talk to you.'

Four o'clock was usually a fairly placid time at the venerable Préfecture in Marseilles. The public desk closed at four and the police shifts changed at five; the DCRI officers were still out in the field; and inside the building the only noises to be heard were of afternoon coffee being brewed.

But now the building seemed to hum with activity as Martin Seurat was waved in by the guard and directed straight upstairs. In the open-plan office, Fézard stood next to a large whiteboard on wheels, a pointer in his hand. Half of the board was covered by a plan of the Korean office building, and he was pointing out the access and exit points on the fifth floor. He looked up questioningly as

Martin entered. When he saw the slight shake of his head, Fézard's expression darkened.

Martin had spent the last hour on the phone. He'd squared the bistro owner by showing him his identity card, then commandeered a table by the front window in case Liz should appear and made his calls from there. First, Isobel Florian after she landed at Marseilles airport – she'd understood his fear for Liz's safety at once, and agreed that the time of the raid should be moved forward. Then he'd rung his own superiors in Paris and explained the situation.

London had rung soon after, and he'd talked to the Director General, assuring him they were doing everything they could to find his officer. The Englishman had been calm and decisive. He had obviously been well briefed by Peggy and didn't waste time asking for the background to the operation in Marseilles. He offered to send out an officer to liaise and give any help he could. Martin said that he would certainly accept the offer if it would help, but for now the police and the DCRI were doing all they could to find Liz Carlyle.

Finally there had been another call from England. 'Seurat,' said a frosty voice, 'It's Geoffrey Fane. What on earth has happened?'

He explained the situation, but it had been an awkward conversation. Each man knew the other had strong personal feelings for Liz, and each of them struggled to sound purely professional. He had discouraged Fane from catching the next flight out or from sending his Station Chief down from Paris. 'Thanks for the offer, Geoffrey, but we're doing all we can – we don't need any more people on the ground. Please just activate any sources you have who might hear anything relevant.'

So he hadn't had time to draw breath, much less worry, and it was only now, as Fézard wrapped up the briefing, that Martin felt again the extent of his own fear. It was four o'clock; in half an hour they'd know whether Liz had been taken to the office of the South Koreans; in half an hour he'd know whether this uncertain agony was over, or would continue. Who could have kidnapped her? This man Dong had never seen her; neither, as far as he knew, had the Russians. But how exactly had they found out about Sorsky's treachery? Could they have monitored his meetings with Liz in Geneva?

He wondered if they'd find her inside the building. Part of him fervently hoped so, but part of him was frightened. If they found her, what state would she be in? If she weren't there, then at least he could hope that she was somewhere else – and alive.

53

FOR A FEW MINUTES Liz thought she was lost. She couldn't be more than a quarter of a mile from the bistro where she was supposed to meet Martin for lunch, but so dense and confusing was the geography of the Old Port that she might as well have been in Mexico. Streets were too grand a name for the little lanes and alleyways that twisted like the Minotaur's maze, and all the sinuous pathways seemed to lie in the shade of tenement buildings that blocked out the sun – Liz couldn't even locate its position in the sky to establish where south lay.

Then suddenly she emerged into a street she recognised – it ran past the Koreans' office building. Not wanting to pass that again, she decided to risk a shortcut down a narrow side road that seemed to head in the right direction. The alley was lined on both sides by the backs of old stone houses, and the smells of midday meals cooking wafted out of windows. The street itself was deserted.

She heard a vehicle turn into the alley behind her. When she looked back she saw a battered blue van, driving slowly. She continued walking and as the van drove past her it struck her as odd that it had no name stencilled on its side. Thirty feet or so in front of her the van stopped, the driver's door opened, and a heavy-set man in a bulky leather jacket and a cloth cap got out, leaving the engine running. Without looking at Liz, he went to the rear and wrenched open the van's double doors. She noticed that the back of the van was empty and at the same time felt there was something familiar about the driver. As she came level with him, the man turned towards her. '*Excusez-moi, Madame,*' he said with a smile, and Liz stopped.

A big mistake: he stepped forward and grabbed her coat with his left arm, then before she could try and pull away he hit her, hard with a clenched fist, smack on the jaw. The cliché was true – Liz literally saw stars, and would have fallen down had the man not been holding her so tightly with his other hand. He turned her halfway round, circling her chest with both arms, squeezing the breath out of her as she tried to wriggle free. Then in one swift motion he lifted her up into the air and dumped her like a side of beef into the back of the van.

She lay dazed on the floor as he banged the doors shut. She heard the front driver's door slam as the man got back in and drove off quickly.

By then she was sitting up, shouting for help, and kicking the rear doors and sides of the van as hard as she could. There was nothing to hold on to; the van was being driven fast, and every time it went round a corner, she slid across the metal floor. But she kept up the noise, though she thought it unlikely that anyone could hear her, and from what she'd seen of the neighbourhood, even if they did hear, they probably wouldn't report it.

After about five minutes the van stopped abruptly, and Liz found herself slammed against the hard wall separating her from the driver's cab. She heard what sounded like a metal garage door opening and closing. What would happen next? Sensing this could be her only chance of escape, she got up awkwardly, crouched under the roof of the van, ready to launch herself out and run for it.

One of the back doors suddenly swung open and a harsh light from a powerful torch shone in Liz's eyes, briefly blinding her. A voice behind the light said, 'My other hand is holding this,' and the light moved down to shine on an automatic pistol pointed right at her.

'Now lie on your stomach,' he ordered. When Liz hesitated he jabbed the pistol at her. 'Do it or I will kill you right now. There's a silencer on this gun so no one will hear me fire.' The English was good, but strongly accented.

Liz did as she was told, pressing her face against the cold metal floor of the van, her back crawling as she wondered what this man was going to do to her. He must have put the torch down; there was less direct light on her now.

'Put your hands together behind your back,' he said, and she obeyed. A moment later Liz felt plastic cuffs go round each of her wrists, then snap shut.

Then he pushed her legs together and what felt like rope was wrapped around her ankles, and tied quickly but tightly with double knots. The man roughly turned her on her side, then on to her back, rolling her like a trussed turkey. She could just make out his features and thought again that she recognised them. From where? Whenever it was, it seemed ages ago.

Leaning forward, he grabbed Liz by the front of her blouse, and hauled her up to a sitting position. She tried to catch his eye, but he ignored her, and reached into the side pocket of his leather jacket, bringing out a roll of surgical tape. 'Stay still,' he said as he tore long strips off the roll, attaching them temporarily to the side wall of the van. He then took them one at a time, pressing them against Liz's mouth and wrapping them all the way around her head. He worked methodically, layer by layer, until the whole area from her chin to just below her nose was sealed tight with tape.

He stared at her, listening to her breathe through her nose, then nodded to himself, satisfied. 'I'll be back in a while and then we're going for a bit of a ride.' He backed out and closed the van door, leaving Liz again in darkness.

With her hands manacled behind her back, she couldn't see her watch, and it was hard to gauge how much time had passed when she heard the garage door open and the man climb back into the cab and start the engine. An hour, she guessed, maybe more.

The van reversed and stopped, then the driver got out and closed the garage doors. When he got back in he drove at speed through the streets, while Liz tried to keep herself from banging against the inner sides of the rear compartment. They paused occasionally for what she assumed were traffic lights, and she could hear street noises from outside. But bound and gagged, there was nothing she could do to let people know that she was being held inside the van.

They drove for almost half an hour, she reckoned, speeding up on what must have been a main road, then slowing and manoeuvring through smaller roads. The man's driving was erratic. He would speed up then suddenly slam the brakes on and turn abruptly, so Liz rolled around like a puppet, sometimes smashing into the sides and the rear doors of the van, unable to protect herself.

At last they slowed down, and then braked so sharply that again she was hurled forwards. She waited for the driver to turn off the engine and then . . . what? If he were going to kill her, wouldn't he have done it in the security of the garage, then taken his time disposing of the body? The body? *My* body, thought Liz, filled with sudden fury. For a moment her fear receded as she determined to get away from this man, and make sure he was caught and punished. She tried to ignore the small voice in the back of her mind that was telling her she'd been brought somewhere private, far from the hubbub of the city centre, away from the eyes of the public or the police, where at his leisure the man could . . .

She was trying to stop herself shuddering when the van moved forward again, this time very slowly and deliberately. She felt a sudden jolt when they hit something – something big enough to jar the whole vehicle. Was it an accident? she asked herself hopefully. But it couldn't be – not crawling forward as they were, and Liz listened as the van's front bumper made a high-pitched grinding noise as it pushed against some large object. Slowly but surely, the van seemed to be winning against this inanimate obstacle, and suddenly it seemed that the impediment had been pushed away and they moved forward freely for several yards.

Then the van slowed and stopped, only to reverse suddenly at speed. This time the jolt came from the rear. Liz found herself pitched into the air, and thrown against the partition. She hit it with the back of her head, then crashed on to the floor of the van, knocked out cold.

54

THE RECEPTIONIST, A PRETTY brunette with ruby-painted nails, stared wide-eyed as an armed, uniformed police inspector led a team of officers into the building, followed by Fézard, three plain clothes officers, Martin Seurat, Isobel Florian, and a mechanic in overalls and stout boots.

'Stay where you are and don't touch the phones,' the inspector ordered the frightened girl, while Fézard and his group crossed the atrium to the stairs and the mechanic set about disabling the lifts. Three police officers were despatched to guard the back exit and disable the service lift.

Fézard and his team took the stairs to the fifth floor two at a time, stopping on the landing to catch their breath; even Isobel, slim and fit as she was, was panting slightly. Fézard, neither slim nor particularly fit, was puffing hard.

Two doors led off the landing. One was half-glazed and bearing the sign: 'Beauchêne et Fils: Négotiants en Vin'. The other, on the opposite side of the landing, was a strong-looking black windowless door with a security keypad beside it, and a small laminated sign on the wall that read 'Technomatics Inc.'

One of Fézard's officers stepped forward and applied a small device to the keypad. After a few seconds the door opened with a click and a buzzer sounded inside the offices. Fézard drew his gun and led the way into a small anteroom furnished with two chairs and a low table piled with a stack of *Time* magazines. Behind an unmanned reception desk an open doorway led to the rest of the offices.

Fézard stood tensely, waiting for a response to the buzzer. But no one came through the doorway and no sound came from within. Covered by his officers, who had now all drawn their weapons, Fézard took three slow steps to the doorway. He stared into the silence, and gradually the expression on his face changed, from alert to puzzled.

Then, jerking his head sideways to his officers, he said quietly, 'Follow me,' and walked through the doorway. As Martin followed behind, he saw in front of him a large open-plan office. Roughly the size of the briefing room at the Préfecture, it held about a dozen desks, each equipped with a black leather swivel chair and a glowing television-sized computer monitor. Soft beige carpet ran wall to wall, and the ceiling was lined with sound-deadening panels in which long lines of lights were recessed. The effect was like the hi-tech trading floor of an investment bank, but instead of shouted phone calls and frantic activity, the room was silent and apparently deserted.

'Where is everyone?' Isobel whispered to Seurat. 'Is it an Asian holiday or something?'

Overhearing her, Fézard said, 'No one's gone anywhere.' He sounded puzzled. 'They all came in this morning and we haven't seen any of them going out. We've been watching the place all day. He started suddenly. 'Wait a minute!' he said, and pointed to the far corner of the room. A young man dressed in a black turtleneck sweater and black trousers sat slumped forward on his desk, his head pillowed on his crossed arms. He looked as if he was taking a catnap, but he must be very sound asleep not to have been woken by the commotion of their arrival. On the screen in front of him a satellite image showed an area Seurat recognised as the Gulf – on one side the sandy shores of the UAE with Oman beneath, on the other Iran north of the Strait of Hormuz.

Fézard walked over to the desk and shook the young man's shoulder. '*Monsieur?*' he said gently. There was no movement. '*Monsieur,*' he said again, shaking the man more sharply. This time the head rolled slightly on the arms but the man did not sit up.

Fézard turned to the others who were watching him and shook his head; there was no point in trying to wake the man – he wasn't asleep, he was no longer breathing. Martin took in the implications and suddenly felt sick. What did this mean for Liz?

At this end of the room there was a little archway, leading to a short corridor with three doors opening off it along one side. Fézard motioned to two of his men to check the rooms. The first contained toilets with no one inside. The second door was kicked open and the two men went in. There was a pause, then one came out and gestured for Fézard. Isobel and Martin followed.

This was a small meeting room. Round a long table sat six young Korean men, all dressed in black turtleneck sweaters and black trousers. They too seemed to be asleep – some sat upright in their chairs, some were slumped on the table. Most had mild expressions on their faces, as if they were dreaming. On the table in front of them were small teacups, all empty or nearly empty. In the middle of the table sat a large Chinese teapot. There were four empty chairs and, stepping into the room, Martin saw two more bodies sprawled on the carpet at the far end.

He counted the teacups around the table – there were eleven. Eight bodies here, one in the open-plan office; that left two unaccounted for. And where was Liz?

'*Inspector!*' one of Fézard's men said from the door. 'I think you'll want to see this.'

Dreading what they might find, Martin and Isobel followed Fézard down the corridor. The third and final door led to a small kitchen, fitted with a wall cupboard containing glasses and plates, a counter top with a microwave, a fridge, and a sink. The tap on the sink was running in a desultory stream.

On the linoleum floor a man was lying flat on his back. His eyes were closed and he wasn't moving. He also looked to be Korean, but he wasn't wearing the office uniform of black turtleneck and trousers – he was dressed in a suit and a shiny silk tie. It became obvious that he wasn't breathing either.

Crouching down, Martin carefully reached into the inner pocket of the dead man's jacket and drew out a wallet and a passport. The wallet contained 400 Euros and several credit cards. The passport was French and named the holder as Dong Shin-soo Wong, a French citizen. The photograph was of the same man who lay on the floor.

Fézard was on the phone, summoning a forensics team, when another of his men appeared in the doorway. 'Sir, we've searched everywhere now. There's no one else in these offices. All we've found is a safe, in a cupboard off the corridor. It's locked.'

'All right. Let's get it open; maybe that will tell us who these people really are.'

*   *   *

It took forty minutes, by which time the silent mortuary was humming with activity. It seemed plain that someone else must have been here and administered the poison. Unless it was a suicide pact, which was possible but seemed unlikely. But how did the killers get in and out without being noticed by the surveillance team? Fézard had sent one of his officers to collect the surveillance logs and photographs, and while the forensics team, pathologist and photographers all went about their business, Fézard himself converted one end of the office into an interview room.

The owner of the building, summoned from his office in the town, said that as far as he knew, Technomatics Inc. was a South Korean computer consultancy. They had had good references and always paid their rent on time by direct debit on an account at a bank in Marseilles. There had been no problem with their tenancy.

The younger Monsieur Beauchêne, the wine merchant from the adjoining office, said he knew very little about his neighbours. He occasionally met one or two of them going in or out. He had the impression that they started work earlier than he and his father did and that they did not leave the building at lunchtime. He did know that they convened in the afternoon in their boardroom – 'I called on them one afternoon when my water supply had stopped working, to see if they had the same problem. They hadn't – it was some-thing to do with our pipes. I found them all sitting around the table like the Apostles, sipping tea from tiny cups.'

The safe, opened at last, was empty except for two large envelopes. One contained 40,000 Swiss francs and $30,000 in hundred-dollar bills. The other held a number of pass-ports. Martin examined them, sorting them into two piles. 'Look at this,' he said. 'There seem to be two passports for each person. One is South Korean all right but the other looks to me as though it's North Korean. The photos in them are identical and the names seem to match, but I guess one is real and the other's a fake. It doesn't take much imagination to work out which is which. This isn't a South Korean computer consultancy at all, it's something to do with North Korea.'

'Bizarre,' said Fézard. 'They claimed their head office was in Seoul.'

'More likely to be Pyongyang.'

'But who murdered them?' asked Isobel. 'I realise they must have been poisoned, and probably by the tea they drank. But how could anyone do it without being spotted?'

'Easily,' said Martin. 'Come have a look.' He led the way down the hall to the conference room. From the doorway he pointed at the teacups on the table. 'There are eleven cups.'

'Yes,' said Isobel, and looked at him a little curiously.

'But only ten bodies.'

'You think we're missing a corpse then?'

'No.' He pointed at the table. 'One of those cups is full. I think our killer was joining these unfortunate gentlemen for tea. Somehow he managed to put poison in the tea, and didn't drink any himself.'

'Oh, at first I thought you meant—' And Isobel stopped.

He got her meaning. 'I don't think Liz was ever here. But the killer was, and I'd bet even money he's the same person who's grabbed her.'

'If you're right, why didn't the surveillance see him?' asked Isobel.

'The pathologist says these men have been dead only a very short time,' interrupted Fézard. 'The logs and photos have arrived, so let's get that receptionist up here and see what she has to say.'

The pretty receptionist looked a mess. She had been crying and her eye make-up was smudged. She had heard what had happened in the building and was shaking with a mixture of excitement and fear. Told by Fézard that her information would be of the utmost importance, she tried to pull herself together.

The Koreans had all arrived before nine o'clock when she started work, and had been let in by the night guard. She had not seen any of them go out again. She looked carefully at the surveillance pictures and was able to identify the workers in the other offices. The pictures showed that at 10.02 a delivery man had entered the building carrying a refill for a water cooler. Yes. That was for one of the offices on the second floor, she said. He had left it in reception to be collected. She had signed for it.

'Were there any other deliveries?' asked Martin. At about two o'clock, she told them, another delivery man had arrived with a parcel for Technomatics. 'Did he leave it in reception?' asked Seurat.

'No, Monsieur. I rang through and they asked me to send him up.'

'How long did he stay?'

'He left not long before you all arrived.'

Isobel was already sorting through the photographs. 14.03. A short stocky man in a cap, worn pulled down over his eyes, was going through the door, carrying a square brown box. At 16.13, he was coming out, without the parcel.

'That must be him,' said Isobel, spreading the photos out on the table.

'Have you seen this man before?' she asked the receptionist.

'Yes. Once or twice, bringing deliveries.'

'It could be Kubiak,' said Martin.

'We have photographs of him which the Swiss sent when they asked us to put surveillance on him, and we have some we took ourselves during the surveillance,' Fézard put in.

Martin nodded grimly. They would wait for the photographs to provide confirmation, but he was already certain of the identity of the delivery man. It didn't help to think that Liz had been abducted by a man who in Switzerland had proved he wouldn't hesitate to dispose of anyone who got in his way.

55

I T WAS 6.30 IN the evening in London, an hour earlier
than Marseilles, and Andy Bokus's expression said *I told
you so*. Geoffrey Fane suppressed a sigh. It was difficult
enough trying to make sense of this business – Liz Carlyle
was missing, ten Koreans were dead in an office in Marseilles
– without having to deal with his American colleague's ego.
He said curtly, 'I don't know why you're looking so pleased
with yourself, Andy. We've got a crisis on our hands.'

'I appreciate that, Geoffrey. It's just that I was thinking,
this is a scenario you and I have seen before. The bloody
Russians are at it again. One of our drones went out of
control and blew itself up. Fortunately no one got hurt –
believe me, we'd be retaliating if they had.'

'Steady on—' Fane began.

Bokus was having none of it. 'I know you're all excited
about this supposed North Korean connection, but I think
this guy Park Woo-jin has been working for our friends in
Moscow, not Pyongyang. I know Carlyle thinks she got
the truth out of him, but it may be that he himself didn't
even know who he was working for.'

'Well, unfortunately she's not here to tell us her reason-
ing. For all I know she's—' And Fane stopped, suddenly

aghast at how close he'd come to saying what he feared most. People died, agents got killed; he was used to mortality. But the thought that Liz Carlyle had been abducted and might have been murdered suddenly seemed too much to bear. What's wrong with me? he thought, trying to pull himself together, which only made it worse. He had an aching sense of unfinished business; he'd never told Liz how much he admired her, and that somehow made the possibility of her death even worse.

Bokus for once was sympathetic. 'I know this is a tough one, Geoffrey,' he said. 'I just thought it best to focus on the larger picture.'

'Of course,' said Fane, regaining control of his emotions. He couldn't bear the thought of Andy Bokus – clever in his way and a representative of Britain's closest ally, but still essentially an *oaf* – pitying him. 'Anyway, I agree with you that we need to lay our cards on the table and see what they have to say.'

Bokus looked surprised. 'Who? You mean the Russians?'

'I do. If you're right, and they're behind all this, then I want to make it clear that they've greatly overstepped the line. And that if they've touched a single hair on Liz Carlyle's head, they'll never hear the end of it. I'll make it my personal mission to hound them all over the world. But I need you shoulder to shoulder with me on this one.' Fane gave what he considered to be his most persuasive smile, gritted his teeth and said, 'After all, you carry a lot more weight with them than we do.'

Summoned urgently, Viktor Kirov left the annual dinner of the British Manufacturing Association readily enough. It was nine o'clock when Bokus and Fane entered the Russian Embassy in Kensington Palace Gardens. They were escorted to a downstairs conference room by two smartly suited young men with holsters visible beneath their jackets. There they found Kirov, formal in dinner jacket and black tie, sitting at a table, sipping a cup of black coffee and smoking a small cheroot. He stood up when they came in, shaking hands before motioning them to seats across the table from him.

They had all met before, but not frequently. Since the murder of Alexander Litvinenko in a London hotel a few years previously, relations between their Services had cooled. Fane knew a lot about Kirov, who had been in London for three years as Head of Station. He was a long-term KGB man, nearing retirement (this would be his last posting), who had been posted in East Berlin during the height of the Cold War, and then in Poland where he had helped hound Lech Wałęsa and his followers. But he was a subtle clever man, not a thug, and had successfully made the transition in the post-1991 years to the leaner, still powerful SVR. A family man, whose grown-up children frequently visited London to see him and his wife Anya – an ex-dancer with the Bolshoi, if the Vauxhall Cross file were to be believed. Like Vladimir Putin, whom he was thought to resemble, Kirov was a diminutive man with receding hair, but like the Russian leader, he was known for his vigour.

All of this would be familiar to Bokus as well, and equally Kirov would know a lot about both of them. Which gave this meeting its oddly surreal element.

Kirov offered them coffee, which they declined. He sipped his slowly, then, addressing Fane, said with a twinkle in his eye, 'Naturally it comes as a great disappointment to leave a dinner at the Guildhall and forgo the company of your eminent manufacturers. So I assume this must be urgent.' He took a long drag on his cheroot and said, 'How can I be of service?'

They had agreed that Fane should kick off. He steepled both hands, like a contemplative don, but when he spoke it was at a rapid pace. 'We recently discovered that a foreign agent had been placed in our Ministry of Defence. His goal was to disrupt a defence project we are working on with Andy's people. It was a cyber-attack.

'At first we did not know who was behind this infiltration. Everything suggested the Chinese, who as we all know are busy waging cyber-warfare against all three of our countries, and many others as well. But by investigation we managed to catch this intruder, and it turned out that he was, of all things, North Korean.'

Kirov's brows lifted momentarily in surprise. The North Koreans were nobody's friends – not even the Chinese whose proximity meant they inevitably had some contact with their neighbour. But the North Korean Intelligence Services had always seemed more intent on defence than attack, and they rarely ventured into the West.

Fane went on, 'We learned a few other things during our investigation. One was that information from our project was being sent to an office in Marseilles. We believe they used this information to sabotage some trials we were running on . . .' he hesitated, again not wanting to say too much '. . . some innovations in aeronautics. We discovered this office was leased and manned by Koreans who were thought to be *South* Koreans – or that's what they said they were. That was puzzling enough, but we've just learned they were in fact North Koreans.'

'Interesting,' said Kirov, with a note of professional appreciation. 'No one would think of Marseilles as a likely place to find North Korean agents.'

'Agreed. But we know that these activities are known to your own Service.'

'Surely not,' said Kirov, looking alert for the first time.

'Not only are they known to your Service, but we believe your Service is actively involved with these North Koreans. Possibly even running the operation.'

'That is a highly unfriendly accusation. I don't believe you can substantiate it.'

'One of your senior officers was seen entering the office in Marseilles from which the operation is being run.'

'That sounds most unlikely. It must have been a mistaken identification.'

'Not at all. He was followed from Geneva to Marseilles. There isn't any question of a mistake.'

The Russian's eyebrows went up a second time. 'Geneva?'

'He is your Head of Security there.'

There was a pause. Then Kirov said, 'I take it you learned this from Herr Bech. The Swiss Service is not one I greatly admire.'

Bokus spoke for the first time. 'Anatole Kubiak.'

There was a long silence in the room. Finally, Kirov stubbed out his cheroot and said, 'Let's accept for the moment that you're right – a Russian intelligence officer has been seen entering an office you believe is occupied by North Korean intelligence agents. So?'

Fane said, 'It would link you to efforts to undermine the US–UK project. As I said, it has already suffered one, possibly two, acts of sabotage. If your country were involved with that in any way, we would take it as a highly provocative act.'

Bokus interjected, 'We sure would. My own government would see it as an act of outright aggression. We are provisionally considering reprisals already.'

Kirov's face was expressionless as he composed his response. Finally, he held up both palms. 'Gentlemen, my wife would tell you it rarely happens, but I am at a loss for words. I have never heard of a North Korean infiltrator in the British Ministry of Defence. Frankly, it sounds preposterous to me. I am happy to relay your concern to Moscow, and tell you their reply in due course. But otherwise, I don't see what I can do, since I don't have any knowledge of what you are talking about.'

'That's not good enough,' said Bokus. 'I notice you didn't say you knew nothing about the project.'

Kirov shrugged. 'One hears a lot of things in our job,' he said blandly.

Fane spoke urgently. 'Events have rather overtaken us. This morning a senior British intelligence officer went to Marseilles to liaise with the French about this Korean operation. They met this morning and were scheduled to meet again at lunchtime. My colleague did not reappear – she's still missing. Something has clearly happened to her.'

'Could the Koreans have spotted her?'

Fane shook his head. 'They had no way of knowing who she was. But there's more: the French raided this office in Marseilles several hours ago; inside they found the Koreans who'd been working there, as well as the North Korean intelligence officer who had been liaising with their covert agent in Britain. All of them were dead.'

'Murdered?' When Bokus nodded, Kirov asked, 'By whom?'

Bokus said, 'We think it was your Head of Security in Geneva.' When Kirov looked astonished at this, Bokus raised his voice: 'He was seen entering the building at the time of the murder and leaving afterwards.'

Fane wished Bokus would calm down. Even though he shared his anger, you got nowhere shouting at the Russians.

Kirov sat quietly, then shook his head finally, as if to rid himself of a bad dream. 'None of this makes any sense to me.'

'Sure,' said Bokus sarcastically.

Kirov ignored him and looked at Fane. There was concern in his eyes for the first time. 'I will make enquiries as a matter of urgency.'

'Please do,' said Fane, trying not to show his own feelings. The Russians were quick to exploit any sign of weakness. He went on firmly, 'If the same person who killed the Koreans is holding our officer, then she's obviously in danger. I want assurances that if indeed an officer of your Service is holding her, then you will ensure that she is not harmed. You can tell your Head Office that if anything does happen to her there will be the most serious repercussions.'

Kirov momentarily bristled, but there was nothing menacing about Fane's threat – it was stated calmly, as fact, and Bokus for once had the good sense not to butt in – so the Russian finally nodded, asking, 'Is it absolutely certain that it was Kubiak who was seen in Marseilles?'

'Without a doubt. The identification was made by the French and the Swiss. '

Kirov shook his head in bafflement. Then he stood up; the meeting was over. Though Fane and Bokus were both six inches taller than the Russian, he had an air of authority which at that moment made him seem the largest person in the room. 'I'll say goodnight now – my aides will show you out. I will be talking with Moscow before you reach the street.'

When they left the Embassy, it was dark outside. Walking towards the guard post at the High Street Kensington end, Bokus turned to Fane. 'So what do you think?'

Fane shrugged and Bokus said crossly, 'My people are going to want to make direct representations to Moscow – we'll be calling in the Ambassador again.'

'Hold them off,' said Fane sharply. Escalation at this point wasn't going to help get Liz back; in fact, it might make it even harder.

'Why?' Bokus demanded. 'I don't trust this guy Kirov an inch; don't tell me you do.'

'Trust isn't the issue now. It's credibility I'm concerned about.'

'You mean you believed him – you think he wouldn't know if the SVR were running an agent in the MOD?'

'Of course he would – *if* they had been doing that. The problem I have is that he may be telling the truth: he has almost certainly heard of Clarity, but I don't think he's heard any of this information about Kubiak before. That's what's worrying me. I'd be less anxious if I thought he had been lying to us about that. At least it would mean he knows where Kubiak is. But I don't think he has any more of a clue than we do.'

56

'CIGARETTE?'

Martin Seurat had stopped smoking ten years before, but he was so tired that he mindlessly accepted Fézard's offer. He borrowed the Inspector's lighter and lit up. It tasted terrible, but he hoped it would help keep him from nodding off. The clock on the wall said 6.15, and daylight was flooding through the windows.

It seemed important to stay awake, though there was nothing they could do – just sit and wait for news. They were both certain that whatever had happened to Liz, Kubiak was behind it. There had been nothing from the hospitals, so an accident could be ruled out. Every hotel, *pension*, and B&B in a twenty-mile radius was being visited by the police, checking the details of every visitor in a desperate search for Kubiak, Liz or anyone suspicious. Railways and the airport had been thoroughly combed over as well, scanning passenger lists and credit-card receipts, checking with Passport Control. Finally, over 400 CCTV cameras were having the contents of their last three days' filing examined painstakingly, in a search for both the Mercedes saloon with Swiss number plates which belonged to Kubiak and the plain blue van in which he had arrived at the Koreans' office, masquerading as a delivery man. Fézard's surveillance cameras had caught only a partial shot of the van as it was being parked a little way down the street, but a couple of digits of the number plate were visible, and these had been checked with all the rental firms in Marseilles, the airport and the outlying areas. Without success.

CCTV seemed likely to be the most helpful source of information, but it would also be the slowest to produce results. Martin didn't want to think how long it would take even the dozen or so who were working on it to scan all the digital video they'd collected.

The phones had been ringing all night. Herr Bech had been one of many callers; he had put out a general alert for any sighting of Kubiak or either of the vehicles in Switzerland. Geoffrey Fane had rung so often that Martin had finally had to suggest that he go to bed, so they could all get some sleep. Not that he himself had done much more than nap for five minutes at a time; he was too tense, too worried that if he closed his eyes he might miss something that could help find Liz.

His phone vibrated. He looked at the screen. 'Now Geoffrey Fane's started texting,' he said irritably. 'He expects to hear from the Russians this morning and will let us know if they have any useful information. I don't expect much from that source,' he added sourly.

Fézard nodded, then said, 'There's a canteen downstairs which will be open now for the early shift. Perhaps we should have some breakfast. It could be a busy day – we'd better eat while we have time.'

As if in rebuke, the phone on Fézard's desk rang with a gentle purr. The Inspector picked it up and said hello, then listened intently, said a quiet *Merci* and put the phone down. 'That was the lab – they have initial results from the first autopsy. The victims were definitely poisoned, and it was in the tea they drank. They haven't identified the poison yet, but they believe it was a kind of venom – there are some that would paralyse a nervous system with just a few sips. It takes a few minutes to work, so provided everyone was drinking the tea at roughly the same time, it would poison them all.'

'Sounds pretty sophisticated,' said Martin.

Fézard nodded. 'It is – that's why they can't identify it yet. The technician said he's never seen exactly this poison before.'

A clever assassin, thought Martin gloomily, which meant he had carefully planned everything. Including, presumably, locating a place to hide Liz which no one could find.

Wait a minute, he told himself, Kubiak couldn't have planned her abduction in advance. He wouldn't have known she was in Marseilles; she hadn't been certain of her plans herself until the day before. So if he had grabbed her, it must have been on the spur of the moment; he might not have had any idea what to do with her. That was where he could have made a mistake, something the CCTV cameras might have picked up. Unless he'd realised the danger, and decided the only thing to do was remove her from the scene altogether.

'How about breakfast?' Fézard began to say again, when there was a light tap on the office door. He sighed. '*Entrez.*'

One of his officers stood in the doorway. He was unshaven and his eyes were red. He'd obviously been up all night as well. 'We've had a call from the CCTV crew, sir. They think they may have found something.'

57

THE CCTV IMAGES WERE from an industrial estate on the northern edge of the city that was scheduled for demolition and redevelopment. They showed a battered blue van driving along a deserted road with a derelict office building in the background. The licence-plate number was half in shadow but enough was visible to identify the vehicle as Kubiak's delivery van.

A few minutes later, they were en route. Fézard drove Martin and Isobel in an unmarked police car. Ahead of them was a police van, containing four armed officers, and the small convoy was escorted by two police outriders on big Honda bikes with lights flashing and sirens going.

They took the Marseilles ring road, their outriders easily slicing a route for them through the heavy early-morning traffic. Martin drummed his fingers nervously on the arm rest while Fézard smoked as he drove and Isobel hummed tunelessly in the back seat. At last they got off the ring road and entered an area of low-lying office buildings, warehouses, and lorry depots. It looked very rundown – at least half the sites had For Sale signs.

'We're lucky there was still a camera operating out here,' said Fézard as they slowed for a traffic light. 'There was a lot of theft in this area – the depots were particular targets – and at one point there were cameras everywhere. In the last three years, as companies have moved out *en masse*, the cameras have been removed.'

'Where was the picture taken?'

'Just there,' said the Inspector, pointing to a junction of the main road they were on with a smaller access road. 'He was travelling that way,' he added, pointing to the smaller road.

He turned and they entered an estate, which was so rundown it made its semi-deserted neighbours look positively prosperous. Here the windows were either smashed or boarded up, and the squares of grass hadn't been mown or the verges trimmed for many months. There were obviously no tenants left in these buildings, though through one set of broken ground-floor windows Martin saw three long-haired men in overalls gathered around a primus stove. Squatters.

They drew alongside the waiting squad car and got out. The senior policeman was shaking his head as they approached him. 'We've checked all the roads here, sir, though there aren't a lot of them. The whole estate's due for demolition. Some gypsies tried to set up camp last month, but we moved them on. There's the odd squatter, but otherwise the only people who've been here are property developers snooping around, looking to buy the land and redevelop when the recession's over. No one's here now – except for the demolition experts and the wrecking crew. They're blowing up one of the office blocks any minute now.'

As if on cue there was a large boom, followed by another, and then another still. Turning round, Martin saw not far away a four-storey office block collapse as if in slow motion – the upper floors crumpled like cheap plasterboard, spewing out dust in a massive cloud as the lower floors followed. It was all over in seconds: a pile of brick dust and mortar now covered the site of what only seconds before had been a 10,000-square-foot office block.

He turned back to the policeman. 'The CCTV caught the van we're looking for as it was turning in. So why didn't it catch it leaving as well?'

The officer looked at him, with the respectful contempt a local policeman shows to higher-ups from outside. 'The camera was only facing one way, sir. If the driver left this estate and turned right on to the main road, the camera wouldn't show it.'

Martin said, 'What else is being blown up?'

'A multi-storey car park.'

'Really?' There was so much space in this ghastly estate that another car park seemed entirely unnecessary – all the buildings had outdoor parking for visitors and employees, with spaces marked out in white paint.

'It's next to what used to be the hypermarket. That didn't last long; it turned out people working here would rather do their shopping where they lived than where they worked. They tore down the store last year.'

'But the car park is still there?' persisted Martin.

'Yes,' the policeman conceded. 'But not for long. They're going to blow it up in about ten minutes.' He looked pointedly at his watch. 'They've prepared it for the charges already. The place is strictly no-entry. There are barriers all over. Believe me, no car could get in.'

'Let me see it anyway.'

The policeman looked at him with undisguised annoyance, then shrugged resignedly. 'This way, sir. But we shouldn't get too close. You never know, they may set the charges off a little early.'

They walked past the remains of what had a few minutes before been an office block, and the officer pointed fifty yards further down the road. Martin saw it then – a three-storey edifice of grey concrete, the same cheap monotonous cladding worn by multi-storey car parks the world over. 'We probably shouldn't go any further,' the policeman said.

'You said we had ten minutes,' said Martin sharply. He hurried ahead, and Isobel and Fézard followed behind.

Nearing the building, they saw that the entrance had been blocked by large concrete tubs – the kind used around public buildings in large cities to deter suicide bombers. Fifty yards away a few foundations were all that was left of the ambitious hypermarket which had once stood next door, and for which the car park had been built.

The policeman caught them up and pointed to the tubs. 'No one could've got through those,' he said. 'And they checked the building for vehicles before they put those in the other day. The place is clean. But we need to get out of here.' He pointed at the stuffed holsters wrapped with ropes around the columns of the car park. 'The charges have been inserted. They're going to push the button in about eight minutes from now.' He looked nervously at his watch.

'Get them to delay it.'

'The man pressing the button is half a mile away. I can try and reach him on his mobile but—'

Martin wasn't listening. 'Where's the exit?'

'Down there, around the corner. But listen—'

He was already running. When he got to the corner he turned and saw the exit, blocked by a wooden barrier with a ticket-machine alongside. Here too concrete tubs had been placed, but they were smaller than those at the entrance. He noticed there were scrapes on the concrete floor around one of them, and when he looked more closely at the tub he saw that one side had been badly chipped as if a careless driver had backed into it. Some traces of paint seemed to confirm this.

'What is it?' asked Isobel behind him.

'Look,' said Martin, pointing down at the concrete tub. 'That's blue paint, and the van we're looking for is blue. Come on!' he said, running past the barrier towards the central staircase.

They raced up the stairs, stopping at each level only long enough to look for a vehicle. The first two floors were empty, and Martin's spirits sagged again. There was nothing on the third floor either, and he was about to give up in despair when Isobel gasped 'Look!' and pointed to a ramp leading to the roof.

He ran on, up the ramp, to the open top floor of the car park. And there at the far end was something large and blue. A van.

Or what was left of a van. Its back end had been badly crushed and the bonnet was squashed like a concertina. Martin ran towards it, sprinting the final yards, with Isobel and Fézard just behind him. He peered into the cab; there was no one inside. He ran round to the crumpled rear doors and pulled on the handle, but it didn't give. Locked.

'Let me,' said Fézard, pulling his weapon from the holster inside his jacket. 'Stand back,' he ordered, as he tilted the gun under the handle of the rear doors, so that the bullet would go upwards into the roof of the van. Then he fired.

The handle seemed to explode, leaving a small hole in the steel door. Martin put his hand in and pulled; the door gave way and swung open. And then they heard it – a muffled groan.

'Liz?' he shouted, his voice breaking. He reached into the van and pulled at two trussed legs until he could see part of a face beyond. The familiar eyes opened above a grotesque mask of white tape, and he saw her blink at the sudden light. He pulled off the tape wrapped around her lower face, guessing how much it must hurt but knowing that there was no time to spare. And he had to be certain she could breathe.

'Ready?' he said, and she nodded. Then he dragged her out far enough to put his arms round her waist and sling her over his shoulder.

'Run for it!' he said to the others, and in an awkward jog he carried Liz to the ramp and down to the third floor. Isobel and Fézard waited for him at the stairwell, holding the door open. Fézard tried to help him with Liz, but Martin shook his head. 'You go on,' he shouted as he started down the stairs. He prayed that the local policeman had reached the man pushing the button; otherwise it was going to be a close-run thing. He tried not to think of what the explosion would do to them all, caught in this claustrophobic stairwell.

He moved as quickly as he could, trying not to stumble on the steps. He reached the second floor, ran across the landing, then started down again. It seemed to take for ever to reach the first floor, focusing on each step, telling himself not to think of how far he still had to go or of the imminent detonation of the charges all around him. He was acutely alert. He could hear the sound of each step Isobel and Fézard took further down the stairwell. He could feel each breath Liz took as she lay over his shoulder.

And then there was only one flight left, and then just half a flight, and he concentrated on keeping his balance, ignoring the weight of the woman he was carrying, the woman he loved. Eight steps, seven, six, and Fézard was waiting, holding the door open, and there were three steps left, then two, then one, and he was out of the door, across the floor and through the exit into the fresh air. He didn't stop running until he was well clear of the building, at least a hundred yards away, and then he put his burden down gently on the soft verge of uncut grass. Isobel came over and began working at the knots of the ropes that were binding Liz's legs, while the police officer tasked with delaying the explosion came over and used a key to remove the plastic handcuffs from her wrists.

'It's okay, Liz,' said Martin, crouching down beside her. 'You're safe now,' and she managed a weak smile but didn't speak. In the distance he could hear an ambulance wail.

He looked at the police officer. 'Thanks for telling them to hold off.'

The man's eyes widened in surprise, just as a loud rumble came from the car park. Turning, Martin saw the roof collapse first, on the side where the blue van was parked, then in a slow one-two-three motion each floor of the building pancaked like a collapsing deck of cards. Dust filled the air, and set them all coughing. But the engineers had done an excellent job, and within thirty seconds the air cleared enough to show a bright blue sky where once the car park had stood.

Martin turned and stared at the policeman. Looking absolutely mortified, the man held up his mobile phone. 'I couldn't get a signal, sir.'

58

L IZ SPENT TWO DAYS in hospital in Marseilles, but except for bruises and abrasions she was remarkably unscathed – physically. She didn't tell anyone at the hospital about the fear she felt every time she closed her eyes and imagined she was back in the van. But a nurse had noticed the terror in her eyes when she'd woken her up to take her blood pressure and had mentioned it to the doctor. He had discussed it with Martin, who visited every day, but at his request they had not told Liz that they knew how frightened she was feeling.

'She is proud and strong and wants to conquer it herself. If she can't, she'll tell me when she's ready,' Martin had said. The doctor had shaken his head, but knowing that this patient would soon be returning to England, he had done as he was asked.

Now, back in London and at work, the terrors were gradually fading. Peggy had offered to come and stay but Liz had turned her down. 'Thanks, Peggy. That's really kind but I'll be fine,' she'd said. And she thought she would be, though she knew she'd only be truly better when Kubiak had been caught.

.She spoke on the phone every evening to Martin in Paris. He was in close touch with Isobel and Fézard in

Marseilles, but though there was a general alert out, there had as yet been no sign of Kubiak or his car. Unbeknown to Liz, Martin was also in touch with DG. He had told him what the doctor at the hospital in Marseilles had said about the trauma she had suffered, and DG had put a very discreet protective ring of trusted colleagues around Liz.

Geoffrey Fane, who seemed to find reasons for frequent visits to Thames House, reported that the Russians persisted in denying any involvement in the infiltration of the Ministry of Defence and had gone completely quiet on the subject of Anatole Kubiak.

In the shallow waters at the edge of Lake Geneva the police frogman missed twice with his hook, thrashing against the water in vain. Third time lucky, he caught the collar of the jacket and drew the thing gingerly towards his two colleagues standing on the shore. When the body reached the gravel, they each grabbed an arm and dragged it up a ramp, where they laid it on its back.

It had first been noticed at about six in the morning by an early dog walker, but by the look of it, it had been in the lake for many hours. The policemen gazing down at it now were used to corpses – fishing them out of the water was almost routine. But this one was more repellant than most. Its jaw sagged open and the skin round its Adam's apple was shrivelled and hanging loose. But above that was only a hideous, sodden mass of bone and flesh. There was no face at all. It looked as though something had smashed it to pulp, and the fish had completed what someone else had begun.

Something odd had happened to the jacket too – both sleeves had been slit from the cuffs up to the elbows. The reason soon became clear: the shirt sleeves were shredded and blood had soaked into them. When they pulled the fabric away from the arms, they could see a series of deep cuts, made with a knife or a razor. There was dried blood on the crotch of the body's trousers as well.

'I've never seen anything like this before,' said one of the policemen, his face screwed up with disgust. 'The guy's been tortured.'

Geoffrey Fane's face appeared round Liz's office door.

Oh, God. Not again, she thought. But he said, 'I have news from Switzerland that you'll want to hear.'

'You'd better come in and sit down. What is it?'

Fane was smiling, clearly enjoying himself. 'Russell White phoned from Geneva an hour ago. The Swiss police pulled a body out of the lake this morning. They're fairly sure it's Kubiak. It wasn't pretty. Apparently he'd been tortured and then shot in the face with a soft-nosed bullet. You know what that means, I suppose.'

'I do,' she replied with a shudder. 'It's classic KGB.'

'Some things never change with our Russian friends. But you see the implication. He was a traitor. Whatever he was doing with the Koreans was unauthorised. He must have killed them all in a panic when he thought he'd been discovered.'

Liz sighed. 'It must have started to go wrong for him when he blurted out to Sorsky that there was an informant in the MOD. After that he knew he could never be safe, and neither was Sorsky.' She added, 'Nor was I – if Kubiak saw me meeting him, that is, which I think he must have done.' She paused, thinking of the stocky man she had seen before her first meeting with Sorsky. 'I wonder if we'll ever know what this was really all about.'

'Let's see what our friend Kirov says,' said Fane. 'He'll know the Swiss have found the body. In fact, it was clearly left for them to find, so he's sure to have some explanation.'

'If only Kubiak had kept his mouth shut, nothing would have happened to Alexander Sorsky.'

'Then we wouldn't have learned about Park Woo-jin and the threat to the Clarity programme.'

Liz knew he was right. In the greater scheme of things, Sorsky was simply the price that had to be paid for detecting a real threat to UK and US security. But it didn't make her feel any better about it.

59

ON FRIDAY EVENING MARTIN Seurat flew into Heathrow from Charles de Gaulle airport. Liz was there to pick him up. They were spending the weekend with her mother and Edward in Wiltshire.

'It's nice not to have to drive down in the dark,' she said as they rejoined the M4. Even now at eight o'clock there was still over an hour until sunset. For the next half-hour her attention was focused on negotiating the heavy Friday evening traffic on the motorway, but as it thinned out after Reading, she noticed that Martin was quieter than usual.

Eventually he said, 'You know, I've been thinking. I'm not sure how much longer I want to stay in this line of work.'

'Really?' Liz was surprised; Martin had never said anything like this before.

'Yes. I'm thinking it might be a good time for a change.'

'What would you do?'

'I'm not sure. Something calm and normal, if that were possible. Something where I didn't have to feel that people's lives depended on what I did.'

'Wouldn't you miss it?'

He shrugged. 'It's not that I'm bored, and I'd certainly

miss the challenge. Though even that seems less exciting. Last week I didn't think about Milraud once.'

'I'd call that progress.'

Martin smiled. 'I'd still like to catch the bastard, but if I don't, it no longer seems like the end of the world.'

This was a side to Martin Liz had not seen before but, listening to him talking, she thought she had a good idea what had brought it on. She said, 'I'm glad they found Kubiak. Though what a horrid way to die. '

'Yes, but remember what he did to you.'

'I don't think he'd planned it at all. I think he panicked when he saw me, and acted on the spur of the moment.'

'Perhaps you're right. But anyway, he's gone now, thank God.'

She nodded. Then, after a pause, said, 'And my nightmares have gone too.'

'Nightmares?' he asked innocently.

'Yes. I know you knew I was having them. But thank you for not mentioning it. I saw the office psychiatrist this afternoon. DG wouldn't let me take on any new cases till she'd signed me off.'

'How did it go?'

'Fine. She said I was clear. But I've got to go back to see her in three months, just to be sure. By the way, I was talking to Isobel this week,' she added.

'Oh, yes. What about?'

'That man Antoine from the commune, the one who's in prison here. They're applying for extradition, but I think he'll be tried here first for the attack on Edward and Cathy.'

'I'm not surprised.'

Liz hesitated, then said, 'And she told me what happened when you raided the commune.'

He said nothing. Liz went on, 'You didn't tell me about René and the gun. Isobel said it was a close-run thing.'

Martin sighed and said, 'I didn't want to worry you. You've had enough to deal with without bothering about me. Anyway, Isobel saved my bacon. Did she tell you that?'

'Not in so many words, but I got the impression that she turned up just in time.'

He didn't respond and she wondered if he was annoyed that she'd mentioned it. There was silence in the car for a few miles, then he said, 'I don't know if René would have killed me. Thanks to Isobel I didn't have to find out. I feel lucky to be here. But my scare was short-lived, yours lasted hours.' He paused then said, 'I'm just tired of having to deal with people like René and Antoine and Kubiak. I can't forget the sight of you tied up in that van. I keep seeing you in there and thinking what would have happened if we hadn't found you.'

So he's having nightmares too, thought Liz. But at least he's talking about it, which must be a good thing.

And having started talking, he didn't want to stop. 'It's funny. I've been in dangerous situations before – including twice in Marseilles, believe it or not. But I've never felt so close to death. I was afraid, I really was. And that makes me angry. Angry with myself; angry with the man who scared me. I've never felt that way before, which makes me think perhaps it's time I got out of the business.'

Liz didn't think there was anything she could say. A few more miles passed, then he said, 'You know, it seems completely surreal to be sitting here next to you, going off for a nice weekend in the country. I can't believe it's true. '

'It is true,' she said. 'This time the bad guys are safely locked away, or dead. We're very fortunate.'

'Yes. You're right. We're very fortunate,' he said happily. Then he placed an affectionate hand on Liz's shoulder. 'Let's stay that way – just drive a little slower, will you?'

60

I T HAD BEEN A lovely weekend. They'd walked along the river in the sunshine after lunch in the village pub, then later had dinner round the kitchen table in the gatehouse. And after dinner, sitting in the garden as the sun went down, they'd talked to Edward about everything that had happened recently to him and Cathy, and – in a censored fashion – what had happened to Martin and Liz. Susan Carlyle sat and listened, shaking her head from time to time at what she was hearing.

She knew by now that Liz needed the excitement, the feeling of playing her part in things that mattered. But she could also see that this time things had been too exciting even for her daughter. Both Liz and Martin looked tired and Edward was still recovering from the injuries that dreadful Frenchman had inflicted on him. Later, Liz and Martin had gone to bed and slept soundly for the first time in weeks, cosily wrapped together, sleeping under a sketch of the pony Liz had ridden as a girl.

Early on Monday morning Liz dropped Martin off at Heathrow on her way back into London. London was sparkling in the late spring sunshine. Tourist buses lined the Embankment, and the boats on the river were already full of Americans and Japanese seeing the sights from the water. The change in seasons had caught her unawares, and she realised how absorbed she'd been in this latest case.

In her office she found a message from Geoffrey Fane, asking if she would join him and Bokus at eleven o'clock for a meeting he knew she would want to attend. Unless he heard otherwise, he'd pick her up in a car at Thames House at 10.45.

She smiled to herself. Trust Geoffrey. How he loved to be mysterious.

They got out of the car at the north end of Kensington Palace Gardens just as Bokus arrived and together walked past the gatehouse and down the tree-lined avenue to the grand Russian Embassy building, where Geoffrey Fane announced their names. The large black door was open by the time they'd climbed the steps. Kirov himself was waiting in the entrance hall, at the foot of the large, impressive staircase. They shook hands, and he said, 'Come upstairs to my office.'

This was no ordinary office but a grand reception room, furnished in a heavy formal style with much gilt and brocade. The large windows overlooked the lawns and trees of Kensington Gardens. After the formalities and the offer of coffee had been completed, Kirov cleared his throat and began to speak. 'Thank you for coming. After our last meeting,' he said, looking at Fane and Bokus, 'I conducted the enquiries I promised, and I have some information for you.'

'Thank you,' said Fane.

Kirov continued addressing him. 'I told you then that

my country had no part in the infiltration of your Ministry of Defence, and I can confirm that information.'

'What about this character Kubiak?' enquired Bokus, unable to restrain himself. 'That's who we want to know about.'

Kirov's discomfort was obvious. 'Mr Bokus, I have to say that that is a different matter.' I'll say, thought Liz, thinking of the faceless corpse dragged out of Lake Geneva, but she said nothing. Kirov went on, 'He was involved, but not on our behalf.'

The three visitors looked at him and waited. There was more to come.

'I think it is important to be frank with you. Ten years ago Kubiak was posted to Pyongyang. Our relations with North Korea fluctuate, as I am sure you understand, but we have a core staff there. At some point during that posting he was recruited by one of the North Korean Services. Kubiak had an unpleasant vice – he was attracted to very young girls. They blackmailed him. He should never have been sent there and those responsible have been disciplined.'

'What did he do for them?' asked Liz.

'A variety of things over the years, we believe. But on this occasion he was acting as the paymaster for the operation to infiltrate your project. I know that you, Mr Bokus, informed your masters in Washington that it was Russia who was meddling with the communication system of your drones. That was not true and it was a very dangerous misinterpretation of the situation.'

Bokus scowled but said nothing.

Kirov went on, 'The North Korean regime has begun to operate in the West more than it ever has before. It had found out about your Clarity project.' He dropped the top-secret codename casually, though all three visitors noted it and knew that nothing he said was accidental. 'The North Koreans wanted to get ahead in the area of unmanned predators, and stealing your latest development seemed to them to be the way to do it. However, secure covert funding for a sophisticated operation in the West was an issue. They needed to move money around without its being detected. That's what Kubiak was doing for them. Laundering their funds in and out through Switzerland and the former Soviet Republics, then moving them into France through a fake messenger service he had set up. By the time the money was actually spent, it was almost impossible to trace where it originally came from.'

Liz knew that what Kirov was saying merely expanded on what Herr Bech had already learned from the Bank Difault-Légère in Zurich. That suggested that Kirov's story overall was probably true.

'With these funds, the office in Marseilles, which was the hub of the North Korean operation, was set up and run. Rent, salaries – these all came from Kubiak.'

He turned to Liz then. 'I understand that you suffered serious discomfort at this man's hands, Miss Carlyle. I wish to apologise on behalf of my government.'

'Thank you,' said Liz. I was nearly killed, she thought but didn't say. She looked innocently at Kirov and said instead, 'I take it that Mr Kubiak is now in the custody of your colleagues. May I ask what will happen to him?'

She knew, as did everyone in the room, that the Swiss police had put out a public request for information about a man with serious injuries fished out of the lake. They all also knew that no response had come from the Russian Embassy in Switzerland, and that on the same day that Kubiak's body had been discovered, a Mercedes car with no number plates had been discovered in a public car park in Geneva. The scratches and traces of paint from Steinmetz's car were no longer there, but from the chassis number Leplan had identified the car beyond doubt as Kubiak's.

Kirov's face was expressionless. 'All loose ends have been tied up,' he replied.

But Liz still wasn't satisfied. There was another person she wanted to enquire about. She couldn't forget that all this had started at a seminar years ago when she, a history student, had attracted the attention of a young Russian visiting lecturer. She knew that Kirov must know about the part Alexander Sorsky had played in setting off this investigation, but she hesitated to mention his name in case it somehow made things worse for him. So she said, 'There was an officer at your Embassy in Geneva who was taken ill and shipped home. Has he recovered?'

'Ah, yes. Our colleague Alexander Sorsky. I gather you knew him some time ago. At the University of Bristol as I understand it.'

Liz's heart sank. She knew what Kirov was telling her. Sorsky had been interrogated and had told them everything. 'Yes,' she said. 'We met quite by chance many years ago.'

'And then again, I think, more recently.'

'Yes,' said Liz. No point in denying it. 'That's true. He is a brave man. He wanted to avoid your country and ours . . .' she indicated Fane and Bokus '. . . misunderstanding each other. He was concerned that there was even a risk of conflict. And judging by what happened,' she said, looking at Bokus, 'I think he was right to be worried.'

'That is perhaps true. But he was not authorised to make those decisions or to take the action he did.'

'Well,' said Liz, feeling her face flush, 'I don't think we will agree on that. Please give him my thanks and my regards.'

Kirov looked at her; his stare was steely. 'That would not be possible.'

'What has happened to him?' she asked, unwilling to let the subject drop.

No one in the room spoke or moved. Then finally Kirov stood up. The meeting was over. He walked to the door, opened it and stood back to let them go through. As she passed him he said quietly to Liz, 'As I told you, Miss Carlyle, all the loose ends in this affair have been tied up.'

A NOTE ON THE AUTHOR

Dame Stella Rimington joined the Security Service (MI5) in 1968. During her career she worked in all the main fields of the Service: counter-subversion, counter-espionage and counter-terrorism. She was appointed Director General in 1992, the first woman to hold the post. She has written her autobiography and six Liz Carlyle novels. She lives in London and Norfolk.

A NOTE ON THE TYPE

The text of this book is set in Adobe Caslon, named after the
English punch-cutter and type-founder William Caslon (1692–
1766). Caslon's rather old-fashioned types were modelled on
seventeenth-century Dutch designs, but found wide acceptance
throughout the English-speaking world for much of the
eighteenth century until being replaced by newer types towards
the end of the century. Used in 1776 to print the Declaration of
Independence, they were revived in the nineteenth century, and
have been popular ever since, particularly amongst fine
printers. There are several digital versions, of which
Carol Twombly's Adobe Caslon is one.